The Battle

Book 8 in the
Combined Operations Series
By
Griff Hosker

Published by Sword Books Ltd 2016
Copyright © Griff Hosker First Edition

Cover by Design for Writers

Dedicated to my two grandson Samuel and Thomas and in memory of my dad who served in Combined Operations from 1941-1945

Prologue

August 1944 France

My men and I had helped to liberate Paris. It had largely been the Americans and Free French who had raced to the bridges of the Seine and captured that fine city intact but we had been with them. To read the papers would give the impression that the war was over. It was not true. The breakout from the Normandy beaches and the closing of the Falaise gap had shown us just how hard the Germans would fight to cling on to their conquests.

When our part was over we returned west. We would not be given a leave. We were too valuable. There were other tasks for which we were well suited and so we had been sent to a holding camp close to Rouen. As we drove west we saw the signs of war across the landscape. The detritus of battle littered the land. There were burned out tanks and deserted emplacements. It had been a hard-fought place of death. Now it was a place to recover and recuperate.

Privates Davis and Crowe were in the temporary hospital in Rouen. We were in the holding camp and we slept in tents again. My section was one of the most experienced in the whole of Combined Operations and they knew, as I did, that we would soon be called upon to go behind the lines, again, and so they used their time well. We went for daily runs to keep up our fitness. We repaired and maintained our weapons and equipment and we ate the food that was in plentiful supply. Letters from England would have helped but they would still be following us around and, although we wrote home, none of us expected letters in reply. So long as our loved ones knew we were alive then all would be well.

I had, as my grandfather might have said, a young lady. Susan worked in Whitehall as part of the team which sent agents and units behind enemy lines. She would know, better than any, where I was. She would know that I was alive. We had both had to put the future from our minds. London was still being attacked by the V1 and V2 rockets and the prospect of me surviving the war grew slimmer with each operation. As Sergeant Gordy Barker, had told me there was only so much luck which a soldier had to call upon. He thought I had used up my own allocation.

As well as making sure we all had enough to eat and drink, we all replenished equipment. We were Commandos. We used the guns, ordnance and equipment which worked for us. Fred Emerson, our mechanical genius, had kept a German halftrack, affectionately named Bertha, going on the chase from Falaise to Paris. Most of my men had German weapons as well as the precious Colts and Thompsons we had been issued when we first joined. The newer Commandos had Lee Enfields and Bren guns. We had grenade rifles and we had German grenades. We were magpies. We clung to the guns which had served us well. My men had been scrounging the precious ammunition we would need. We hoarded it like a squirrel hoards nuts. We did not know how long it would last but we would make the most of it. In our line of work the next operation was always just around the corner.

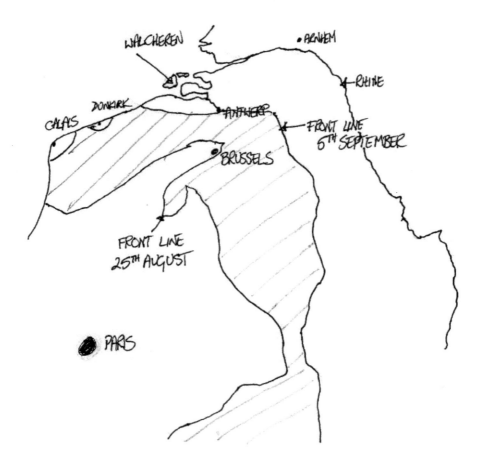

WALCHEREN

ARNHEM

RHINE

DUNKIRK

CALAIS

ANTWERP

FRONT LINE
6TH SEPTEMBER

BRUSSELS

FRONT LINE
25TH AUGUST

PARIS

Part 1
The Road to Antwerp

Chapter 1

"Sir, there is a jeep here for you. Major Foster needs you at Headquarters."

"Thanks Shepherd." I left my tent and the half-written letter to Susan. That was how I wrote my letters; a little each day. They had become a sort of diary. I folded it and put it in the side pocket of my Bergen. Going outside I saw the jeep. Since D-Day they had been brought over in rapidly increasing numbers and the American vehicle was a godsend. I waved over Sergeant Poulson as I clambered aboard. "I cannot imagine that this is an invite to a cocktail party, Sergeant, better make sure we are ready to go at a moment's notice. It is major Foster who has sent for me."

"I think you are right, sir. Crowe has been released from the hospital. That is a sure sign that someone wants us at the sharp end again."

"Where else would we be, eh?"

Headquarters had been the local German Headquarters before the previous owners had fled. As I entered I saw that they had taken everything with them. The lighter patches on the walls showed where pictures had been. I had no doubt that one would have been a martial posed painting of Adolf Hitler. The Redcap corporal scrutinised my papers before admitting me. The sergeant at the desk looked up, "Ah, Captain Harsker. If you would like to take a seat. The Major is with Major General Roberts at the moment. They are in the conference room there, sir." He pointed to some double doors opposite. "They won't be long."

"Thank you, Sergeant."

"Tea sir?"

"If there is one on the go."

He grinned, "Wouldn't be the British Army without tea on the go would it now, sir?"

It was a busy headquarters. Clerks scurried back and forth with sheaves of paper. Harassed looking officers entered and left. Since our return from Paris I had had little news about the war. All that I had was gleaned from newspapers. As Reg Dean often said, '*The best use for newspapers was to wrap around your fish and chips!*'

The tea was dark, strong and heavily sweetened. Sergeants knew of no other way to serve it. I had just finished it when the double doors opened and a huddle of officers emerged. I recognised Major Foster. He was talking to a Major General. When he saw me he waved me over.

"This, Major General Roberts, is Captain Harsker. He will be leading the unit which will help your tanks take Antwerp."

He nodded, "Good. I have heard good things about you, young man. The Free French, Canadians and Americans all speak highly of you. I expected you to be older. Still you don't get so much fruit salad sitting on your backside eh?" He turned to Major Foster, "I shall stay in touch. This officer and his men do not have long!"

With that he and his officers left. Major Foster took me into the conference room and closed the doors. There was just a sergeant who was collecting discarded papers.

"Have long for what, sir?"

"Take a seat, Tom." He sat opposite me. "I know you need a rest. Good heavens you have not stopped since D-Day but the General needs you. He needs Commandos, at any rate. There were other units available but they didn't have your experience. Besides which, you know the area."

I pointed to the map, "Antwerp? I have never been there in my life."

"True but the land to the south you know. We both crossed it in nineteen forty!" He smiled, "We have started this the wrong way round. Wilkins, a pot of coffee and see if you can rustle up some biscuits eh?"

"Righto sir."

He left and Major Foster stood and went to the map which was on the wall. "The race to Paris was a great success, Tom. Eisenhower thinks it might shorten the war by years but the trouble is we can't land enough supplies. Now that Mulberry is wrecked there we are in great danger of running out of steam. We need a port. More particularly we need a port which is inland to shorten our supply routes to Germany."

"Antwerp?"

"You have it in one." The door opened and the sergeant returned. "Thanks Sergeant. We don't need you for a while. Make sure we aren't disturbed eh?"

"Righto sir."

After he had gone Major Foster became serious. He lit a cigarette and sucked deeply on it. "Our American cousins want to get to the Rhine as soon as possible. Monty has cooked up an airborne operation which might do that and get us there quickly but unless we have a port then we can't move fast enough to supply the troops who will be racing to get there. Even if it does succeed then they will be hung out to dry unless we can keep them supplied. As we get deeper into enemy territory Hitler's supply lines get shorter as ours get longer. His aeroplanes can stay over a battlefield for longer periods and ours shorter. I don't need to tell you, your father will have told you. The further we are from the sea then the longer our lines of communication are. Antwerp is further inland and if we take it then we can supply our armour."

"I can see that, sir but where do we come in? I mean you must have plenty of aerial photographs. Don't they show you what you need to know?"

5

"To some extent yes but we want to use you like a scalpel. You go in before the armour. The resistance is already doing a sterling job sabotaging but Commandos like your section can do far more. You can survive behind the lines. We want you to act like old fashioned scouts. You will stay in touch with the armour which will be on the road behind you. You will tell them the roads to avoid. We are not intending to advance along a broad front. This will be a heavily armoured column with infantry support racing to capture Antwerp. That will be phase one."

That was ominous. It was more than one mission. I nodded, "How long do we have then sir?"

"There is the rub, Tom. The attack on the Seine bridges begins on the 29th of August."

My mouth must have dropped open. I regained my composure. "Tomorrow?"

"I told you this was a rush job and that is why it has to be you. You are here and in position already."

"That is more than a tall order, sir."

"Look the armour will not be in Belgium until the 3rd or 4th of September. That gives you a couple of days to sneak behind the enemy lines. We have new radios and you can keep the armour on the straight and narrow so to speak."

"More likely the twisted and bent, sir. If we use the straight and narrow, we will be in trouble."

"That's the spirit. Now we think that the armour should be able to get through most things that Jerry can throw at them except for here." He pointed to a place called Boom. "There is a railway bridge and a bridge over the Rupel. If the Germans have them mined and blow them, and we think they might, then they would hold up the advance and give Jerry the chance to make Antwerp unusable as a port. We have not got time to make a Monty type slow advance. This has to be a lightning thrust. We are taking a leaf out of Guderian and Rommel's book. Your main mission is to make sure the two bridges are there when the Shermans arrive. After that you accompany the tanks into Antwerp."

I went to examine the map. It looked to be a good two hundred miles from our present front line. It had taken us a couple of months to reach our present position. "So, we get them into Antwerp and that is it?"

"Not quite." He stood and used his pointer to indicate a couple of pieces of land which jutted into the sea west of Antwerp. "As I said that was Phase One. There is a Phase Two. Even if we have the port in our hands we still have the problem of the German batteries at Flushing and Westkapelle." He tapped a little island which looked to be almost part of the mainland and lay at the mouth of the Scheldt. "The RAF are sending as many sorties as they can in an attempt to knock them out. However, as we discovered in Normandy, bombers are not particularly effective at knocking out batteries. Especially these which appear to have been made with ten feet thick concrete. We will be using the battleship '*Warspite*' and the monitors '*Erebus*' and '*Roberts*'. We have more hopes for their efficacy. They are steaming towards Walcheren even as we speak. They will take time to get there. However, we need someone on the ground who can tell us the effect of their fire. We don't want another Pont du Hoc. The American rangers scaled an impossible cliff only to discover that the guns were gone. The three ships are not on station yet. That part of the operation may have to be delayed. First, we take Antwerp, intact. When that is done, we send you down river to scout out the island and its defences."

"Let me get this quite clear then, sir. You want us to drive through enemy lines to help secure the bridges they need to take Antwerp. When that is done, we toddle off to the west of Antwerp and see how effective our battleships' fire power is." He nodded, "Without getting ourselves killed in the process."

"Yes, Tom and there is something else. There is an amphibious landing planned, should the bombardment fail. Your lads, the Special Service Brigade, will be tasked with an amphibious assault on Flushing and Westkapelle."

He had me there. I could not refuse. It was vital that we made it as safe as possible for our fellow Commandos to land with as few casualties as possible. Amphibious landings were unpredictable. I think he had saved that ace until last. He knew me well. There was a bond between Commandos and I would not break that bond.

Major Foster saw my answer on my face, "Good fellow! You can do this. I know you can."

"How do we get behind German lines sir? German uniforms?"

"Not this time. We had some chaps who were in German uniforms. They were close to where you broke through near to Paris. They were all captured and shot."

"It doesn't seem to make much difference. We are Commandos and they shoot us anyway!"

"Perhaps not. It seems that fewer line officers are obeying that particular order. The S.S. and the Gestapo are different. Intelligence does not have the S.S. in the area around Antwerp. In fact, the nearest elite unit is the 6th Parachute Regiment in Holland." He smiled, "This has come from the top, Tom. Go in your regular uniform."

I wandered over to the map and studied it. "Sir, what about Calais, Boulogne or Cherbourg? Surely they must be easier to take?"

"Cherbourg and Le Havre are just too far away from the Rhine to be of much use. As for the other two, the Germans are making life hard for us and both ports have been badly knocked about. No, it has to be Antwerp. If we have Antwerp, then we open up Germany's heartland."

I continued to study the map. The only thing we had going for us was the labyrinth of roads. The flat country meant we could escape if we were pursued. Against that were the canal bridges which would be easy to block.

"How many jeeps have we?"

"We can let you have two and a Bedford."

I shook my head, "No sir, a lorry will only slow us down. Better we take just two jeeps. Six men should be enough for the job."

7

Major Foster stubbed out his cigarette, "You are probably right. I will bring over the jeeps, radio and equipment this evening. The codename for this operation is Cinderella. The larger operation is Infatuate. You will liaise with Lieutenant Colonel Silvertop and Major Dunlop. The Colonel will command the 11th Armoured Brigade and they will be in the lead Shermans on this operation."

"Do I get to meet them first, sir?"

"Afraid not. They are being refitted after Falaise. They are at Amiens. They are having their tracks renewed and wrecked tanks replaced. Don't worry though, Tom, they are both fine chaps. They did well at Falaise."

"It's not that, sir. I like to see the faces of the men I am fighting with. A disembodied voice is not the same."

"Sorry, Tom, can't be helped. It is possible you may get to meet them at Amiens but speed is of the essence. Oh, by the by, that Canadian Major has put you in for the M.C. They were really impressed by you and they are part of this."

"One big happy family eh sir?"

He missed the irony and beamed, "That's the spirit. Here you are then, the maps and call signs you will need." He handed me a manila folder bound in string. "I don't need to tell you to burn the call sign sheet as soon as you have memorised it."

"Yes sir."

As I headed back to camp I thought about the Major. When I had first met him he had been a line officer and he was the reason I had joined the Commandos. He had been a different person then. Once he became a planner he started to change. He would never be as bad as Colonel Fleming but he was no longer an officer I admired. As I was driven back to the camp I made my selection of the men I would take. They almost picked themselves. The recently wounded men were not yet recovered and I would leave them at camp and give them more recovery time. Gordy Barker had been wounded and I was not certain that he was totally recovered. He was the oldest member of my section. I would leave him. The one who would be most disappointed to be left behind was the newest member of my team, Joe Wilkinson. It could not be helped. Two jeeps meant a maximum of six. Even then we would be overcrowded.

Our jumping off point would be Amiens. We would then have a hundred and sixty miles or so to go. It was a reassuring thought that the armour would be leaving Amiens soon after us. The Sherman was a fast tank and we would not be as isolated as we had been in North Africa and Italy. There we had been behind the lines and waiting. The problem we would have was carrying enough equipment. How long would we be behind the German lines? As we approached the camp I realised that had been the reason that we had been chosen. We could live off the land if we had to.

My men were experienced to know that a summons to headquarters meant we would soon be in action and they were all hovering close by. After dismissing the jeep, I waved my men over and we headed for the mess tent. It was empty for it would be a couple of hours before it was needed for lunch. "Gordy, could you pop and tell the sergeant cook that we will need the mess tent for an hour."

"Right sir."

"Sit in a circle chaps and I will brief you."

Sergeant Poulson grinned, "Something tells me we are off again and really quickly this time sir."

"You have got it in one. We leave tonight."

"Tonight? That is even quicker than I anticipated. sir."

Gordy returned, "What is, Polly?"

"We are leaving tonight!"

I held up my hand. "Some of us are leaving tonight." I saw the look of disappointment on some of their faces. None of them wanted to be left behind. "It is not my choice to leave anyone behind but we will be taking two jeeps and that means just six of us. The back seat can only take one if we have Bergens with us. Eight is too many for the two jeeps to carry but, as we will be behind enemy lines again, I want as much firepower as we can manage and the six of us will be well armed. I will brief you all and then tell you who will be coming."

"We could always find another Bertha, sir."

"Sorry, Emerson, we have to use our vehicles. I was offered a lorry but that would slow us down. We are going to scout the road to Antwerp for the 11th Armoured Division. We have to ensure that the bridges are in place and to warn them of any build-up of enemy forces."

"What about the RAF sir?"

"They can take aerial photographs but that won't show the demolition charges and we know how good Jerry is at hiding himself. They are giving us a new radio and we will be just one step ahead of the Shermans. They want to capture the port intact. Speed is of the essence."

"We won't be blowing anything up then sir?"

"Unlikely, Beaumont. We will just take Thompsons, Colts and grenades. We will need food for five days and petrol too."

"How do we cross the lines then, sir?"

"We go at night and we find a small road and just cross."

"That sounds a little mad sir!"

"Not really Fletcher. There is a bridge close to Vecquemont. I had a look at the aerial photographs. It is a small bridge. It looks to be medieval. I think it is only as wide as a car. It certainly can't be used by tanks. There may well be guards there but I doubt that they will expect two fast little vehicles to come flying over the bridge. We have plenty of firepower. If we strike in the middle of the night there will, in all likelihood, just be a handful of men there. Once we are through then we use the back roads and then lie up for the day."

Fletcher nodded, "Fair enough sir. We have done that sort of thing before."

"Who gets to go then sir?"

"I will tell you who and the reason I chose them. Corporal Fletcher is the first commando I chose. He is the radio expert. Private Emerson will look after the vehicles. Lance Sergeant Hay has the language skills and Sergeant Poulson will be second in command. Private Beaumont will be the sixth." I saw the disappointment on the faces of those not chosen. I knew that they would not try to persuade me to take them. They were a team. "Gordy, I want you to have the rest of the section ready for the second part of the mission."

"Second part, sir?"

"Yes, Private Beaumont. We have to scout out the defences on the islands of Flushing and Walcheren. Our lads are going to make an amphibious assault there and we have to spot for the Navy. If we do take the road to Antwerp and capture the port, then the rest of you lads can join us there. We might not need the jeeps for that part of the mission. But I am getting ahead of myself. Job number one is to make sure the armour gets through to Antwerp. Any questions?"

My men had enough information and I took their silence as my answer.

"Right. I want us ready to leave before dark. The vehicles and Major Foster will be here by this afternoon. Gordy get the rations sorted eh?" As he was leaving I waved Fletcher over, "Here are the radio frequencies and call signs. Memorize them and destroy them."

"Right sir. Who is my oppo?"

"We all knew that any of us could be killed and everyone needed a backup. Mine would be Polly. "Make it Lance Sergeant Hay."

"Right sir."

I had as much to prepare as my men. I took out my old Bergen and emptied it. It was a ritual I did for each mission. It ensured that I missed out nothing. I packed my wire cutters, spare compass, lighter, flint, toggle ropes, sap, torch and binoculars first. They would be at the right side pocket of the bag. Then I packed my spare socks and underwear. They went in the bottom of the bag with the camouflage netting. I took all the grenades I had and placed them in the bag. I put the ammunition for the Colt, Thompson and Luger in the left hand side pocket. I had decided to leave the Mauser sniper rifle at camp. I took the coins and notes I kept for emergencies and put them in the back pockets of my trousers. I had German and French coins and notes. Most of them came from the Germans we had either killed or captured. Fletcher called us dustbin rats. Then I put in the torch. Finally, I put the maps in the pocket at the rear of the bag. I still had room for the rations.

I changed from my better uniform and donned the one without medal ribbons. It was old but it was comfortable. More importantly, it had faded and that made it harder to see. I strapped my dagger to my lower leg. I found it easier to carry it there. Finally, I fastened my holster. Then I took the half-finished letter and signed it. I put it in an envelope. I would give it to Major Foster when he arrived. If anything happened to me at least Susan would have my last letter.

I had just finished when Gordy came in. He named each item as he placed it on the cot, "One tin of Spam, one pack of biscuits, plain, one block chocolate, vitamin fortified, one sachet of boiled sweets, two tea blocks, one pack of biscuit, sweet, one pack of plain matches, one pack of latrine paper, one pack of oatmeal, instant, two packets of meat broth, two packs of chewing gum, one pack of sugar tablets."

"I don't use the gum. Give them to the lads who do use it."

"Right sir. Do you mind me asking, sir, why Polly and not me? Just wondering like."

"Two reasons, Gordy: one, you haven't fully recovered from the wounds you got at Falaise and two, I need the rest of the team to be able to pick up the baton in case we drop it. If we get stopped then Major Foster will send you in. You are our back up."

"Fair enough sir but you have never dropped the baton yet, sir."

"There is always a first time. At least this way you and the lads can just drive if you need to replace us. You don't need the Navy or the Air Force eh?"

"Aye you are right. Did you say that the Major offered a Bedford sir?"

"He did."

"When he comes, I shall get it then. That way we can get moving quicker. If the armour clears the road, then we can follow on behind." I smiled. Gordy hated missing out on anything.

It was just after lunch that we heard the sound of the jeeps. I was pleased to see that Major Foster had had the foresight to get us jerricans of petrol and they were strapped around the rear and sides of the two vehicles. They were a danger if we had a firefight but then again, we were supposed to be clandestine. As soon as they stopped Emerson had the bonnets up and was checking out the engine. Fletcher and Hay took the radio and checked that.

Major Foster shook his head, "Your boys don't waste time, do they?"

"In our business wasted time can be fatal!" I pointed to the Bedford, "Is that your transport back, sir?"

"It is as you don't appear to need it."

"We would like to use it for the support team. If Gordy comes back with you and drops you off, we can have it can't we sir?"

He laughed, "Very well." He waved me over. "Just one thing, Tom. The two monitors have had a wee bit of bother. Their part in the operation will be delayed until the last week in October. Put that part of the mission on hold. Antwerp is the key."

"Right sir. So, our job is finished when we get the armour to Antwerp?"

"It is but there will be no leave. You will still have the reconnaissance of the batteries to complete."

"I know sir but we could pull back from the fighting zone couldn't we? There will be quiet areas we can use."

"Of course."

"And is there any chance of talking to the tankers, sir?"

11

"Major Dunlop of C Squadron, 3rd RTR will be laagered just south of Amiens. He knows you are the liaison. But the thing is Tom, we need you behind the lines as soon as you can. I think that once the armour breaks through it will be like corn through a duck."

"Don't worry, sir. We will be behind the lines as soon as possible."

An hour later I had the latest aerial photographs studied and we had the vehicles loaded. Gordy and my support team boarded the Bedford along with the jeep drivers and Major Foster. "Good luck, Tom. You will do a fine job, I know."

"We'll do our best." I handed him the letter. "Could you see this gets posted sir?"

"Of course, Tom."

As they drove off Fletcher said, "Aye sir, off we go into the wild blue yonder! If me mam knew what we got up to she would go hairless!"

Beaumont grinned as he started the jeep, "Scouse, the way you are I am surprised your mother has any hair left at all!"

Chapter 2

The first sixty or so miles were easy. If it had not been for the road blocks and security checks, we would have done it quickly. The jeep was faster than the Kubelwagens we were used to and slightly more comfortable. Even so, after a few hours, we were ready to stretch our legs. We were flying for I hoped to reach Amiens and actually speak to one of the officers in the Armoured Division. We would then try to slip across the border at night. I had studied the aerial photographs and found a forest north of Mons. We could hide there.

As we drove towards Amiens and the Armoured Division I said, "Are you happy with the radio, Fletcher?"

"It looks alright sir. It is smaller than the old machines. The battery looks sound." He shrugged, "It depends on the radio traffic. If we are a long way behind their lines and the tanks aren't close enough then Jerry might jam us."

"So, we need to stay as close to the column as we can?"

"In a perfect world, yes sir."

I knew that once over the Somme the tanks would have little difficulty until they reached the main railway line and then the Rupel. They would hit both just south of the town of Boom. The railway bridge was a viaduct bridge and if it was destroyed then it would stall the tanks. I estimated at least four days for them to get there. We had to find the German armour for them. That would be the hard part. We could find them but could we avoid being destroyed by them?

We were south of Amiens when we spotted the tank laager. Difficult to see from the air we saw the muzzles of the tanks. We turned to enter and speak with the officers. We did not get beyond the barrier. The Redcap sergeant major refused to allow us in.

"Sorry sir but I have my orders. You could be Jerries wearing Commando uniforms!"

I sighed. I had met men like this one before. They were not combat troops but they knew Kings \regulations back to front and inside out. "Look Sarn't Major, just send a message to Major Dunlop that Captain Tom Harsker is here. That is all I ask."

He nodded and said to his corporal. "Keep your eyes on these. They could be Jerry in disguise. What are six Commandos doing here in Yank jeeps eh?"

As he wandered off Scouse said, "Bloody Jobsworth!"

"Just doing what he has been told. We have used disguises often enough, haven't we?"

"I suppose so sir."

Major Dunlop arrived a short while later. A young lieutenant was with him. The major shook his head, "Sorry about this Captain Harsker but we can't be too careful." He gestured me to one side. He said, quietly, "To be honest old boy I thought you would be busy trying to get behind the lines. We push off tomorrow."

"I know, sir, but I wanted to meet with you. I have found that putting a face to a voice on the radio helps."

"You have done this sort of thing before then?"

"A few times. We will get behind the lines. I intend to camp close to Mons tomorrow."

"That is a hundred miles behind the enemy lines!"

"I know sir. There is a wood there and it will make a good place to lie up. Tell me sir what is it that you want us to do?"

"Make sure that all the bridges we need will be there and will be intact. The infantry who are following us don't need them but we do. Intelligence doesn't have too many German tanks in our way but if you spot any then let us know."

"Will do sir. We will wait for you south of the town of Willebroek. It is close to the railway bridge. By the time you get there we should have scouted it out."

"And if it is mined?"

"Then we will find another way around or disarm the explosives. If we can't we will let you know."

He smiled, "You make it sound easy, Captain."

"Not easy but I know my men and their abilities. What about Brussels sir? Is that to be taken by your column?"

"No, the Guards Division have that duty. Our priority is Antwerp. We skirt around it. Don't take any chances, Captain. We aim to catch Jerry with his trousers down."

"Then we had best be on our way sir. I am glad I met you and when you hear a Liverpool accent on the radio it is Fletcher here."

"That's good to know. I will have Lieutenant Ditchburn here keep you informed of any changes eh?"

"Thanks sir."

I climbed back in the jeep and we headed back down the road towards the east and the river crossing I had chosen. We drove slowly along the narrow, hedge lined road. It kept the noise of the engine down to a minimum and would allow us to see the crossing more easily. I spied the lighter area which showed that the hedgerow had ended and I waved Beaumont towards it. I saw the bridge. It was fifty yards to our left. I tapped Beaumont on the arm and he cut the engine. When Emerson did the same in the second jeep the night became as silent as it was dark.

Then two soldiers appeared from the undergrowth, their Lee Enfields aimed at Beaumont.

"Halt who goes there!"

"Friend."

14

"What is the password?"

Scouse said, "Loophole!"

The two soldiers walked from the cover of the undergrowth grinning. "If you have a Scouser with you then you can't be German." The corporal of the Green Howards saw my pips and snapped to attention. "Sir!"

"At ease, Corporal." I climbed out of the jeep. I led them further from the road where we could talk quietly. "We are going to cross the river. What is the opposition like?"

"Over there?" I nodded. "Same as here. There are a couple of German sentries and a bit of barbed wire." He gestured to the rolled wire which stood across the narrow bridge. Now that my eyes were accustomed to the dark I could see that the bridge was even narrower than I had thought.

"Are there other Jerries nearby?"

He pointed to the left. "There is a farmhouse over there sir. It is three hundred yards down a little lane. Jerry has a command post there."

I remembered seeing the farmhouse from the aerial photographs. I had not seen any vehicles. "Any armour?"

"No sir, quiet little neck of the woods is this. After Falaise this is almost a holiday camp, sir!"

I nodded, "Well I am afraid, Corporal that we might make it a little noisier soon." I turned, "Hay, Beaumont; come with me. Bring your Colts." They appeared next to me. I opened the right-hand pocket in my Bergen and took out the sap. "Bill, slip across the river. I want to take the two sentries on the other side. Beaumont and I will walk across the bridge. Don't shoot unless you have to. We will take them prisoner."

The Corporal asked, as my men prepared themselves, "Just walk across sir?"

"Of course, Corporal." I took off my beret." Come on Beaumont. If we are challenged, then speak German."

"Right sir."

We walked to the barrier and moved it so that we could walk across. The bridge had a hump in the centre of it. That and darkness made the other side invisible. I watched as Bill slid silently towards the water. He slipped silently into the inky blackness. I held my Colt behind my back and my sap was in my left hand. Our rubber soled shoes did not make a sound as we approached the bridge. I had been right; it was medieval. It looked barely wide enough to take an ancient cart. We had reached the humped middle when a German voice asked us to halt or he would fire.

I replied in German, "Thank God we have found our lines. Hans and I have been wandering around the Tommies' lines for days." I kept walking.

"What?" It was curiosity which prompted the German's question and not suspicion.

"We escaped from a Tommy transport. We have been walking for days. We are starving. Have you food?"

I saw that the two of them had rifles but our German had made them less suspicious and their barrels were pointed away from us. When we were ten yards from them I saw a shadow rise from behind them. I pulled my gun from behind my back and pointed it at them. "Drop your weapons. You are my prisoners."

One of them, a corporal, began to raise his gun until Bill Hay rammed the barrel of his gun into the back of his head and hissed, in German, "You heard the Captain, drop the weapon."

The two guns fell to the ground. "Take them and their guns over to the Green Howards. We will shift this barrier."

"Come on my lads. For you the war is over." He pushed them towards the bridge.

Beaumont and I picked up the barrier. The middle was barbed wire but the ends were made of wood to make removal easy. We threw it to the side and then I went to the small brazier and guard hut. This was more organized than the one on the allied side of the lines. They even had a flask of acorn coffee. Satisfied that there was no telephone connected to the farmhouse we returned to the others. I took the flask with me.

"Right Corporal. I suspect that Jerry will be none too pleased with the situation. When are you relieved?"

"The Sarge will be along in an hour sir."

"Right." I turned to the German Corporal, "You are now prisoners. If you try to escape you will be shot. You will be treated well."

The Corporal nodded, "You are Kommandos?"

"Yes."

"Then we are lucky to be alive! We will behave. We have both had enough of this war. This is not even our land! My father died not far from here in the Great War. That was a waste and this is too."

I nodded, "You are a wise man." I turned to the Corporal. "They should give you no bother but keep an eye on them eh?"

"You off over there sir?"

"We are indeed, Corporal." I handed him the flask. "Here is some of their coffee. It will keep you warm eh?"

I climbed back into the jeep and both vehicles were started, "Right, Roger, take it slowly over the bridge. It looks a little fragile. If we can avoid waking the neighbours then that would be spot on!"

"Right sir." Keeping in it in first gear we climbed up the humped back bridge. There was barely a hand span between the side of the jeep and the bridge. I could see why security on both sides was so lax. This would not be where a breakout would take place. Once on the other side the engine stopped straining and Beaumont slipped it into second gear. The road headed north but I kept my eyes to the left and the farmhouse. We had just passed the end of the track leading to it when I saw the flicker of a light inside. Someone had heard the two vehicles.

"Right, Roger, a little faster eh?"

Both Emerson and Beaumont were good drivers but the narrow country lane which was lined with tall, untrimmed bushes was a challenge. Without lights, I could not see the speedometer but I doubted that we were making above twenty miles an hour and even that seemed too fast. Bushes and branches occasionally scraped us and the jeep as we made our way north. It was with some relief that we found the main road just five miles after crossing the river. It was still black but it was straighter and we were able to travel faster. I had the map below the dashboard and I used the shaded torch to check out the route. We were going to miss Arras which I knew had a large German presence. Crespin was a less dangerous option. I had seen no German vehicles on the aerial photographs but it was a relatively large village. After that it would just be tiny clusters of houses. Crespin was the last obstacle before we had to skirt Mons and find my wood.

Before we reached it, however, we had to get around both Cambrai and Valenciennes. They both involved long detours using the smallest of country lanes. We stopped, just after we had managed to get around Cambrai, to refill the tank. "How is the fuel holding up, Emerson?"

"We have enough to get there and a bit to spare but if you want to get home we had better find some more."

"These vehicles are only to get us close. If we run out, we abandon them and take to Shanks' Pony!"

"That is a comforting thought sir."

Bill Hay said, "That is one thing they aren't sir, comfortable!"

"And we still have over a hundred miles to go before we get some rest."

I nodded, "Sergeant Poulson is right. Stay sharp. Keep weapons to hand and your eyes open. Freddie, you will have to watch what we do. Just follow our jeep. We will have to leave the main roads at some time and then you will need the reactions of a cat."

We did meet traffic on the road; it was coming in our direction. Luckily, they were driving with dimmed lights. They were just enough of a warning for us to take side roads and wait. They did, however, add to the time it took to progress north. I had given plenty of time to be in the woods before dawn broke but each delay made it tighter. Valenciennes was a harder place than Cambrai. I spied a column of vehicles heading south. We had to drive into a side street and we barely made it as the column headed south. There were no tanks but the half-tracks suggested men. When we stopped, I would pass that information on to Major Dunlop. Motorized German infantry were tough. The Shermans were notoriously easy to set on fire. I knew, from my briefing, that the infantry were not travelling with the Shermans. The plan was an audacious one. The aim was to reach Antwerp as quickly as possible. Major General Roberts was only concerned with the port. Everything in between could be left to support units to mop up.

After Valenciennes, it took us some time to reach the main road again. Crespin could not be avoided. Every other inhabited place on the route had either had roads we could use to get around or was so small that it was not an obstacle. Crespin had a number of side roads. It could be blocked easily.

I checked the map and saw that we had just a mile to go before Crespin. I turned to Beaumont, "Put the lights on, Beaumont, and drive steadily through the village."

"Bit risky sir?"

"I don't think so, Fletcher. All the vehicles coming south had lights. It would be more suspicious for us to be travelling without them. In the dark they might take us for a pair of Kubelwagen."

I took out my silenced Colt and took off my beret. I saw, in the dark ahead, the glow of a brazier. There were Germans ahead. They were not in the village. There looked to be some sort of camp to the right. As we drew close I saw that there were at least four Mark IV Panzers. I hoped that they had no armoured cars or Kubelwagen with them.

"Ready with a grenade, Fletcher, just in case."

"I have two, sir, and they are potato mashers!" We liked to use German grenades whenever possible. They made a different sound to the Mills bomb and often confused the Germans.

As we drew closer to the brazier I saw a figure rise and hold his hand up. I said, quietly, "Slow down Beaumont but be ready to floor it!"

"Sir."

I saw that there were two men seated around the brazier and a third who had stood. When we were thirty paces from him I saw his eyes widen as he recognised the vehicle. He was beginning to shout as I fired two bullets into him. "Now!" Beaumont jammed his foot on the accelerator. He had already dropped down to second gear and our departure was rapid. I fired the rest of my bullets at the other two. It was more to make them keep their heads down than anything else.

Fletcher shouted, "Grenades!" It was for the benefit of the second jeep. Emerson would take the jeep to the left of the road.

We drove into the dark of the village and then it was lit up by the light from the two grenades. There was a rattle of German gunfire and then we were back in the dark. If the Germans did not know it before they knew now that there were enemy soldiers and they were well behind their lines.

"That's blown it sir."

"Not necessarily, Fletcher. They were tanks we saw. I can't see them wasting fuel to chase us. They will just try to stop us up ahead."

"That's just as bad, isn't it sir?"

"No, Beaumont. I will find us a way off this main road." I took out the torch and saw that, up ahead was a side road. It passed through a hamlet called Hautage-Etat. It would take us to the woods. We would not be at the exact spot I had chosen but we had to improvise. I knew that the turn off was a narrow one and I saw it at the last minute. "Here Beaumont, turn!"

He dropped a gear and threw the jeep over. The tyres squealed and lifted, dangerously. We crashed down as he made the turn. Emerson's tyre squeal was less dramatic. Beaumont said, drily, "I am not certain that did the jeep any good at all, sir."

"Sorry about that, Beaumont. Pull over and turn off your lights."

As he did so I heard the squeal of brakes behind as Emerson had to stop suddenly. Then there was silence. There was the smell of burned rubber and brakes but it was silent. Then I heard the sound of a Kubelwagen, closely followed by the sound of an armoured car. It sounded like a RAD 6. It was a good job we had left the road. We could have been easily caught when we tried to get through Mons. I had no doubt that there were roadblocks ahead of us now.

"Right Beaumont, let's go. Take it steady and no lights again. You can take it slowly and as quietly as possible. I think we only have a few miles to go."

He laughed as we set off.

"What so funny, Beaumont?"

He pointed at the sign. The Germans had taken it down to confuse allied soldiers but they had just left it by the hedge. It said, 'Rue des Bats'. "Sounds perfect for us sir! We like the night and we are as unpredictable as a bat."

"Aren't they blood suckers sir? I mean like Dracula and all that!"

Roger laughed, "I don't think so Scouse. They are only as big as your little finger!"

"They have teeth, though don't they?"

Fletcher was a town boy. Beaumont looked at me and rolled his eyes.

The tiny hamlet was asleep as we passed through it but it would not be for long. Dawn would be breaking in a couple of hours and we needed to be under cover before then. I was grateful when I saw the woods ahead. "Beaumont, just find a track and when you are inside then stop."

He took the corner slowly this time and stopped thirty yards in. "Right, everyone out and cover our tracks."

I think everyone was grateful to be able to get off the seats. Using the broken branches from the last storm we first walked over the tracks of our tyres and then used the branches to scrape away our footprints. I collected some of the early fallen leaves and used those to cover up the track. It would take an expert tracker who knew where we had turned to find our tracks now. We boarded the jeeps again and I consulted the map. The clearing I had seen on the aerial photograph was two miles to the north of us. I took out my compass. We would have to find it by dead reckoning. It was time consuming. Dawn was just beginning to break when we finally reached the clearing.

"Park the jeeps under the cover of the trees and rig the camouflage netting. Emerson, Beaumont refuel. Fletcher, get a fire going for a brew."

"Are you sure, sir?"

"Yes, Lance Sergeant Hay." I pointed to the middle of the clearing. There was a blackened area. "Charcoal burners use this clearing. It is why I picked it. The smell of smoke will not seem unusual. The petrol and our exhaust fumes are a bigger giveaway."

While they busied themselves, I took out my binoculars and waved Sergeant Poulson over. "Fletcher can report to the Armoured Division and then you can arrange a rota. In pairs. Two hours on each. That way we can all have at least four hours' sleep."

"Right sir."

I took out my notepad and wrote down what we had seen and where. The armour was a worry as were the personnel carriers. I was not certain that the column would find it as easy as Major Foster had made out.

"Fire's going sir."

"Right Fletcher, get on the radio to Major Dunlop. I have the positions of the enemy forces we saw. I will dictate them and you repeat them."

Although this would take longer it ensured that we gave the right information and we kept the security of using Fletcher's distinctive voice. Even if the Germans had vehicles searching for radio signals they would need at least three to triangulate on our position and as we were in the middle of the woods I thought that unlikely.

The atmospherics must have been perfect or the new radios more efficient than the old ones for Fletcher had his call answered quickly. He asked me questions and I answered them. When he had finished, he said, "They have made good progress sir. They have two bridges over the Somme and are heading up the road to Lens. Sounds like it has been fairly easy, sir. Major Dunlop said that as long as he could have his bridges he would be happy."

"Good. "Let's get some grub and then some shut eye."

We had the broth and the plain biscuits. It was hardly filling but we knew it would fill a hole. We would eat the wrong way around. We would have oats before we left after dark. The tea and a sweet biscuit rounded off the al fresco feast. The smokers smoked and sipped their tea. Hidden under the camouflage netting we would be invisible and so we chatted.

"When I was in camp sir, one of the lads reckoned that the war would be over by Christmas. I mean we have got Paris already. What we saw last night won't stop the lads in the tanks. What do you think?"

"I think Freddie, that we have a long way to go. Remember how hard Jerry fought to hold Falaise and that was just France. The closer we get to Germany the harder he will fight. It is like us; we would fight harder in England than over here."

"I don't know sir. We fight pretty hard here."

"I know, Sergeant Poulson, but you find hidden reserves when you are fighting for the ones you love. No Fletcher, I wouldn't make any plans for after the war just yet."

"I think I will stay in sir."

"A career soldier, Polly? I never took you for one."

"I like the life and I like the excitement."

"After the war is over will it be so exciting?"

"There's always wars, Bill. Besides what about the Nips? They are still fighting. Singapore, India, Burma; I reckon they will send us there as soon as this is all over."

"I won't mind if I never fire a gun again in my life."

"You prefer your engines, eh, Emerson?"

"Too right, sir. I was a fair hand before this started but looking after the Kubelwagens, Bertha and now these jeeps, well I think I could turn my hand to anything now. A nice little garage would suit me down to the ground."

"I have no idea what I want to do."

Beaumont laughed, "I think, Scouse, that whatever you do will be on the shady side of the law!"

He adopted an outraged expression, "You never know. I reckon I might be a teacher!"

"A teacher?"

"Hey Rog, when I was at school you just got a clip behind the back of the head if you lifted it. We learned nowt that was any good. I reckon I would make a good teacher. I mean a teacher is supposed to teach you useful stuff. Well I know a bit of German and French. My geography has improved. I know loads of stuff. It's either that or open a shop repairing radios."

"Well I will be back to University. This war has been about destruction. I want to build things. I want to make it a better world."

"What about you sir? Any plans? You have a young lady now eh sir?"

I shook my head, "No Sergeant Poulson, I have no plans. If you have dreams, then they can be shattered. We have a job to do and until Adolf surrenders that is all that is on my mind. When that is done, I will think about going home, getting married and planning a life. As to what that might be… I haven't the foggiest. And on that note, I will get my head down. Wake me in two hours Sergeant."

"Will do, sir."

We all had the ability to curl up and sleep, almost on command. Petty Officer Bill Leslie had sworn that he could sleep on a clothesline! As for me I was out for the count as soon as my head hit the Bergen. I was awake as quickly when I heard the aero engine.

"I was just coming to wake you, sir. It's Storch." Sergeant Poulson looked down at me.

I looked up but could see nothing. "It was to be expected." I checked my watch. It was just ten minutes off my duty anyway. "You two get your heads down. I will wake Beaumont in ten minutes."

The German spotter stooged around for half an hour, criss-crossing the forest and then it disappeared north. I woke Beaumont. He looked at his watch, "You let me sleep in, sir."

"I was awake. Get a brew on eh? I will go and fertilise the forest and see if we have company."

After my ablutions, I walked a complete circle around the clearing. I saw no other recent tracks. I had not expected to see any but it always paid to check these things out. When I got back to the camp my tea was waiting. "What do we do, sir, if these bridges are mined?"

"We stop them blowing them but I have looked at the aerial photographs. I am certain that we could get around them. The secret is to act quickly. I like this plan. Too often we have waited until we had all our ducks lined up. This has more chance than most of the plans."

"And then?"

"And then we tag along behind the armour. When Antwerp is taken we rejoin the rest of the boys and wait for the Navy to bring their ships up."

"Like you say, sir, sounds simple but I don't think it will be."

My men were realists. They knew that the planners could plan all that they liked but at the end of the day we would be the ones to adapt and survive.

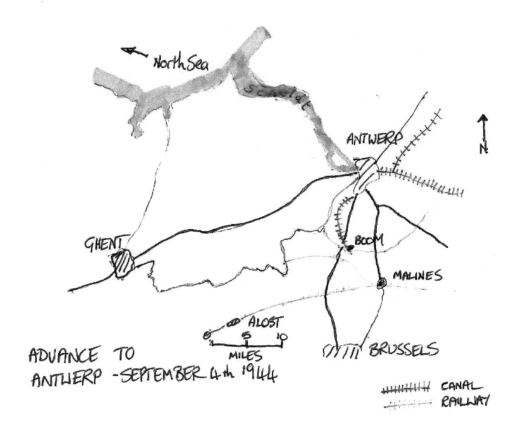

North Sea

Schelde

ANTWERP

N

GHENT

BOOM

MALINES

ALOST

0   5   10
MILES

BRUSSELS

ADVANCE TO
ANTWERP - SEPTEMBER 4th 1944

|||||||| CANAL
.... RAILWAY

Chapter 3

We left before dark had fallen. I decided to risk the track in the dusk. I had explained to my men the next part of the mission in case I was incapacitated. I intended to swing up to the Scheldt itself. There were woods which were close to the river and as it was only ten miles or so to the bridges we could hide the vehicles and go on foot. You could disguise a Commando but a jeep was harder to hide.

We left the forest and headed up the main road to Soignies. I intended to skirt the town but events conspired against us. Even as we approached the town I heard the heavy bombers overhead. Their target was not Soignies. It was somewhere further east but the anti-aircraft fire was intense on the western side of the town. They were obviously protecting Antwerp. The sky was suddenly lit up as one of the Lancasters was hit. The shell hit the inner port engine and I watched, in horror, as half of the wing broke off and the aeroplane spiralled down to earth.

Fletcher said, "It's gonna hit us sir!"

"No, it won't but it will stop us going around the town. He is going to crash close to the road we were going to use." I had the map open and I could see the road marked on it.

The Lancaster still had a full bomb load and, when it hit, we felt the concussion from over three quarters of a mile away. The stricken aeroplane must have hit a petrol station for there was a second wave of explosions and flames shot high in the sky. In the light of the fire I saw houses nearby. It had not been intended but civilians would die.

"Through the town, Beaumont. Berets off. If you see Jerry, then wave!"

We heard the sound of bells as fire engines and ambulances raced from Soignies. It actually helped us for we were going in the opposite direction. No one seemed to notice us and we appeared to bear a charmed life. I thought that we had made it unseen when, as we left the main square and were passing the town hall a policeman saw us. Putting his whistle to his mouth he blew. He then turned and ran into a building. I guessed it was the police station. It was too little, too late. We were through the town and into the dark. Behind us I saw the glow in the sky which marked the final resting place of a Lancaster and its crew.

Ahead of us lay Brussels and that had to be avoided. It meant we drove further than was necessary and we headed north west towards Enghien. It meant leaving the main road and using the smaller side roads. It was getting late and there were fewer people about for the air raids would increase the later it got. And then it began to rain. The jeep did have a canvas roof but we had not put it up. I dared not risk stopping and so Fletcher and I struggled to put it up as the rain pelted down on us. All three of us were soaked. The roof was not to protect us but the radio. If the radio failed, then we would not be able to get word back to the tanks.

"How is it, Fletcher?"

"I think we managed to stop the worst of it, sir. I'll have a butcher's when it is daylight."

The rain was our friend for it kept the few people who might have been out, indoors. The canvas also disguised our shape. We looked a little more like a Kubelwagen. We covered the seventy odd miles in just over two hours.

We headed for Luipegem. It was a huddle of houses not far from the Scheldt. More importantly there was a road which led to the Scheldt and passed alongside the forest. Once we had passed the houses I intended to disappear into the woods. By my watch, it was after midnight when we passed through the sleeping Belgians. The road was very small and I was looking for a track. Beaumont slowed down. "There sir. I can see a gap in the hedge."

When we stopped, I saw that it was not a gate but it was an open field which lay next to the forest. We drove across it. "Take it steady, Beaumont. Drive along the furrows. It might disguise our presence. But slowly eh? I don't want to get bogged down."

"Right sir."

There was no path between the trees but there was a gap big enough for the jeep. We headed gingerly, north towards the Scheldt. After ten minutes I decided we had come far enough. "We will stop here."

When Sergeant Poulson climbed out I said. "Set up camp here. I am going back for a recce. I want to see our tracks."

The rain was still bouncing down but the canopy of leaves above us absorbed most of it. When I reached the edge of the forest, however, I saw that the field was rapidly becoming a quagmire. In the fifteen or so minutes since we had passed it the heavens had opened. There would be no sign of our passing. On the other side of the coin, however, we would find it hard moving across such a muddy landscape.

Once I reached the camp I saw that my resourceful men had managed to get a fire going. "That is impressive."

Emerson shook his head, "Fletcher wasted some of our petrol sir! We might need every drop we can get."

"We will steal some. A fire is more important. Fletcher, radio. Hay, tea!"

I rummaged around in my Bergen for my notebook. When we had been putting the roof up it had been thrown around. I began to write what we had seen. It was good news for we had seen few German vehicles and German soldiers had been confined to the larger towns.

Fletcher gave me the thumbs up. The radio worked. He put on the headphones and began to speak. He put his thumb up again and I gave him the report to dictate. When he finished, he said, "They are really moving, sir. They were north east of Arras. The Major seemed pleased that we had not met much. His operator reminded us about the bridges."

"That is tomorrow's task. We will have some food and then get some shuteye. We won't bother with sentries. Just rig a couple of booby traps a hundred yards into the forest, Beaumont. We will disarm them before we leave."

"How long are we here for then, sir?"

"Until the armour gets here. They might be here as early as the day after tomorrow. They have made good time up to now."

Beaumont returned half an hour later. "I spread six of them out, sir. I will lead tomorrow. It would be daft if we blew ourselves up eh sir?"

I took the opportunity to change out of wet underwear and socks. I placed the wet ones by the fire. They would dry out. Sleep would be uncomfortable as the ground was damp. We used our waterproof capes as a ground sheet and managed as best we could. Although I fell asleep quickly enough my mind was full of the operation and I awoke before dawn. I got the fire going again and put on a dixie of water for some tea. My socks and underwear had dried and I packed them in my Bergen. We would not be taking our Bergens. I wanted us light and mobile. I would take grenades, my pistols and my binoculars. They would hang from my battle jerkin.

Early the next morning we prepared to leave. I wanted to be out at first light. We needed daylight to examine the bridges. We left the radio in the camp with Fletcher. He was not happy but I pointed out that the last thing we needed was for anything to happen to the radio. I led them to the river. My intention was to walk down the river bank until we came to the Rupel. We would approach the bridges from the Antwerp side.

We did not have far to travel. Half a mile from our camp we discovered the canal which ran alongside the Rupel. There was enough cover there to allow us to see that there was a lock at the mouth of the canal. There was no lock keeper's house and it looked to be unguarded. I saw some discarded crates and a coil of rope some bargee had left there. Seeing no one on the opposite bank I ran across the lock gates and we threw myself on the ground on the other side. Waving my men forward I scanned the opposite bank I could see the Rupel to our left. Ahead of me was scrub land. I could see no sign of habitation nor activity. More importantly there was no sign of military activity.

I turned to my men. "Follow me and move quickly. Five seconds between each man."

I rose and ran, crouching. My eyes moved from side to side the whole time. It did not matter if I tripped. Lying flat I would be harder to see. Speed was more important. I saw, ahead, that the land narrowed until there was just a thirty yard strip of land between the canal and the river. The river side had bushes and trees. There was no one there to spy us. The river and canal traffic was also absent. Then I saw, half a mile ahead, the railway line. When we were three hundred yards from it I heard a train. We threw ourselves into the scrubby long grass. I kept my face buried in the earth until the sound of the train disappeared in the distance.

"Let's go."

We rose and ran to the railway line. It was single track. We were safe for a short time. We scrambled over it and I saw that there was a gasworks and a factory on the other side of the river. A cinder track ran along the side of the river on the canal side. We ran towards the cinder track. There were enough trees there to give us cover. We dropped behind the trees and into whatever cover we could find. I took out the binoculars. I had a good view of the railway bridges. There were two: one across the canal and one across the river. The river bridge was longer. I used the binoculars to scan the river bridge. I could see the explosives under the central spans and the leads which ran up to the guardrail and thence towards Boom, in the distance.

I turned and looked at the canal bridge. I could not see any leads on the guardrail but I had to be sure. "Sergeant, take Emerson and Hay. Go to the canal railway bridge and see if there are any explosives. Then go down to the road bridge over the canal and check that for explosives too. I will meet you back here."

"Sir."

"With me, Beaumont." Before I left I scanned the other side of the river with my glasses. The gasworks and the factory appeared to be busy. However, there appeared to be neither windows nor observers on the river side. We ran down the cinder track. I could see the bridge. I wanted to get closer to it. Half way along we stopped. I used the binoculars. I saw that the bridge was mined. I saw the cables on the guard rail but I could only see explosives on one span. We had to get closer. There was only three or four hundred yards between the two bridges.

Forty yards from the Pont Van Enschodt was a piece of cleared ground. I threw myself to the ground just shy of it. I wriggled my way to the river and, peering through the grass and reeds, checked out the bridge. I had been right. They had only mined one span.

"Beaumont, keep your eyes open. I am going to get closer."

I began to crawl towards the road and the bridge. When I neared the road, I saw that there were people walking towards the bridge. It was early. Were they on their way to work? I crawled back to the safety of the hide where Beaumont waited. I took off my battledress and holster. I handed my binoculars to him. I had my Luger in one pocket and my sap in the other. My dagger was still strapped to my leg.

"Wait here."

"Where are you off to sir?"

"A little stroll amongst the locals."

"Be careful sir."

"I may be some time. If you hear firing, then get back to the clearing and tell Sergeant Poulson he is in command."

"Sir."

Instead of crawling back towards the road I crouched and ran a little way back down the cinder track. Then I rose and walked up towards the canal bank. I walked along the canal bank with my hands in my pockets. I tried to be as casual as possible. As I approached the road I saw two women pushing bicycles. They had sacks hanging from them. I guessed they were farm produce; either vegetables or cheese. The two looked to be young women in their early twenties. Their red hands bespoke hard work. I joined the road and walked just twenty yards behind them. I did not look back. That would have raised suspicion. The problem I had was that it was a little chilly and I was dressed in just my shirt and trousers. The rain had stopped but there was still a cold wind blowing. I looked under dressed. It could not be helped.

There were few people coming the other way. There was a slight bend to the road but, as we neared the bridge, I saw that the bridge was guarded. There was a moveable barbed wire barrier and Germans. It was too late now to turn around. That would have looked suspicious. Instead I hurried forward to catch up to the two women. As I neared the rear of their bicycles they looked around. I smiled at them. They looked at me and then turned around and carried on walking. If they were collaborators, then it would be capture and the Gestapo for me.

I forced myself to do my job and analyse what I saw. There were two machine guns; one on each side. It looked to be two sections of Germans. There was a gap between the barbed wire but it was only large enough for one vehicle at a time and it was angled to make any vehicle have to turn. Thankfully there did not appear to be any check on people. The Germans did not even look at us as we approached. I saw that these were not young men. They had the world weary look of men who have served some time. They had a fire going and a pot of coffee on it. That appeared to be their priority.

As we began to cross the bridge I breathed a sigh of relief. The relief was tinged with the worry of how I would get back. I was desperate to turn around to see if anyone followed me but that would have been a mistake. Suddenly one of the women spoke English, "English or American?"

I hesitated but briefly, "English. Commandos."

"You stand out. You should have a jacket."

"I know."

"Are you alone?"

"For the moment, yes."

"Are you an escaped prisoner of war?"

"No." Until I knew more I would keep my answers monosyllabic but I was hopeful that I would have some help.

"They sometimes ask questions on the other side. Do you speak Dutch?"

"Just German or French."

"If we are asked anything then speak French. I will say you are from the south. You live in Diksmuide. You are my cousin. Here, push my bicycle."

I took the handlebars and pushed. I could now see that there was a tower just beyond the bridge and it afforded a fine view down the bridge and the road beyond. They would easily spot any advancing tanks. I needed to get closer to the tower to see if they controlled the explosives. As we passed the mined section I saw the cables which ran to the Boom side of the bridge. There were more trenches and Germans on the other side of the bridge. I saw a German scrutinising the faces of those who crossed. I knew that the worst thing I could do was to avoid eye contact. I affected a neutral expression. Suddenly I found myself linked by the woman who spoke English. She began to speak Dutch to me and when I turned she was smiling at me. I smiled back and just said, "Merci." She giggled as though I had said something funny.

We were nearing the man who was watching faces. The woman spoke again and pulled me a little tighter and so I laughed. Then we were through and I was in Boom. I glanced down at the cables and saw that they led to a sandbagged concrete pill box. They did not lead to the tower which was some fifty yards away.

I had a dilemma. I had seen all that I had needed to see but I could not go directly back. That would look suspicious. The Dutch girl made the decision for me by gripping my arm tightly and propelling me into the town. She turned us down a road which ran parallel to the river. I saw that it was called the Windstraat. Then we turned left. The two young women had been chattering away in Dutch since we had left the bridge. I recognised the odd word. 'English' and 'Commando' were two of them. I was in their hands now.

I saw a market being set up ahead of us. It now became clear that the two young women were bringing farm produce to be sold. A white haired man frowned when he saw me with the two young women. The one who spoke English relinquished her hold on me and went to speak to the man. He seemed satisfied and he smiled. He held out his hand and said, quietly, in English, "Welcome!"

The woman said, "We can talk here. My uncle has heard that the British are coming. The resistance has been alerted but we did not expect them until tomorrow at the earliest."

"I am reconnaissance. I came to see if the bridge was mined and it is."

"My name is Anne and this is Elsa, my cousin. Come there is a café nearby. We will have coffee and then go back."

"Why not now?"

"We do this each market day and the sentries will be suspicious if we return too quickly with you. Besides, my uncle will get you a hat and a jacket to disguise you."

They laid their bicycles against the market stall and led me to a smoky café. The tables inside were full for there was a chill in the air but we found a table outside. A waiter came to take the order and Anne rattled off what we wanted. He returned inside and Anne leaned in conspiratorially.

"What is your name, Englishman?"

"Tom Harsker."

"You are a brave man. You were willing to risk walking through Germans without papers. Or perhaps you are foolish eh?"

I smiled, "I take risks but I have done this before."

"We have heard of the Commandos. The Germans both hate and fear you. We have a section of German soldiers who guard the crossroads close to our farm. They often speak of the men with the daggers."

"Where is your farm?"

"Four kilometres from the bridge. We are on the road from Breendonk and close to the cross roads."

"How many Germans are there?"

"Just twelve. They have seven tents that they use. We only have two rooms. I think they thought about taking over the house but, in the end, they put up their tents."

"Have they been there long?"

"The ones at the farm arrived in July. They man a machine gun. They built a concrete shelter for the gun when they first arrived. My mother says it will make a useful store when the war is over."

"And your father?"

Her face clouded, "He was killed when the Germans invaded. He was part of the army which tried to stop them."

The coffee arrived and, as Anne, took out her purse, I shook my head and brought out a handful of notes and coins. She smiled and chose the French coins. She handed them to the waiter who grinned and gave me a wink.

Anne said, "Do not worry about, Albert. He is in the resistance." She nodded at the market. "Most of the people you see are loyal. We know who the collaborators are. When the war is over they will reap their reward."

Her words chilled me. I had seen French women in Caen with their heads shaved. They had been driven from the town. No-one had any time for such traitors. I sipped the coffee. My men would have hated it. The only coffee they enjoyed was milky and sweetened. This was strong and black. I enjoyed it. We stopped talking, as did everyone else, when the German patrol marched down the street. After they had gone Anne said, "They are going to the bridge. During the day they double the guards there. We know the Germans here. They arrived when they invaded and they have stayed here ever since. They have grown fat on Belgian beer. Some of them have taken Belgian women. That will be remembered." Her words were, once again, cold. She drained her coffee. "Come, we can go."

When we reached the market stall where her uncle was serving he handed me a dirty, dark blue jacket which had seen better days and a crumpled flat cap. It was the sort my granddad had worn. I donned them both. Her uncle shook my hand.

I said, in French, which I guessed he would understand, "We are coming. Soon you will be free once more." He nodded and his eyes began to fill.

"Tom, you push the bicycle and I will be your cousin again."

The streets were busier now and when we reached the bridge I saw that they had added firepower. They were now setting up two new machine guns; one on each side. If the general populace knew that the British were coming, then it was obvious that the Germans would too. The officer who had scrutinised us as we had first crossed glanced at the girls and the bicycles and then returned to his conversation. I saw that the gasworks and the factory hid the cinder track from the bridge and the tower. If the tanks approached that way, then they would be invisible until the actual bridge. The Sherman was fast enough to race across the mined section and reach the command post. I had seen no anti-tank guns. Machine guns would not stop a Firefly.

When we reached the other side of the bridge Anne gripped my arm in case I tried to slip away. She did not relinquish it until we had crossed the bridge over the canal. Then she stopped. She turned and pointed up the road. "The Germans cannot see us here. The bend in the road and the buildings hide us. Our farm is at the next crossroads."

"The tanks will be here soon. If there are Germans at the farm, then you will be in danger."

She shrugged, "We are always in danger but I thank you. We will not stay if there is fighting."

"You say I am brave but I think you have far more courage." I leaned down to kiss her on the cheek. She put her hand to her cheek and then grabbed me and kissed me full on the lips.

"Be safe, Englishman!"

With that the two of them turned and left me. I walked over the bridge noting that there were no explosives. Sergeant Poulson would have seen that but what he would not have seen was the fact that the tanks could cross this bridge and, if they headed left to the railway line, then they could cross to the bridge undetected. I had the information that Major Dunlop and Colonel Silvertop would need. I strolled down the road and then ducked into the undergrowth to my left. I crawled the last part to where Beaumont waited.

"Strewth sir, you had me worried. I thought you were in the bag. What happened?"

"I will tell you later. Come on let's get back to the others. I think Sergeant Poulson will be even more worried than you." I quickly changed back into my battledress and beret. I took the jacket and hat with me. Who knew when I might need them again. We scurried down the cinder track more confidently for I knew that we could not be seen.

Sergeant Poulson looked like a mother whose daughter has come back late from a night out. "Sir! Where have you been? It has been hours."

"Wait until we are back in camp and I will tell all. I have vital information for the tanks."

I led them back to the canal lock. It was later now and there were more people about on the other side of the river. We dared not risk running across the lock gates. We would be seen. I crawled to the edge and saw a metal ladder going down each side. I rolled over and climbed down a couple of feet. Turning, so that my back was to the ladder, I threw myself at the ladder, eight feet away on the other side. I managed to catch hold of a rung although I scraped my hand as I did so. I climbed up to the top and, rolling over, found the rope I had spied before. I climbed back down and said, "Sergeant Poulson, catch this rope and tie it off on the ladder." I tied it to my side and then the men climbed over using the rope.

Half an hour later Beaumont led us through his booby traps to the camp.

Fletcher was waiting with a gun pointed into the woods. He was smoking a cigarette, "Next time, lads, let me know you will be late after a night on the tiles! Your mam was worried!"

Chapter 4

While Fletcher set up the radio I told the others what I had learned.

Sergeant Poulson nodded when I had finished, "Yes, sir, we found that they had not mined the bridges as well. We were worried that we might be seen by the civilians but it seems we had no need."

"I am not certain. The two ladies suggested that, while most of the Belgians and Dutch are loyal, there are some who are not. I was just lucky."

Fletcher waved and said, "Got them, sir. They are just down the road at a place called Wolvertem."

"Good. Here is what I discovered."

I told Fletcher what to say and when I had finished he said, "That sounds good to him, sir. But he is worried that the Germans at the crossroads might alert the bridge."

"Tell him that we can show him a way to get close to the Germans without being seen. We need to rendezvous with them."

He spoke into the microphone and then nodded, "Major Dunlop asked if we could meet them down the road. They will leave at dawn. What is this place where the Germans have a pill box sir?"

I grabbed my map, "Tell him a couple of miles from Breendonk."

He repeated my words and then said, "He wants to know if we can disable the machine gun, sir?"

I did not like endangering the two girls and their family but the attack came first. "Tell him yes."

When he had finished reporting I said, "Get your heads down. We will leave just after dark. I will need to warn this Belgian family of the danger so that they can leave."

"Isn't that risky sir? What if Jerry rumbles. They might bring reinforcements down."

"Then I will have to make sure that does not happen." I spent the half hour while we prepared food and ate thinking of a safe way to do this and I could only come up with one. It was risky but I did not think we had a choice.

Beaumont disarmed our booby traps and we loaded up the jeeps. "We only have enough fuel for twenty or so miles sir."

"That should be fine. We are meeting up with the Shermans. Either they will have petrol or we can cadge a lift." Private Emerson nodded. He was not happy but he would live with it. He liked a full fuel tank. He worried about the bottom of a tank fouling the spark plugs. "Now my plan is to hide the two jeeps just down the road from the farm. I seem to remember seeing a half destroyed house. That should make good cover. Fletcher, you will need to come with us. We will need the radio. That makes you Tail End Charlie. When we are within sight of the farm then you hide. I will don a disguise and head down to the farmhouse. I will get back to you when it is safe. We take out the Germans."

"How sir?" Lance Sergeant Hay asked, "I mean kill them or just incapacitate them?"

"Good point. If this attack fails, then I don't want any repercussions for the farm. We try to do it without killing but if we have to then we shoot. Those of us who have Colts with silencers will do the shooting. We are too close to the bridge to risk them hearing firing."

Sergeant Poulson asked, "Sir, what if they take you? What do we do then?"

"You carry on with the mission. Those in the farm and I will have to take ourchances."

"Righto sir. I just wanted to be clear." I could rely on my sergeant. He was like my right arm.

We drove the reverse route out of the farm. Luipegem was not asleep as we passed through. There were two men smoking pipes outside one of their homes. They stared at us as we passed. I waved at them. "That's blown it, sir."

"Not necessarily, Fletcher. Besides it couldn't be helped."

Night had fallen when we reached the road leading to the bridge over the canal. We turned right and drove slowly down the road. This was the riskiest part of the whole mission. I knew that it was a busy road and well-used by Germans. Lady Luck was on our side. We saw no Germans. In fact, we saw no one. Beaumont pulled in behind the half damaged building. We quickly covered the two vehicles with camouflage netting and bits of debris. I was satisfied that only a close examination in daylight would reveal them. Fletcher hoisted the radio on his back and we set off down the road.

It would, largely, be guesswork which led us to the farm. There were no signs nor were there mileposts. When I estimated that we were half a mile or so away I stopped the section and waved them behind the overgrown wall which abutted the road. I took out the binoculars. It was dark but I was looking for the tell-tale light of a brazier. It was September and the nights were drawing in. It was cold. I spied it as soon as I looked south. The glow was like a beacon. The farm was a dark shape to the right. I estimated it to be six hundred yards away. We would not be overheard.

I took off my battle dress and beret then I donned my disguise. I handed my weapons to Bill Hay. He smiled, "You be careful eh, sir? We are too close to the end of the war for any heroics and, besides, you have all the fruit salad you can carry!"

"I thought Fletcher was my mother!" I turned to Emerson, "Freddie have you still got those god awful German cigarettes?"

"Aye sir. I have a packet left. I keep them for emergencies. So far I haven't been that desperate."

"Well, light one for me and then give me the rest of the packet."

"You don't smoke sir."

"I know Beaumont but the Germans do."

Fred lit one and handed it to me. I kept it in between my forefinger and thumb trying to adopt the cupped posture that sentries used when trying to avoid being seen smoking. I shook my head, "I don't know how you lads smoke. Just holding it turns my stomach." He put the packet in my jacket pocket.

Fletcher said, "Practice sir, lots of practice!"

I headed for the German post. I guessed that a sharp eyed German would spot the glowing butt of my cigarette as I swung my cupped hand. I didn't want to alarm them. I needed them to see me before I saw them. I heard voices ahead and I lifted the cigarette and hung it between my lips. I just let it rest there. Suddenly a German voice ordered me to put my hands in the air. I took the opportunity of throwing the cigarette to the ground and then said, in French, "I am just visiting my cousin Anne in the farm!"

A light was brought close to my face. There were four Germans and they had guns pointing at me. "Anne? And what is her cousin called?"

I smiled, "The lovely Elsa! Are they at home?" As I answered I checked the position of the tents and the machine gun. I saw barbed wire and trenches too. When we came to take them it was vital that I knew where everything was.

The sergeant said, in German, "Let him visit. He looks harmless. If anything he looks simple to me."

Another German said, in French, "You can go in but first, have you any cigarettes?"

I affected an outraged expression, "I only have a few left!" He snapped his fingers and held out his palm. "This is not fair. Leave me one, at least!" I handed over the packet. He took one out and gave it to me. I put it behind my ear as I had seen my men do. I turned and walked up the path to the farm house. I noticed that it had seen better days. It looked as though some bomb damage had taken out some outbuildings. It explained why the Germans did not want it. I saw that the road which led to the crossroads was alongside the south side of their home.

I knocked on the door. Anne opened it. There was surprise on her face and then she said, loudly, "Cousin! How nice to see you. This is a surprise. Come in. Mother, it is cousin Jean from Diksmuide." She hurried me and then slammed the door shut. "What has happened?"

"Tomorrow the tanks will be here. I came to give you warning so that you could leave."

Anne shook her head, "If the end of the war is close then we will stay. We do not want our belongings taken. We have seen it happen before. What are you going to do?"

"We are going to disarm these Germans and wait for the tanks."

"Then we will be safe here."

"No, for if the attack fails then there might be repercussions."

"We stay."

"Is there a cellar here?"

"Of course. It is where we store our wine and our hams."

"Then go there until the fighting is over. Please, I beg of you."

She smiled and shook her head, "You are an odd soldier! You are nothing like the Germans. Very well but you must tell us as soon as it is safe to come out."

"I will. Is there a back door?"

"Come, it is close to the cellar door." She led me to the back. I saw that the back door and the cellar door were at right angles to each other. As I opened the door she said, "Be careful!"

Stepping out into the dark I reflected that everyone but me seemed concerned with my well-being.

I slipped out of the lit kitchen and into the black of night. I made my way around the damaged outbuildings and headed back to my men. I did not use the road. A Commando is like a cat at night. He can move in the dark without being seen and without being heard. Beaumont, however, heard me; I realised that I must have been careless. I heard the safety slip off the Colt as I stepped behind the jeep.

"The family is safe. There are four German soldiers watching the road south. The rest are sitting around the brazier or sleeping. I didn't see any field telephone. Fletcher, leave the radio here. We will need all of us for this." I took off my coat and hat and began to dress. "Fletcher, you and Emerson take the Thompsons. I think the sight of those will cow them. Hay and Beaumont; I want you to slip around the far side of the farmhouse. Use the reverse of my route. It will bring you to the road from the west. I want you two to sneak up on the men watching the crossroads. Wait until you hear me order them to surrender before you appear. If they think we will shoot them if they disobey then we might be able to pull this off. If not..." I tapped the barrel of the silenced Colt. "Right Hay and Beaumont, off you go."

I gave them a five minute start and then we left. This time there was no glow from a cigarette to give me away and we kept to the side of the road. Sergeant Poulson and I were in the middle. I could rely on the other two to flank them and cover us at the same time. I heard the Germans as they talked. They were playing cards and money was involved. The light from the brazier showed where they were and the darkness hid us. I spied the sergeant. He was close to the brazier and he was reading by its light.

We moved purposefully but we were silent and we used the shadows as cover. When I stepped quickly into the light my Colt was instantly pressed against the side of the sergeant's head. "Nobody move and you will all live!"

I heard, from ahead of me, "And that goes for you four too! Hands up and move towards the light." I heard a 'phut' as Bill fired a warning shot into the ground and then the four Germans walked towards us. I gestured for them to raise their hands and then there were two ominous clicks as Emerson and Fletcher cocked their Thompsons. I think that they had been unaware of them until that moment.

The sergeant undid his belt and dropped his pistol, "Do as they say. They are Commandos. They will slit our throats as soon as look at us." He glared at me as he said it.

I gave him a thin smile, "Having seen your S.S. at work I feel like a choirboy in comparison. Tell your men to take off their boots."

"Our boots?"

"I want to make sure that none of you run off. In the night."

He nodded, "Boots off."

"Freddie collect the weapons. Beaumont take Fletcher's Thompson. Fletcher fetch the radio."

I looked at my watch. It was one o'clock in the morning. This would be a long night. When the weapons were all safely gathered, I said, "Now sit around the fire. I wouldn't want your little feet to get cold." I saw that there was a large pot of water bubbling on a second brazier. "When Fletcher gets back we might as well have a brew."

The Germans outnumbered us but these troops were not front line troops. I guessed, from their uniforms, that they had been garrison troops. They were outmatched by us. To be fair to them if I was in their position with two machine guns facing me then I might obey too. Fletcher returned with the radio and set it up. None of us moved from the circle of guns we held on the prisoners. I admired the sergeant; he picked up his book and began to read again.

"What is the book, sergeant?"

"A Farewell to Arms. It seems appropriate somehow."

I nodded, "I met Hemingway; we all did. He was with us when we took Paris."

The sergeant laid down his book. He looked to be about the same age as Reg Dean, "You are lucky. I would like to have met him. He is a man. He writes like a warrior."

"He certainly does." The sergeant nodded and I added, "You and your men will not be harmed, sergeant. You will become prisoners of war. Despite what you have heard we do not kill for pleasure."

"No, but you do kill and kill very well."

I pointed to the book, "This is war and in wars, men die."

"That is true."

"Got 'em sir. They had to wake the Major up."

"Tell him that we hold the crossroads."

"That all sir?"

"That's all he needs to know."

Fletcher spoke into the microphone. Then he said, "Major Dunlop is bringing an armoured car and two Shermans ahead of the rest of the column. He will be here in two hours sir."

"Good then we have time for that cup of tea. Come on Freddie!"

"Coming right up sir. I had to let it brew a while. It's not right if it isn't stewed!"

Emerson brought the tea around. He had made enough for the Germans although some chose not to drink it. As we were drinking it the sergeant said, "The family in the farm; you warned them?"

There was little to be gained from lying. "I did. I did not want civilians harmed. If you had fought...."

He nodded, "That was kind of you."

"And now that you have reminded me I will get them from the cellar. They should not be deprived of their beds, even if we are." I stood. "By the way sergeant, my men speak German. No tricks."

"Of course not. I surrendered. I will not go back on my word. It is against the Geneva Convention."

"Sergeant Poulson, take charge. I won't be long."

I went through the front door and into the farm. I went to the cellar door and opened it. I shouted into the darkness, "You can come out Anne. We have captured them without injuries."

I waited until they ascended and then headed back to the front door.

"It is over?"

"This part is. The tanks will be here in less than two hours and then it will be. At least I hope it will be."

We heard the three vehicles as they trundled up the road. We still looked around expectantly. It could have been German tanks but the Sherman has a distinctive sound. They pulled up outside the farm and Major Dunlop clambered out. He grinned and pumped my arm, "Well done, old boy! You have done better than I hoped. The rest of the column will be an hour behind us. The Colonel asked me to make sure we capture the bridge intact. If we wait for daylight, we risk Jerry aeroplanes."

"Right sir." I turned to my men, "Emerson, Beaumont, fetch the jeeps." "Sir!"

"We will only take one jeep. Sergeant Poulson you and the rest of the men can guard the prisoners until infantry arrive. I will take Beaumont."

"Right sir."

Major Dunlop lit a cigarette, "You were unduly modest the other day weren't you?"

"What do mean sir?"

"A V.C. and M.C. Someone had heard of you and your exploits. Damned impressive and you are so young."

"The medals don't make me do my job any better sir. I will enjoy them when the war is over."

I heard the sound of the jeeps as they returned. I walked over to the German sergeant and shook his hand, "I am sorry we had to meet under these circumstances. I think in peace time we might have got on."

He nodded, "At least this way my men and I may get a chance to enjoy the peace. I fear many of my comrades will not. I think, Captain, that, like Hemingway, you too are a warrior."

I climbed aboard the jeep and said, "Nice and steady, Roger. We have tanks for company!"

"Right sir. Then I might as well use the headlights eh? They will hear us coming."

"No keep them off. The sound will be distorted but the headlights will mark our position." As we drove up the road I saw the sky becoming lighter to our right. Lights would soon be unnecessary. While we drove, I put spare magazines in my pockets and hung grenades from my webbing. I took the silencer from the Colt. We would not need silence.

When we reached the road to the railway bridge we halted and I went back to explain to Major Dunlop what we intended. He nodded, "Lieutenant Maguire is in the armoured car. As soon as we get to the bridge he will race across to this command post you mentioned and stop them setting off the charges."

"Right sir. It will be daylight by then."

"I know. We had better get a move on then, eh Captain."

"Right sir." Having just two of us in the jeep meant more room for us and I picked up my Thompson and cocked it. "Right Beaumont. Along the cinder track and you can use all the power we have." I pushed the folding windscreen flat and laid my Thompson across the bonnet. We were the leading vehicle and when the Germans opened fire I expected us to draw the lion's share of the bullets.

We drove down to the bridge and then turned right to reach the river and the cinder track. The weak sun was bright enough to show us what lay ahead but not to blind us. It seemed impossible that the Germans would not see us. The tanks threw up clouds of dust but then I remembered that we were hidden by the buildings on the side of the river.

When we neared the Germans at the end of the bridge I saw them jump up and point their weapons at us. I fired the Thompson from side to side. I soon emptied the magazine and I jammed another in just as Beaumont threw the jeep to the left and the tyres screamed as we left the cinder and hit the tarmac. He managed, somehow, to make the gap between the barbed wire. The sides of the jeep smashed into the wood and pushed them to the side. Bullets began to smack into the vehicle as the Germans we had passed tried to hit us.

"Go, go!"

Behind me I heard the machine gun on the armoured car as it kept down the heads of the Germans who had recovered from the shock of our arrival. Suddenly the jeep slewed to the side.

"Sir! We have lost a tyre."

"To the side and bail out! Follow me."

Grabbing my Thompson I jumped from the jeep. Ahead of me I saw that the Germans on the far side had seen us. We did not have long. I saw the cables leading to the demolitions. They were just twenty yards away. As the German machine guns and rifles opened fire I ran crouching towards them. In the half dark of dawn I was difficult to see. Behind me I heard the sound of the machine guns from the Shermans and armoured car as they fired at the defenders. There was a crack as the tanks' guns fired. I had no time to look at its effect. I reached the wires, and putting the Thompson down, I took my dagger and, lifting the first cables, tore the sharp blade through them. I turned and saw that Beaumont had gone to the far side of the bridge.

Picking up my Thompson I ran to the next cables and repeated my action. The Shermans rumbled past me. I saw, from the corner of my eye, that the armoured car was almost at the barrier on the far side. Its two pounder fired at the command post at almost point blank range. It was well made. The gun barely made an impact but I knew that the concussion would have incapacitated those inside. I reached the last cables and I severed them. The bridge was now safe but we had just an armoured car and two Shermans to hold it until the main column arrived.

The three armoured vehicles had formed an arrow at the end of the bridge and were engaging the Germans. I ran up to the left hand Sherman and took shelter behind it. I saw that the concrete command post was resisting the fire of the armoured car and the tanks. I also spotted that there was a slit and the shells had enlarged it. Taking a grenade, I left the shelter of the tank and sprinted across the body littered ground to the concrete command post twenty yards away. I bore a charmed life. The smoke from the guns helped to obscure me although what I was doing seemed impossible. I threw myself at the base of the post and took the pin from the grenade. As I looked up I saw the face of the driver of Major Dunlop's tank through his slit. A thumb came up. I slid my back up the bullet pocked concrete and when the top of my head was level with the slit I released the handle and threw the grenade inside. I dropped to the ground and covered my ears.

The sound of the explosion was muffled but I saw pieces of shrapnel flying out of the slit and heard the shouts from within. Grabbing my Thompson I rose and ran around to the back of the post. I reached it as the blast door was opened and the three survivors, blood pouring from their wounds staggered out coughing and spluttering. Blood str eamed from hands and faces where shrapnel had torn into them.

I shouted, in German, "Hands up!"

Stunned and shocked they obeyed. I heard the rumble of the tanks as they moved forward. The two machine guns sprayed the road ahead. I saw grey uniforms running up the Windstraat. We held the bridge.

The hatch on the Sherman opened and Major Dunlop's head appeared, "You are as mad as a fish Captain but thank God you are on our side!" He pointed behind him. "Lieutenant Colonel Silvertop is ten minutes away. We have done it!"

Just then we heard the sound of a loud explosion. The other bridge had been blown. I looked up at the Major, "But only just sir!"

Chapter 5

Beaumont wandered over. I saw that he had a cut to his cheek from fragments of stone. "That was exciting, sir!"

"I know. I half expected the bridge to go up when we cut the cables."

"They were slow, sir. If I had been in charge, then I would have blown the bridge as soon as I saw the jeep."

As we wandered back to the jeep I said, "I think they were complacent. That girl, Anne, told me that these soldiers have been here since the invasion. They weren't ready to fight. We haven't stopped since the war started. These Germans were a blade which had become dulled and rusted. If we have the same opposition in Antwerp, then this might be easier than we thought."

I saw the column of tanks. They had not taken the cinder track. They were coming down the road and I saw that the other jeep was leading them. We reached our jeep and Beaumont set to work on the wrecked tyre. We had one spare and that was all. Emerson pulled the overcrowded jeep up leaving plenty of room for the tanks to get by.

"When we heard the explosion, we thought you had been blown up too."

"No Sergeant, we were lucky."

Beaumont didn't lift his head as he said, "The captain rode his luck again Sarge, took out the command post with a grenade."

I heard the tanks ahead as they began to move off. They could now begin to clear the town and prepare for the advance on Antwerp. With Emerson helping we soon had the tyre changed. Fletcher had the radio going. He had been listening to the chatter between the tanks. "They are pushing on, sir but there is some resistance around the main square. They have asked for infantry support. It is still on the road, sir."

"We were still infantry the last time I looked. Come on lads let's get back into the war. Fletcher tell them the Commandos are on their way."

As we drove I took out the rest of my grenades and ammunition from my Bergen. I would soon need it. We easily overtook Colonel Silvertop's Shermans and reached the armoured car. They had suffered the same fate as us and had a puncture. Lieutenant Maguire said, "They are using the narrow streets to slow us down, sir. The Major is reluctant to use the big guns to fire at the buildings. He is not certain if there are civilians inside."

"Right. We did this at Normandy. Sergeant Poulson you take your men up the left hand alley. Fletcher and Beaumont come with me."

I led the two of them to the right hand side of the Sherman. I saw that Germans had occupied the upper floors and there was a hastily erected barricade blocking one of the streets leading from it. The café was the obvious target. There would be a back door and an alley. If we went through it we could flank those in the alley. The problem was crossing the killing zone of the square. I shouted towards the driver's visor. "Give us some covering fire to help us reach the café!"

I heard a voice shout, "Righto sir!"

The heavy machine gun's bullets smacked into the café and we ran. We did not run in a straight line but crabbed across the open square. My Thompson was ready to fire but I was looking for a target. The machine gun's bullets had shattered the window and only the frame remained. I hurled myself at it and it shattered. Bullets smacked into the door and I fired a burst from my Thompson. Then Fletcher fired and I heard a cry as he shot the German.

"Upstairs sir?"

"No Beaumont. The tanks can deal with that. Straight out of the back and then down the alley to the right."

We ran past the bottom of the stairs leading to the upper floors. I saw Scouse pull the pin from a grenade. As we ran into the cooking part of the café he hurled it and shouted, "Grenade!"

We did not break stride. In five seconds you can cover a lot of ground. We had just burst into the back yard when the grenade went off. The concussion brought a shower of dust through the open door. Reaching the gate, I opened it. I could hear a machine gun to my right. I peered out. I saw ten Germans hunkered behind the barricade. I turned to my two men and held up my left hand twice to tell them how many men there were. I pointed to the grenades on Beaumont and Fletcher's webbing. They nodded. I opened the gate and then leapt out. I emptied the magazine at the barricade. My two men were out almost as soon as I was and the two grenades sailed the twenty yards to the Germans. The three of us threw ourselves to the ground and covered our ears. The narrow alley channelled the explosion. As we raised our heads I saw that my bullets and the grenades had cleared the obstacle. The Germans were finished. I heard explosions from the far side.

"Let's go back and make sure that the café is cleared eh?"

As we went back into the café I saw Germans descending with their hands in the air. Resistance in Boom had ended. We had the town.

The first elements of the Rifle Brigade arrived. They had the prisoners from the farm and quickly organised a search for any more Germans left in the town. The locals poured from the streets to welcome us. I recognised Albert from the café. He had a bottle of brandy in his hand and a handful of cups in the other. He came directly to me. "Thank you! I did not think it would be so fast! We are indebted to you." He would not take no for an answer and the six of us enjoyed a cup of brandy at ten o'clock in the morning. Albert jerked his thumb at the café. "The kitchen is ruined but my friends are bringing hot food from our homes for you! It is the least we could do." He suddenly became serious, "Anne and her family?"

"They are safe, Albert."

43

"Good, I will tell her uncle. George is helping out in the bakery!"

As he went off I heard Major Dunlop, "Tom, have you a minute? The Colonel would like a word."

I handed my half-finished cup to Fletcher. He would see that it was shared out. "Sir."

The Colonel said, "A good job this morning. You have done all that we asked. What are your orders now?"

"Go into Antwerp with you, sir."

"Good, that is what I hoped. G Company of the 8th Battalion Rifle Brigade will be with you but as John here speaks the language and knows the town a little I am sending him and his squadron ahead. We have to wait for the Hussars and the other elements of the Rifles. They are held up at Malines. I want you to clear the way to Antwerp. We need the docks in our hands."

"Yes sir."

"Get some food and then I want you on the road within the hour before Jerry can react to this strike. We have them! By God we have them!"

With that he turned and left the Major and myself. The Major waved over another major. "This is Major Noel Bell of the Rifles. Major, Captain Harsker of the Commandos."

He shook my hand. "Some of your chaps are following in a lorry. Couldn't wait to get here. Speaks volumes about the esprit de corps you have."

I nodded, "Yes sir, they were annoyed to be left behind."

He pointed to the two jeeps. "They are damned handy and damned fast. I take it you will be the scouts?"

I looked at Major Dunlop who nodded, "I think so. We haven't much firepower but we can draw fire."

"No tin lids eh?"

"Never got used to them sir."

Major Dunlop said, "We have less than seven miles to go. In fifty minutes, we go. Are you happy to be leading, Tom?"

"I think so. We have done this before and the last time we didn't have a squadron of Shermans behind us. With your permission sir, we will go and sort out the jeeps."

When I reached the jeeps, I saw Fletcher brandishing a Mauser sniper rifle. "See what I found sir? The machine guns killed the sniper in the café before he could use it." In his other hand, he had a bag. "I also found some food, sir. A shame to let it go to waste."

"A shame indeed, Scouse." I took the rifle and the bandolier of ammunition. "Right lads we have forty five minutes then we lead the column into Antwerp. We will be a little crowded. Fred, did you get the tanks filled up?"

He grinned. "Yes, sir I found a couple of jerricans and they did nicely. I reckon we have another thirty odd miles in the tanks now."

"Good. I want the Bergens strapping over the bonnet to give some protection from the front. We will lead and watch the road. Sergeant Poulson and Lance Sergeant Hay, I want you two and Fletcher to watch the sides." I held up the

Mauser. "If they have one sniper they will have more. Did we get any German grenades?"

Beaumont held up a hessian sack, "Yes sir, I collected twenty from the prisoners and the dead."

"Good, then share them out." He began to do so. "If you need to pee then now would be a good time!"

We were in position before the start time. I had noticed that the Shermans drove with their turrets open and the tank commanders exposed. They were brave men. Lieutenant Maguire said, as we passed him, "If we have another puncture then we have no spare and no inners either."

"Don't worry, Lieutenant, we are so close that we could walk!"

"We are armoured Captain! We never walk!"

Major Dunlop shouted, "Let's go."

"Off we go Beaumont. Put some daylight between us and the tanks. That way we can do our job and spot danger before it happens."

We reached the outskirts of Boom successfully and there was a short patch of open country. It was as we approached the outskirts of Antwerp that we found trouble. Someone had organised a road block and there were Germans on both sides of the road. Amazingly they did not fire at us. That made me think that they had the Panzershreck rocket launchers and were saving them for the tanks.

"Fletcher get on the radio and tell the major I think there are anti-tank guns on the outskirts of Antwerp."

"Sir."

"Beaumont pull over."

As soon as we stopped the Germans opened fire with rifles and sub machine guns. The Bergens absorbed the bullets and we dropped behind the jeep. Scouse was half exposed as he gave the intelligence to the tanks. The other jeep had also stopped and they opened fire. I took the Mauser. I had had no time to adjust the sights but I was a good shot with or without a telescopic sight. I rested the barrel on the bonnet of the jeep. Behind me I heard the armoured car as it advanced. Suddenly there was a flash and a rocket flew towards the armoured car. I fired at the operator. I managed to hit him in the shoulder and the tube fell on our side of the sandbags. As a soldier reached over to retrieve it I shot him too. Even as I fired the armoured car's front was struck and flames leapt up. Lieutenant Maguire would not have to worry about punctured tyres. His crew bailed out but I saw that only two of them had survived. Then there was a crack from Major Dunlop's Sherman and the Germans on the right were hit. The shell damaged the wall behind which crashed down on them. The ones closer to us raised their hands and stepped forward.

"Back in the jeeps! We still have a job to do."

The Germans had done their job well. They had delayed us. As we went further into the city I saw a tram coming towards us. Beaumont said, "What the hell is a tram doing here!"

I caught sight of German uniforms. "It is full of Germans. Stop! Fletcher get on the radio and warn them!"

"I know sir! I am on it."

"Open fire!"

The tram was a hundred and forty yards away but was such a big target that it was worth the risk. I did not bother to leave the vehicle. I rested the Mauser on the Bergens and aimed at the officer who jumped from the tram and began to order his men into the houses. My bullet spun him around. The range was a little too far for accuracy from the Thompsons but the effect of four sub machine guns sending bullets at them made them take cover. I guessed that there were forty men on the tram. They were too many for us but all we had to do was keep their heads down until the tanks arrived. This was where we missed the grenade rifle.

The Germans set up a heavy machine gun which sent bullets towards us. I could not see the gunner and so I sent five rounds towards the machine gun. I must have hit it or one of the gunners for it briefly stopped. Then the machine guns on the turrets and in the cupolas of the tanks began a withering fire. I saw a white flag being waved and shouted, "Cease fire! They have surrendered."

This time we had suffered no casualties.

"Let's go."

I knew, from the buildings around us that we were less than three quarters of a mile from the docks. We were tantalizingly close to our first objective. Three hundred yards later I saw that the two sets of Germans we had met had been sacrificed to buy time to build this road block. The barrels of anti-tank guns as well as barricades were a barrier across the road. Most dangerously I saw the unmistakeable skull and crossbones sign. They had laid a minefield across the street.

As the barrels swung towards us I shouted, "Reverse! Find cover. Fletcher, warn the major."

The two jeeps reversed and we almost made it into a side street. However, Emerson's jeep was struck by a rocket. He was lucky that it only struck the right hand side of the bonnet but that was bad enough. The wheel was destroyed and my three men only saved by their Bergens. They rolled from the stricken jeep which was now burning and hurled themselves after us. We were just twenty yards down the side street when the jeep exploded. Hay and Emerson were thrown from their feet.

Beaumont and I raced to help them up. Fred staggered to his feet, "By hell sir that'll smart in the morning!"

"Are you hurt, Emerson?"

"Something hit me in the back sir. I'll be fine."

I turned him around and saw that a piece of masonry had struck his back. I could see the dust where it had hit. "I think you have been lucky, Freddie. If that had been shrapnel, it might have been worse."

Fletcher said, "Sir, the major said to take cover. They are sending the Rifles up."

"Tell him that we are Commandos and we fight our own battles. Beaumont, see to Freddie. Anyone else hurt?" They shook their heads. "Then let's see what we can do. Bill, see if we can flank them down this side street eh?"

"Right sir."

I slung the Mauser over my shoulder and left the Thompson in the jeep. Bill Hay came rushing back. "You are right sir. There is a building which we can enter and the second floor will let us shoot down into their positions."

"Great! Let's move!"

"Trouble is, sir, if they know we are there then they can send men in after us."

"We will have to make life hard for them then Lance Sergeant. Fletcher, just tell the Major what we are doing and then follow us. Bring all the spare grenades we have."

Sergeant Poulson and I hurried after Bill. There was little damage where we were. We were still far enough away from the docks so that the bombers had not made the landscape desolate. I could not see any people and I assumed they had fled. I hoped so. Bill suddenly darted to the right and disappeared into the back of a two storey building. I had my Colt out in case we saw any enemy but we did not.

We raced up the stairs. I heard footsteps behind me and knew that Fletcher had sent the message and followed. Bill stopped us at the door. "We have to crawl, sir. There are three windows. I thought we could each take one. Jerry is at ten o'clock!"

"Right, I have the Mauser I will take the window furthest from them. Wait for my command to fire. The Rifles will be moving soon. Let's try to disrupt their firing. Fletcher, spread the grenades out."

We flung ourselves to the floor and crawled to the three windows. I did not make the mistake of sticking the barrel of the Mauser out of the window. I moved a chair in front of the window and rested my gun across it. I placed the four grenades Fletcher gave me on the seat and then I looked through the sight. The Germans had a good position and they were there in numbers. I saw the tell-tale pins of the mines forty yards in front of them. They looked dangerously close to us. The Germans had used sandbags and old cars to make the barricade. When the Rifles attacked, there would be a metal barrier before them. They had four 88mm guns as well as smaller anti-tank guns and four rocket launchers. With five machine guns, there would be a killing zone for the Rifles to cross.

I saw a command post. It was nestled next to a building and protected by sandbags. However, I could see the insignia of the officers. There were three of them and a radio operator. I had targets for my first our bullets. The firth was the radio itself. I targeted the most senior officer first.

"When I fire then open up. I will take the command post. Kill the gunners on the machine guns and then the anti-tank weapons."

Fletcher said, "What about when they start firing at us, sir?"

Sergeant Poulson said, "Bite the bullet and take it. We have a job to do, Corporal, and if we don't do it then men will die. There are four of us here. We are Commandos." Sergeant Poulson had grown in the last few years. He was a leader now.

"I just asked Sarge."

They would do their job. I knew that. We were British soldiers and we didn't know how to fail. Even when badly led, as at Balaclava and Isandlwana, the British soldier did his job and died facing the enemy. It was who we were.

With that thought in my mind I squeezed the trigger and then fired a second at the radio operator. My third took out a second officer before the others took cover. My men each threw a grenade and then fired their Thompsons. My next two shots were aimed at the radio. I hit it with both. The ceiling above me was suddenly struck by machine gun bullets and rifle bullets as the enemy sought our position. I had a chair to give me some protection for it was in front of me. I was hard to see. I smashed the porcelain cap of the German grenade, pulled the lanyard and hurled it blindly through the window.

When the grenades went off there was a lull in the firing from below. My men reacted quicker than I did and their Thompsons chattered through the smoke. I heard firing from my right and knew that the Rifles were advancing. The four of us were an itch the Germans could not scratch.

After ramming another magazine into the Mauser I peered through the sight. Smoke obscured the enemy but I was patient. I caught a glimpse of the gunner who was aiming the 88. I squeezed off a shot and then moved my gun slightly and fired four more shots into the smoke. Suddenly the ceiling cascaded down on my head as the Germans launched a rocket through the window and worsened the damage. I was covered in plaster and pieces of the ceiling but none did any damage. We were winning. If they used the rockets against us, then they could not use them against the Shermans.

My men hurled more grenades through the open windows. It was safer than raising their heads and when some of the grenades exploded in the air the metal scythed through the gunners. I reloaded. The sound of Bren guns was reassuring. The Rifles were adding their firepower. I heard a noise behind me. I whipped around with my Luger out. It was Beaumont and Emerson, "Steady sir. We thought we might help!"

"Good lads! Keep your heads down though. Jerry knows we are here."

Beaumont said, "I know sir. I made a couple of booby traps at the two doors." He shrugged. "We will have a little bit of warning at least."

The last remnants of the ceiling were suddenly struck by two more rockets. This time it was wrecked and a large piece of the ceiling fell, missing Bill Hay by inches. "This is getting personal, sir!"

"Right, on my command I want us to lay down a barrage on their positions. As soon as you are empty throw every grenade we have. Let's buy time for the Rifles to get closer." I had four grenades left and I laid them out before me. I cocked my rifle. "Now!" I aimed the gun at the furthest Germans. It was a machine gun crew. I emptied the magazine and then laid down the rifle. I threw

48

the four grenades as far as I could. The German grenades were better suited for throwing in the air and our elevation meant that some of them exploded in the air making air bombs. Beaumont fell clutching his arm.

Fletcher, see to Beaumont!"

"Sir!"

Just then I heard a double explosion downstairs. "Bill with me! Sergeant, keep them pinned down."

I flung open the door and saw the smoke rising from the booby traps they had set off. I still had two Mills bombs. I took them out and laid them before me. Suddenly a fusillade of hopeful shots came up the stairs. They hit neither of us. I took one grenade, pulled the pin and released the handle. I counted to two and then dropped it. Bill had seen me throw the grenade and we both dropped like stones. The grenade exploded half way up the stairs and I heard the screams of the dying and the wounded.

There was a hiatus. Officer training told me that the officer in charge was assessing the situation. After five minutes or so there was a sudden whoosh as the Germans sent a wall of flame from a flamethrower up the stairs. The banister bore the brunt of the flames. I gave a very theatrical scream and then sent my last grenade down the stairs. It was nearly our undoing. The grenade exploded the tank on the back of the flamethrower. A volcano erupted before us. Bill and I threw ourselves into the room. The flames leapt up to the roof. The banister was now an inferno. We had trapped ourselves. Standing, I slammed the door shut. I banged the wall next to the door. It was not brick. The fire would catch. It was a wood and plaster interior wall. That gave me an idea and I ran to the wall which adjoined the next house. I banged it. It just appeared to be a single course of bricks.

. "Sergeant Poulson, get the men to use their bayonets and make a hole to the house next door. We have done all that we can here. I will cover you from the window. How is it, Beaumont?"

Roger Beaumont held his pistol up, "It is fine sir. It is my left arm. I can fire my pistol. I will give you a hand!"

I returned to my chair and picked up the Mauser. I had to throw caution to the wind and kill as many officers and sergeants as I could. I half stood and began to fire at every semblance of a target that I could. My first bullets hit two officers and NCOs. The rest dived for cover. Not all that I hit died but they were hit. I ignored the bullets which zipped around me. Beaumont's pistol fired twice as quickly as my bolt action rifle. Our shells kept down the heads of the Germans. Even blind shots could send chips of brick, mortar and stone to inflict wounds. Behind me I heard the sound of the wall being destroyed. The men had hacked away the plaster and were now gouging out the mortar from between the single course of bricks. I could feel the heat from the landing was growing and smoke was seeping under the door.

We had no more grenades but, as I risked a look out of the window, I saw that three of the four 88s had been incapacitated and only one machine gun was firing. I loaded another magazine and fired at the machine gun crew. That was more of a threat to the Rifles than the 88.

"Sir, we have made a hole!"

"Let me know when it is big enough for us to escape. I don't think we have too much time left."

The Germans used their last two rockets to bring down the ceiling. A huge chunk hit me on the head. For a moment, I saw nothing. The dust and the plaster surrounded me and then Beaumont pulled me to my feet. "Come on sir. We have done enough. The lads have almost finished the hole."

By the time, I reached my men Fletcher had squirmed through the hole. Sergeant Poulson said, "Stand back!" He ran at the hole and hurled himself at it. He fell through the enlarged hole.

Scouse Fletcher laughed, "Bloody hell, Sarge! You could be a prop forward for the Saints!"

We all scrambled through the hole as the door to the room caught fire. "Right lads, everyone out and back to the jeep. We have done our bit!"

With Fletcher in the front we hurtled down the stairs. My radio operator was the first out of the gate at the rear and I heard his gun bark twice. "We have company sir!"

Sergeant Poulson ran out and he emptied his Thompson down the side street. He shouted, "Clear!"

As we came out I saw two wounded Germans who were trying to crawl back into a house lower down. We backed up the road until we reached our jeep. "Sort out Beaumont." I went to my Bergen, laid the Mauser in the jeep, and took out another magazine for the Thompson. Returning to the side street I peered down. There was no sign of the Germans. I ran down the street to see how the Rifles were faring. I saw that the tanks had used smoke. Our diversion had bought them enough time to get into position. They were now advancing under the cover of the smoke. The tanks fired at their positions. The anti-tank gun which remained, fired blindly through the smoke.

"Take charge, Sergeant. I will go and speak with the Major."

I zig zagged across the open ground towards the Shermans. The smoke which they had laid drifted towards us. I was confident that I was hidden from the sights of any potential sniper. The Major's head was out of the turret. "Good work, Tom."

"We lost one of the jeeps and two of the lads have slight wounds."

He jerked a thumb behind him. "Apparently, there is a Bedford at the rear of the column! There is a sergeant who does not appear to understand an order to wait until the road is clear."

I grinned, "Yes sir, Gordy Barker is a Bolshie little bugger!"

"When we have this clear I intend to push on to the docks. We have been in touch with the Resistance. They have risen in the town. They are already attacking the Germans on our flanks. They have taken over Boom. Lieutenant Colonel Silvertop is leading the rest of the Brigade towards the Central Park. Once we have the docks we will consolidate our position."

"Right sir."

There was little that we could do to help. We would have only been in the way of the Rifles who were clearing the mines and winkling out the last of the defenders. I passed the tanks and half-tracks. I spied the Bedford at the end of the column. Gordy was leaning from the cab, smoking. When he saw me he waved and jumped down.

"Good to see you sir! I brought the rest of the lads! Thought you might need us."

"Was Alan Crowe discharged?"

"Yes sir, he is in the back with the rest of the lads. What is the SP?"

"The Rifles are clearing out the Germans who held us up. We have lost one jeep and Emerson and Beaumont have slight wounds. Hewitt go and take a look at them. Shepherd and Wilkinson, come with me."

"I'll just get my medical kit."

The two of them jumped down and, with their Thompsons over their shoulders, marched protectively next to me. "Have we ammo in the lorry?"

"Yes sir. Sergeant Barker said we might as well fill the lorry. We have rations, petrol, water, grenades and ammo."

"Good." We soon reached our jeep. "Emerson and Beaumont, go with Wilkinson and Shepherd. Hewitt is in the lorry and he can deal with your wounds. Take back the Bergens. Give us all of your ammunition. There is more in the lorry. The four of us will be a little crowded in the jeep but it can't be helped. We only have a couple of miles to go."

"Right sir."

The four of them left. "Bill, you drive. Fletcher, you had better keep the radio on your knee. I want to be in constant touch with the Major. Get the cans on now Fletcher. Keep an ear open for chatter."

As Bill familiarised himself with the jeep and Scouse set up the radio, Sergeant Poulson said, "This was easier than I thought, sir. These Germans aren't the same ones we fought at Falaise."

"I know. I am wondering if it will get any tougher the closer we are to the centre but so far so good. Let's not get complacent though. It only takes one moment of carelessness and it could end in disaster. At least we have the Bedford now and the rest of the section."

We now had to wait for the Rifles to do their job.

Chapter 6

It took another hour for the road to be cleared and then we set off. By now word was out that the British were coming and the civilians appeared as soon as we began to drive down the road. The men pumped our hands and the women planted kisses on us as we made our tortuous way into the centre of the city.

Bill Hay said, "Are these on the German side sir? They are slowing us down more than the Germans."

"You can't blame them. They have endured occupation for four years." Just then a fusillade of shots rang out. The civilians scattered. Bullets pinged off Major Dunlop's tank which was now just thirty yards behind us. I grabbed the Mauser. I scanned the upper floors of the buildings. The puff of smoke showed me where some Germans were.

"Two o'clock on the second floor. Sergeant, use your Tommy gun. Fletcher, tell the Major where they are." I fired four bullets at the puff of smoke and the helmet I could see behind the parapet.

"Grenade!"

Bill had spotted the grenade being thrown and even as he shouted he floored the jeep and we leapt down the now deserted street. We crouched as low as we could. The grenade exploded behind us. Pieces of metal clanked into the back of the jeep but none hit us. Then there was a crack from the Sherman and a shell took out the corner of the building. I saw bodies falling with the masonry.

"Well done Bill. Let's get down the road as quickly as we can now."

We managed another mile before we were once again inundated by a wave of grateful Belgians. I had four cigars thrust into my hand. Sergeant Poulson suddenly found himself the owner of a bottle of Champagne and a woman threw herself on Fletcher to kiss him passionately. Bill managed to force a way through the crowds and Scouse grinned, "I could get used to this conquering hero bit!"

Once again it was the Germans who disrupted the party. They opened fire, indiscriminately hitting civilians. Scouse was rarely angered but his face became a mask of hate as he saw the woman who had just showered him with kisses scythed in two by machine gun bullets. His Thompson sprayed the German section. I emptied my magazine and the German patrol was finally silenced by the machine gun of Major Dunlop's Sherman Firefly.

We drove the last mile to the docks in grim silence. Fletcher still had the headphones on and he said, "The Major said this is our target; the Bonapartdok. He said we should take cover. The tanks will clear the area."

I looked around and spied a building which was close to the canal. "Bill, park it over there. We have some shelter."

As we disgorged I saw the first four tanks as they drove towards the canal side. I saw a coastal steamer and it was filled with Germans. It began to sail towards us. The tanks began to fire at it. The single gun on the steamer was outmatched. One of is shells hit a Sherman but it did no damage. After ten or so hits the steamer began to sink beneath the water. I watched the Germans as they floundered in the water, weighed down by their equipment. Many drowned.

I led my men to the side of the canal. As a half dozen or so of the survivors climbed up I said, "Hands up."

The half-tracks of the Rifles arrived and began to spread out. The Bedford arrived. My men leapt out. "Beaumont, Emerson, take charge of these prisoners. Sergeant Poulson, have the men ready." I pointed to the lock gates. "We have to secure those. That is the way across the docks."

Fletcher said, "But the major said that they would clear the area, sir"

"And they have done. It is now up to the infantry and the last time I looked Fletcher we were still infantry!"

"Yes sir."

"You can leave the radio here."

He was about to take the headphones off when he said, "Sir, Major Dunlop wants you and Major Bell at the command tank."

"Right. Be ready to move when I return."

The two majors were smoking a few yards from the tanks. "Lieutenant Colonel Silvertop and the rest of the column are approaching from the east. Our orders are to secure the bascule bridges and make sure that they do not blow the Albert Canal. I am afraid that is a job for you chaps."

Major Noel said, "I am down to less than eighty men at the moment." He looked at me. "We need your help, Captain Harsker. It looks like we will have to winkle out the groups of Germans who are on this side of the city."

I nodded, "I think we caught them with their trousers down. They have not had time to organize. Where would you like us to patrol?"

Major Dunlop took out a pre-war tourist map of Antwerp. He grinned, "Never thought I would need this again. I came here as a school boy before the war and cycled around here. Picked up some Flemish too. I am going to send two tanks to the Kattenijkdok. That is about as far as tanks can go. If you take your section there and raise the bascule bridges then my chaps can guard it."

"Will do."

"When that is done you and your lads can get your heads down. You deserve the rest."

I waved the men over, "Climb aboard these two Shermans. We have some bridges to raise."

We clung to the backs of the two tanks as they headed north towards the canal gates which were our targets. As we neared them there was the sudden chatter of sub-machine guns and rifles. Bullets pinged off the glacis of the tank. The commander sensibly ducked into the cupola.

"Right lads. This is work for us now."

We slithered off the backs of the two Shermans as the tanks' machine guns sprayed the area in front of them. I cocked my Thompson and moved along the side of the tank. I shouted, "Keep us covered!"

A disembodied voice from inside shouted back, "Will do. Get the bastards!"

I saw that there was some sort of barricade around the mechanism to lift the bascule gates. I had Wilkinson, Fletcher and Hewitt with me. "Wilkinson go left, Hewitt go right. It looks like they are behind those sandbags ahead."

"Sir."

The tank's machine gun opened up and ripped across the fifty feet long sandbagged defence. It was forty yards away. As soon as we passed in front of the tank then the machine gun would have to stop firing and the Germans would be able to fire back. We had to be quick. I had the gun cradled in my arms at waist height. It would not be guns which eliminated the Germans; it would be grenades. The machine gun stopped firing and I ran. Scouse was as fast as I was and we had covered half the distance when the first Germans rose. I sprayed from left to right without breaking stride. Fletcher fired in short bursts. I saw one German pitched backwards. Fletcher and I were the focus of their fire. To my right I heard the guns of Sergeant Poulson and his men.

I dived to the ground twenty feet shy of the sandbags. Fletcher emulated me. I took a grenade and pulled the pin. The machine gun in the tank opened fire and the bullets zipped overhead. I suspected the gunner had aimed high but they felt alarmingly close. Fletcher also had a grenade and I saw, out of the corner of my eye that Joe Wilkinson did too. I shouted, "One, two, three." On three I rose and hurled the grenade into the air towards the sandbags.

As we dropped to the ground the tanks fired again. The grenades rippled as they exploded. We were all below the blast but we heard the cries and screams from the other side. Although deafened I was on my feet and clambering over the sandbags before the Germans could recover. We had caused carnage. I saw Gordy Barker at the far end of the sandbags. He fired at the officer who raised his Luger. The bullet hit him in the shoulder and spun him around.

I shouted, "Drop your weapons! Surrender!"

There were ten survivors. They were lucky and just had cuts and minor wounds. The rest lay dead. "Lance Sergeant Hay, take Wilkinson and escort them to the rear."

"Sir. Come on Hans! Get a move on."

Emerson and Beaumont were my mechanical experts. "Shepherd, get these bridges raised."

"Sir."

It was as my men were slowly raising the bridges that the Germans began to fire at us. They were beginning to set up guns across the Scheldt in the northern part of the city. I walked over to the tank. "You had better warn Major Dunlop that this could get a little hot when those guns begin to fire and start to get our range."

"Right sir."

With the bridges raised we could move to the edge of the river. Right now that did not seem like a good idea for I saw machine guns being set up. Soon it would be dark and I felt we had done enough.

The tank commander stuck his head out of the turret. "You are being stood down, sir. We are being kept here as a deterrent."

"Thank you, Lieutenant. Right lads, back to the Bedford!" We jogged back the way we had come on the back of the tank.

Gordy Barker had used his experience to bring more in the lorry than might have been expected. He and Hewitt pulled out a brazier and began to break down a partly demolished wooden fence. "We might as well have a fire, eh sir? Cosy like!"

With the extra rations they had brought we ate well that night. When our men returned from taking the prisoners to the rear they told us that hundreds of Germans had surrendered. "But, sir, it seems the rest of the advance did not move as quickly as we did. We are the furthest north. There is just one section holding the Albert Canal. The Germans aren't putting up much of a fight south of the river but north…. There was a rumour that they were moving heavy tanks to meet our attack."

I shook my head, "I doubt that Bill. The better stuff was either destroyed at Falaise or pulled back east of the Seine. There may be armour but these Fireflies can handle a Mark IV."

Hewitt had done a good job fixing up Emerson and Beaumont. We had missed his medical skills. I was glad to have my whole team back together.

Joe Wilkinson, our newest member of the section said, "I heard that the German Paratroopers are based in Holland." We had been lucky to get Lance Corporal Wilkinson back. He had been due for a promotion in his old unit but he had made such a nuisance of himself that he had been transferred back. He had been waiting for us when we returned from Paris. I had persuaded Major Foster to make him a full corporal. He acceded and now we had a well-balanced team once more.

"They will be tough buggers sir."

"They will Freddie but I think we are as tough. And our airborne are even better. Remember Belleville?"

Gordy nodded at the memory, "Aye that was a hard fight but we showed the S.S. that day!"

"Well I am going to turn in. Sergeant Poulson arrange a duty roster eh? I will take the two a.m. slot."

"Righto sir."

Leaving the men to play cards, smoke and talk, I clambered into the back of the lorry. I would be dry at any rate. I was woken at midnight by Lance Sergeant Wilkinson, "Sir, sorry to disturb you but we have prisoners."

"Prisoners?"

"Yes sir. Half a dozen Jerries walked up to the tanks and surrendered."

I got up and saw that the six were led by a corporal. When they saw my rank, they saluted. "Are there others who wish to surrender?"

The German corporal nodded, "Yes sir. The war is lost. Your bombers have played havoc with our supplies. We are hungry and we have little ammunition."

"I thought the First Parachute Army was based here." Now that I had him talking I would see more information. You never knew when it would come in useful.

"No sir. They are north of Eindhoven."

"Right Joe, take them off to the holding area." Hay had told me that they were using the city zoo. The animals had all been eaten by the populace and it was a perfect place to hold prisoners. "It will be nice and cosy there. I will stay up now."

By the end of the night thirty Germans had surrendered. This was not the same army which had fought us in Normandy. Perhaps Walcheren and Flushing would surrender too. It would save an amphibious assault.

The next morning I was summoned, along with Major Bell, to the command tank. "It looks like someone has put a rocket up the back-up troops. The Monmouths and King's Shropshire Light Infantry are joining us. The Resistance are doing a sterling job and the Colonel wants you chaps to go and help them to clear the Banque Hypothecaire. There are over a hundred Germans there." He paused, "I am afraid that we have orders and cannot risk the tanks."

Major Bell snorted, "But my chaps are expendable eh?"

"Don't be like that. It isn't the colonel. The orders come from on high." He lowered his voice, "I have heard a whisper that something is going on north east of us. The Guards armoured have all been withdrawn from the front line. The 11th Armoured is all that we have left. If it is too hard then wait for the Monmouths and the KSLI."

"Of course, we will do it!" He shook his head, "Typical cavalryman! Thin skinned! Just grumbling! We will have it in our hands by this afternoon. That's right isn't it Captain?"

I gave him a weak smile, "If you say so, sir."

The maps we had were not the best and so the Major gave us directions. The Banque was close to the Central Park. As we marched our sixty men towards it Major Bell said, "These resistance chaps are damned tough men. They are going against Jerry with Sten guns and Molotov cocktails! But when they catch Jerry they are reluctant to take prisoners. I think that is why we have been asked to go. It might keep more of the Germans alive."

I agreed with the major. The Belgians hated the Germans. They had been occupied in two world wars. I think I might have wanted a little retribution if they had done that to my home. We heard the firing in the distance and the Major had us double time. There were not only Germans in the Banque from which fluttered the swastika, there were others who were well protected behind barbed wire and concrete emplacements. When I saw the anti-tank guns I realised why they had not risked the tanks. We would have lost irreplaceable Shermans. Until we got a port then we could not land as many tanks as we needed.

A civilian sporting a German sub-machine gun ran over to us when we arrived. He grinned. When he spoke, his English was excellent, "I am Edouard Pilaet. I am a colonel in the resistance. I am pleased you have come. Our best weapons are the ones we take from the Germans. Now that you are here with your tanks…"

The Major shook his head, "No tanks, just us."

He looked disappointed but shrugged, "It will take a little longer but with the Rifles and the Commandos what cannot we achieve?"

The Major looked at me, "Well Harsker, any ideas?"

"Have you any mortars?"

"Fraid not."

"Grenade launchers?"

"Half a dozen."

"Then, sir, if we send smoke over and then have the six grenade launchers keep lobbing grenades we can work our way closer to them. The old light infantry tactic of pairs of men moving and firing should do the trick."

"That sounds good to me."

"And what shall my men do, Major?" The colonel was keen to take part in this attack.

"Keep out of our way. You have done a fine job up to now but we are the professionals." The Major waved an irritated hand at him as though it would make him disappear.

The Belgian shrugged and smiled, "I am sorry but I cannot do that. We will let you attack first but we will follow. This is our city and we will fight for it."

I admired the little Belgian. It would be up to us to ensure that they were safe. "I will take my men and we will attack on the right flank. If you and yours take the centre and the left, then we should divide their fire."

"The Banque is on the right flank."

I took out my Colt. "My men have these. If we have to clear the building, then these are much easier to use than a rifle."

"Fair point. Good luck then Captain."

I waved my men around me. "We are going to take the Headquarters. There are up to ninety men inside. The Rifles will lay down smoke and then use grenades. We go in under the smoke. We fight in pairs. Fletcher, you are with me. Once we get in the building then use your hand guns and grenades." I gestured with my thumb. "And watch out for civilians. The Resistance are coming in after us."

I had not bothered with the Mauser. I needed firepower. I had four spare magazines for the Tommy gun and four for the Colt. My Luger was fully loaded and I had two spare magazines. I had six grenades with me as did most of my men. The battle jerkins we had allowed us to carry them much more easily than on our battle dress.

The Rifles sent over twelve smoke grenades and, as the explosive grenades dropped behind the Germans, we advanced. We ran crouched. Machine guns fired into the smoke but they fired too high. We felt the bullets zip overhead but so long as you were crouched you were relatively safe. We did not fire. That would only tell them where we were. I would wait until I was close enough to see their muzzle flashes. The smoke made it hard to breathe and to see. I kept my mouth shut as we ran into the fog like smoke. Fletcher was close on my heels. I saw the flash of a gun through the smoke. I stopped and knelt. Fletcher did the same. I waited until I saw the flash again and then fired a burst. As soon as I had fired I ran forward and Fletcher fired. There was too much gunfire to know if I had hit anything. I ran twenty feet and then dived to the ground. I saw barbed wire in front of me. I took a grenade and, pulling the pin, threw it from a prone position. I had just shouted, "Grenade!" when Fletcher threw himself flat on the ground beside me.

This time I did hear the shouts and cries from those I had wounded. We both stood and sprayed our guns through a hundred and eighty degrees. Then we ran at the wire and in true Commando style leapt and did a forward roll over the top. Once across I was on my feet in an instant. I pulled the trigger at the four men on the machine gun. I had only two bullets left and so, when it clicked empty, I swung the barrel across the temple of one of the three who had survived. Holding my Thompson in my left hand I pulled my Colt and even as the barrel of the machine gun swung towards me, fired five bullets into the two gunners.

Fletcher loomed up followed by Edouard Pilaet. I pointed to the machine gun, "You now have a decent weapon."

"And we will use it well, my friend!"

The building we had to attack was fifty feet from us. The fact that we were sheltered amongst the German defences afforded us some protection but I knew that as soon as we headed toward the building then the defenders would throw everything at us.

I turned towards Edouard, "Could you throw everything you have at the ground floor of the building?"

"It would be a pleasure."

I turned to my men. "We run at the windows on the ground floor. I want us to attack the centre windows. Forget the door, they will expect that. We move through the building as a team. They will outnumber us and I want to hit them with such firepower that they will not know what hit them."

They all shouted, "Sir, yes sir!"

"We go in pairs. The resistance will give us enough cover to reach the building. Most of those inside will be clerks or staff. We are Commandos."

Edouard said, "Ready!"

"Then unleash hell!"

The three heavy machine guns we had captured and every rifle suddenly opened up. The walls and windows were assaulted by bullets. We ran towards the building. None of us wasted any bullets. We would wait until we were inside. Miraculously, the fusillade kept the guns inside from firing and we reached the wall unscathed. I took a grenade from my webbing. The rest of my men did the same. The bullets kept hitting the wall. I held three fingers up, then two and then one. I stood and hurled my grenade through the broken window. My men copied my action. Dropping to the ground I waited for the explosion. When it came it was spectacular. Parts of the brickwork were thrown over our heads. It was as though half of the building was thrown out. Leaping up I dived through the open window. I did a forward roll and came up with the Thompson in my hand. I blindly sprayed in front of me. The handful of survivors fell to the .45 bullets from my men's Thompsons.

The room in which Fletcher and I had landed along with Hay and Hewitt had no one left alive. We hurried past the scattered files, broken furniture and bodies to the corridor. I popped my head out and then back. Bullets rattled down the corridor. There was a German body next to the door. I pulled a grenade from his belt and smashing the porcelain, threw it down the corridor. There was a flash and then an explosion. I leapt out and ran down the corridor. Fletcher was hard on my heels. I put my shoulder to the next door and threw myself inside. I just sprayed the Thompson in a semi-circle. Fletcher did the same.

"We surrender! Do not shoot! We have had enough!"

I shouted, "Hands up! Down the corridor and go out of the door!" They were so terrified that they obeyed. When they had all left we followed them.

Sergeant Poulson said, "That is the ground floor sir. What now?"

"Let's clear the building. Sergeant Poulson take half the men and deal with the far stairwell. The rest with me." I changed my magazine and led my men to the left hand stairwell. I opened the door, dashed in and fired a burst up the stairs. Fletcher followed me and did the same.

"Hewitt, Wilkinson, up the stairs. We will cover you." I emptied my magazine up the stairs. The two of them ran to the first floor and opened the double doors. They sprayed their guns from side to side. We followed them and burst through the doors.

I was about to fire when a German voice said, "No, no! We surrender! Do not shoot!"

"Wilkinson and Hewitt, reload and go upstairs. Fletcher take these prisoners downstairs."

As he stepped out Hewitt said, "Sir, I think it is all over. There are seven officers here and they have a white flag. I think we have won."

We kept our guns trained on them as they trooped down the stairs. Their appearance in the Central Park had an immediate effect. Those who just moments before had been fighting the resistance and the Rifles now stood and joined those from the Headquarters.

Edouard Pilaet had a beaming smile as he walked over to me. "I have heard of you Commandos. Now I have seen you in action I can see that your reputation is truly deserved."

Major Bell was organizing the prisoners and his men were collecting weapons. I said to Sergeant Poulson, "See if you can get any grenades, and ammunition for my Luger."

"Right sir."

I turned to the resistance leader, "You and your men are brave fighters. You can be proud of what you have done."

"When the city and our country are back in our hands then we will be happy." He pointed west. "And this is not truly returned to us until the fortress islands are taken." He looked at the German prisoners as they marched past us. "The soldiers you will find there are a little tougher than these men."

"Perhaps with Antwerp captured the garrisons may well surrender."

"I tell you, my friend, we tried to sabotage the building of the casemates for the guns. We lost many men doing so. I do not know how you will manage to capture them."

"We have clever men planning how to do so."

"It takes more than clever men. It takes brave men, such as you and your Commandos. It will take men who can kill and not falter."

Major Bell came over, "Two hundred and eighty prisoners! A good haul. How many did you lose, Harsker?"

"None sir."

"Remarkable! Our orders are to hand over the park and the headquarters to the resistance." He pointed to the pile of weapons. "The weapons are for you, sir. We are to take these to the zoo and then prepare for the next phase."

The resistance leader nodded, "Across the Albert."

"Across the Canal, indeed."

It was late when we arrived back at the Bonapartdok. Major Dunlop was waiting for us. "Well, Captain. It seems your part in this is all over."

"Really sir? But the Germans still have half the city."

"I know but they are sending fresh troops. The 4th Canadian Infantry Brigade is coming to clear the rest of the city. You and your chaps have done enough and besides," he lowered his voice, "you and your chaps are ordered to Ghent. One of your fellows, a Major Foster, is setting up his headquarters there and he needs you and your men." He smiled, I think you are going behind the lines again, Tom." He held out his hand, "It has been a pleasure and an honour serving with you Captain. I now see that the medals you won do not tell the whole story. I wish we had time to sit and chat about what you have done. After the war, eh?"

"I hope so, sir, I hope so." I turned, "Gordy, get the Bedford. We will leave the jeep for the Major. I am sure he can find a use for it."

"We off sir?"

"Yes, Sergeant Poulson. Major Foster has need of us."

Part Two
Terneuzen- Behind the lines- again

Chapter 7

Although we had less than forty miles to go it was a tortuous journey. It was like trying to swim upstream. All the traffic was heading to Antwerp as the Canadians were rushed north to make the final assault and take Antwerp. We discovered confusion when we reached Ghent. No one knew where Major Foster was to be found. It was almost ten o'clock and so I took a decision. "Park up wherever you can Gordy and we will sleep in the lorry again. Let's see what daylight brings."

With no sentries to set the back of the lorry was a little more crowded and I was awake early. I am not certain if it was Wilkinson's snoring or Barker's wind which finally woke me but I clambered over the section and dropped out of the back of the lorry. There was an early morning chill in the air. Gordy had parked close to Sint-Michielskerk, the huge church which dominated the square we had found. I donned my beret and decided to find a café. Although only recently freed from the German jackboot, the city had quickly picked itself up. I found a café which was open and busy and the sight of my uniform brought me smiles and handshakes.

I ordered coffee and was delighted when it arrived with a croissant. It was the most civilised breakfast I had had in a long time. They were going to refuse payment but I insisted. I never felt that the money I handed over was real money. This was the war time money taken from our enemies. It was like the money Mary and I had used as children when we were playing 'shop'. After discovering where the main square was I headed for it. I saw the Union Flag and the sentries and knew that I had found Headquarters.

The sentry saluted but his face showed that entry would be difficult without some sort of paperwork. I had met this type of soldier before. They were almost professional sentries. They were not front line troops; his uniform was far too smart for that and his rifle still had factory grease in the barrel. Reg Dean would have had his guts for garters. "Corporal I would like to leave a message for Major Foster." I took out my notepad and wrote a note for him. "Could you see he gets it please?"

The Corporal said, "I don't know the officer you mean...sir."

I nodded and put my face a little closer to his, "Then I would make it your business to acquaint yourself with him. He has ordered me and my unit here. If I have to return then I can assure you, Corporal, that neither you nor your greasy gun will stop me gaining entry. Understand?" I had used my old sergeant's voice. I did not like to use it but soldiers like this corporal only understood such threats.

"Yes sir. Sorry sir."

I found a bakery as I walked back to the section. The smell of fresh bread drew me there and I used the last of my money to buy twelve baguettes. As I drew near to the Bedford the smell woke my men.

"Sir, you are a hero! Fresh bread!" Scouse suddenly rummaged in his Bergen and, like a magician, flourished a pack of butter and a pot of jam.

Gordy said, "Bloody hell Scouse, where did you get that!"

"When we were at the docks I found a cupboard where the lock man had his lunch. There was bugger all else there, not even a bottle of wine, but I put these in my bag. I knew they would come in handy! Rog, get a brew on eh? Can't have jam butties without a pot of tea."

Beaumont shook his head, "I hardly think that French bread and conserve count as jam butties, Scouse!"

"Anything between two pieces of bread counts as a butty! Were you too posh for that?"

As Beaumont filled the kettle from the jerrycan can he said, "We had sandwiches, yes."

Fred Emerson lit a cigarette with the match he had used to light the brazier, "Aye but did you have a chip butty from the chippy?"

"Chip butty?"

My men stared at him as though he was from outer space. I smiled, "It is a northern thing Beaumont. You pack as many chips, heavily soaked in salt and vinegar, as you can between two pieces of buttered bread; a chip butty."

Gordy said, "Sir that is cruel! We are miles from home. There is no chance of a chip butty here."

Beaumont had finally filled the kettle and he handed it to Emerson to put on the brazier. "Actually, Sergeant, chips come from Belgium. They were invented here. It is why the Americans call then French Fries. They are almost the national dish of Belgium. I would not mind betting that there will be a shop somewhere selling chips here in the town."

Joe Wilkinson said, "Then we will have to find one! Fish, chips and mushy peas! Now that is proper food!"

My men were happy. They were not talking of the war they were talking of those things which gave them pleasure, food and drink.

"And they have decent ale here in Belgium too. My dad was in the Great War and he reckoned that Belgian beer was almost as good as Greenall's beer."

Fred shook his head, "I am sorry Lance Sergeant but Newcastle ale is the best or, possibly Vaux even though they are a Sunderland beer."

Gordy shook his head, "You northerners! It's Marston's that's the best ale. A pint of best bitter… now that is proper beer!"

As they smeared butter on French bread and drank hot sweet tea they chatted and argued as though there was not even a war on. They were true warriors.

When they fought then they fought like tigers but when they talked they talked as brothers. I knew that I was lucky in the men I led.

Major Foster arrived at noon. The men were busy washing their clothes. It looked like a Chinese laundry. They had improvised a makeshift boiler and had boiled their underwear. Using our climbing ropes as washing lines they were drying them around the brazier.

Major Foster waved his hand at the nearby church, "A little bit sacrilegious isn't it Tom?"

I shrugged, "The locals didn't seem to mind."

Scouse chirped up, "No sir and it's not as though we used the holy water to wash them now is it?"

"Fletcher!"

"Sorry sir."

I said, "There is a café around the corner. I will let you buy me a coffee while you tell me what we have to do."

He shook his head, "No, Tom. I am afraid this is top secret. Let's find a quiet corner close to the church and I will give you the gist. My driver will bring the papers and maps you need later on."

"Right sir. Sergeant Poulson, take charge eh?"

"Yes sir."

There was a bench close to the church and we sat on it. There were no other visitors to the church and we were alone. "Monty has come up with a plan to bring the war to a sudden conclusion. Operation Market Garden. At the end of next week, the Airborne of the British, Poles and the Americans will be dropping behind the enemy lines to capture the bridges at Eindhoven, Nijmegen and Arnhem intact. The plan has been around for some time but when the 11th managed to get into Boom then the operation was given the green light. That meant the left flank of the assault route was secured and we are closer to capturing a usable port."

"So, we don't need to land on Walcheren?"

"I am afraid we do. We now have Antwerp and Brussels. That is why I am a little late getting to you. There is some mopping up but we have the port. The trouble is the German batteries at the mouth of the Scheldt mean we can't use it. The bombers we were going to use to help the warships have now been diverted to disrupt the movement from Germany to the bridges we will be attacking."

"So, what do you want of us?"

"A Motor Launch and a number of landing craft are being sent across from Ostend. They will be lifted into the canal. The mouth of the canal at Terneuzen is in our hands. The Canadians are going to attack the last enclave from land and sea. You and your chaps are going to spend the next week going to Walcheren, Flushing and Westkapelle. Your mission is to assess the beaches."

"They did that at Normandy but they took months over it!"

"We haven't got months; we have weeks, at the most. Monty wants the land south of the Scheldt occupied by the middle of October. D-Day is November

64

the 1st. That is when your lads go in. They are training down at Ostend; using the beaches there. The Canadians will be going in as well."

"But if the guns aren't destroyed then it will be a massacre."

"Now you see why your job is so important."

"What if we are spotted? Won't that alert Jerry?"

"From Intelligence, we know that they are expecting us to attack. They have mined the Scheldt and beefed up their defences. This will not be like Normandy. This time they know we are coming and all they need is the time to make them even better defended."

"Then instead of sending the paras to take the bridges why don't they use them at Walcheren? They might be expecting an amphibious assault but there isn't a great deal they can do about an aerial attack."

"Market Garden is Monty's baby. Operation Infatuate is a side show. That's why they didn't risk the armour in the advance to Antwerp. The 11th cannot be reinforced. What they have is what they get!"

"I am sorry sir but I have a bad feeling about this."

"And I agree but what can we do? You have a maximum of ten days and then you will rejoin your unit at Ostend. You will be going in a day before the attack. You will be there on October 31st."

"Halloween! There is a certain irony in all this, sir."

"That's the spirit. Keep you sense of humour. Once the motor launch arrives then you and your men will head down the canal. I will accompany you and I will be based at Terneuzen; for a while at least."

"Any idea when the boat will arrive?"

"It left Ostend this morning. I think tonight is the earliest. But if there are raids from German aircraft then it might be delayed."

"Thank you, sir. I had better go and tell the men. Any chance of rations and ammunition? We used most of ours at Antwerp."

"I will send that with my driver this afternoon. Are your chaps happy to stay in the Bedford?"

"If it is just for one more night then that will not be a problem."

"Right I will get back to headquarters." He turned back, "By the way, what did you say to Corporal Taylor?"

"I just asked him to pass a message on to you, why?"

"He just asked whose side you were on. I think you frightened him a little. He is used to staff officers like me." The major laughed, "I had better tell him that you won't be visiting any time soon!"

He climbed into his jeep and sped off. My men knew that something was up and they naturally gathered around me. "We have one more night in the Bedford and then we are catching a Motor Launch to the sea. We are going back to war."

Fletcher sniffed, "Don't get much time off do we, sir?"

Beaumont laughed, "Probably safer to have us closer to the Germans, Scouse."

"The Major is sending ammo and rations over this afternoon. If there is anything else you need you had better get it here. We are going to the front line and I doubt that there will be much there."

Sergeant Poulson said, "Right, you heard the captain. Get your gear sorted out. Er sir, a couple of the lads' Bergens have holes shot in them."

"I can't see us getting them replaced yet. But we shouldn't need them for a while. We are meeting up with the rest of the battalion after this mission. We should be able to replace them then."

"Fair enough sir. And here is your washing sir. It is almost dry!"

As I put my clean clothes in my Bergen I wondered how they would be able to transport the landing craft. I doubted they would be the big ones we had used at Normandy. I guessed they would be the smaller Landing Craft Assault.

The equipment came in the afternoon. Major Foster had been as good as his word. We had plenty of ammunition and rations. He even sent some haversacks, anticipating our needs. Not as good as a Bergen they were, at least, a stop gap. The maps and written instructions were also there. The Sergeant who drove the Bedford said, "Sir, Major Foster said that rather than unload it here and then reload it to take it to the canal we ought to take you to the canal and unpack there." He smiled, "It makes sense, sir."

"You are right, sergeant. Right lads, load the Bedford. We will follow the sergeant."

We headed north to the basins on the canal. I sat in the cab with Emerson and began to read my instructions. Our first mission was to scout out the Elleswoutduke. It was just across the Scheldt from where we would be based. Then we were to go to Flushing on Walcheren and finally Westkapelle. I could see that it would be hard to perform the missions in under seven days. I had no doubt that there would be mines and that the Germans would be prepared for us. This would not be easy. As we neared the canal I wondered about the Motor Launch. It had been some time since we had used one. When we had had the 'Lucky Lady' we had the luxury of a German E-Boat and a top-notch crew. I had no doubt that the crew of the boat we would use would be a good one but we didn't know them and that familiarity often greased the wheels of a mission. I knew that I was being pessimistic but this mission had a bad feel to it already.

When we reached the canal, I saw that there were some transports already being unloaded from large tank transporters. They were the Landing Vehicle Tracked or Buffaloes. They could land twenty four men and looked like a floating tank but they had no gun and they were vulnerable to fire. It was, however, a start.

"Sergeant, get both vehicles unloaded. I am guessing that Major Foster would like his Bedfords back."

"Yes sir. He said to go on without him if the launch arrives before he returns. He will join you later. Something has come up."

"Right sergeant, get the gear out of the back. We no longer have the Bedford Hotel!"

"But sir, what if it rains! We'll get wet!"

Gordy snarled, "And will that spoil your hair do? Get the lead out. The sooner we are unloaded the better."

With many hands to make light work we soon had the two lorries unloaded and they sped away. Sergeant Barker said, "You lads who don't have a decent Bergen take one of the haversacks. Beaumont distribute the ammo. Shepherd and Wilkinson do the same for the grenades."

We were half way through when the first of the tank transporters arrived. There were six of them and they each had a Landing Craft Assault on their backs. They could carry thirty five men. I could see now that this operation would be much smaller than the Normandy landings. There was a huge crane and I watched as each one was unloaded. A lorry pulled up and spilled out their crews. They had five per boat. I saw them watching fearfully as the craft were lifted from the tank transports and then lowered gently into the canal. It was a Belgian crane driver and I knew that the Navy would have preferred their own personnel. When the first five had been lowered into the water they were all moved down the canal.

The men were sitting on the bollards by the side of the canal. The smokers were smoking. Gordy pointed towards the south. "Must be some more coming sir. I can see vehicles."

The first four all contained an LCA but the fourth one had the unmistakeable shape of a warship. It was a Motor Launch. "I think our ride has arrived, lads. Better get ready. You know that Navy likes to move quickly."

The first of the LCAs was being lifted off its low loader when the two lorries pulled up. I saw the crew of the LCA. They raced across to watch their ship as it was raised. The petty officer who commanded scowled at the driver, "You should have waited for us! We don't want just anybody handling our Lucy!"

It was an army driver and he laughed, "Bloody sailors! It is just a tub."

One of the ratings moved across and had to be restrained by the Petty Officer. I rose. "Corporal if you can't think of something pleasant to say then I suggest you keep your mouth shut and if you don't I will put you on a charge!"

I saw his face as he considered saying something but my rank, Commando flash and the men who rose behind me made him reconsider. He stuck his head outside of the cab. "Are we clear?"

The Belgian who was directing the crane driver gave him the thumbs up and he drove off without another word. I guessed that he would complain when he returned to his unit. There were warriors and there were soldiers. He was a soldier but the five sailors, I could see, were warriors.

The Petty Officer said, "Thank you sir. I would have given him a bunch of fives!"

"He is not worth it."

The second lorry disgorged and I heard a familiar voice, "Captain Harsker and Sergeant Barker, well, well, it is a small world and that's no error."

I turned around and saw Chief Petty Officer Bill Leslie striding towards me. I smiled. This was the best news I had had in a long time. "I was wondering who we would have to take us on this mission. I am happy it is you."

He turned and I saw an incredibly young looking lieutenant, "This is the captain, sir. Lieutenant Williamson."

The affable young man saluted and said, "Lieutenant Samuel Williamson sir. This is my first command! Exciting, isn't it?"

I remembered when I had found it all exciting. "It is indeed, Lieutenant, and you have a good Chief Petty Officer there. I have served with Bill more times than I care to count."

Bill said, "I had better go and see to the boat sir. The last thing we need is a sprung plank. Come on you lot. Stow your bags near to the Commandos. They'll keep their eye on them."

The Lieutenant looked lost. He made to follow Bill. "I should let the Chief get on with this, Lieutenant. There isn't a great deal you can do."

He nodded, "I volunteered for this sir. I wanted to be part of Combined Operations. Is it exciting work?"

"That's not the word I would have used but the work we do is important." I put my arm around his shoulders and moved him away from the canal. "It is tricky work. You will have to negotiate minefields and close with the shore. You might have to wait off shore and avoid detection. If I were you I would listen to any advice which Chief Petty Officer Leslie offers. He knows his business."

"I know sir. Captain Hargreaves gave him to me for that very reason. I know I am young sir but I am more than willing to learn."

I smiled, "You will be fine!"

It took two hours to offload the boats. Bill made sure there was no damage before he allowed the Lieutenant and the crew aboard. They then had to be fuelled which took more time. It took another half an hour before he was satisfied enough to allow us and our gear on board. The Lieutenant looked appalled at the quantity.

Bill said, "Don't worry sir. There's bags of room and when we get to the other end some of it can be stored ashore. We'll manage." He winked at me.

Sergeant Poulson and Gordy were old hands at this and the whole process took less than thirty minutes. The next tank transporters had arrived. Our berth was needed and Lieutenant Williamson said, "Ready to leave, Captain?"

"We are in your hands. Right lads, let's go below decks and leave the Navy to do their job." I saw the grateful smile on the young Lieutenant's face.

As I passed Bill he said quietly, "Thanks sir. It will just be until we have travelled a little ways down the canal sir."

"It gives me the chance to speak with the men."

We jammed ourselves into the mess. It was empty for the crew were busy on deck. "Right lads, this is our home for up to ten days. We are not heavily armed. Those who haven't sailed on one of these before you need to know that if we are attacked then all of us become part of the crew. Our guns will be the ship's guns. Familiarise yourself with the layout. We will be operating at night. You will not have the luxury of lights. The skipper will just need an hour to get used to the ship and the canal and then we can have a look around."

Sergeant Poulson nodded, "I am glad that it is Bill who is the Chief. We are in good hands."

I went back to reading my orders and studying the maps. We had done this sort of thing in Normandy. It was not the sort of work which garnered glory but it was vital. The lives of the men who would be attacking depending upon it. From what I had been told and what the orders implied I guessed that the first part of the attack would be the Canadians. They had the job of completing the subjugation of the mainland. It was the island of Walcheren which would be the target for the Marines and Commandos.

It was forty minutes late that a hand came down, "Skipper says it is okay to walk about, sir." He grinned, "It gets a bit whiffy down here!"

"Right, lads, familiarise yourselves with the boat but don't get under their feet."

I went to the bridge where the chief and skipper were talking. Lieutenant Williamson pointed ahead, "I am afraid we are travelling at the speed of the landing craft. We could overtake but the canal is still a little narrow and our wake could swamp the Buffaloes."

Chief Leslie pointed to the fuel gauge, "Besides, sir, this conserves fuel. I am not certain how much they have at this, Terneuzen."

"I have been studying the maps. The first trip should be relatively short but the others will be much longer. You will need fuel."

Lieutenant Williamson said, "Sir, how long has this port been in our hands?"

"Looking at the map it is hardly a port. It seems to be a small town at the end of the canal. A few days at most. When we travelled south it was still in German hands." I tried to work back and work out when we had first been sent to Boom but the days all melded into one another. "We are pushing hard."

The Lieutenant nodded, "You alright here Chief?"

"Yes sir."

"I thought I'd have a walk around and see how the chaps are doing."

He disappeared through the hatch. Bill said, quietly without turning his head, "He is a good officer sir. Just a little young."

"I wondered about his experience for this."

"Aye sir well most of the ones who had experience were whipped off to the Med. With the French coast largely in our hands there was more need for them down there. Southampton and Newhaven are almost empty now, sir. The days when there were MGBs and MTBS in huge numbers is gone. They just have the RAF air sea rescue and a few older boats. We were lucky that this was a new one." He sighed, "I get the impression, sir, that this is a sort of backwater. If it wasn't for your lads training at Ostend, then I would have thought it wasn't that important."

I could talk to Bill. When I had first met him we had been of almost equal rank. My rank didn't come into it although he insisted on calling me, sir. "It is the age old story, Bill. The generals have their own views and ideas." I did not mention Operation Market Garden to Bill but I knew that had had an effect on the resources being allocated to this attack.

"Aye well it is the poor buggers on the ground who have to pick up the pieces. Doesn't it annoy you, sir? We are just a glorified taxi driver but you and Gordy and the others, you are the ones who take the risks."

"We are Commandos, Bill, and the risk comes with the flash."

He nodded, "I can't see us docking until just before dawn, sir. These landing craft are like old ladies!"

"There is no rush. I have no idea what we will find when we get there. It has only been in our hands for a few days."

Lieutenant Williamson returned and he was beaming from ear to ear, "All going splendidly!" he turned to me, "Your chaps are mucking in too, sir."

"We get on well with Navy, Lieutenant, we always have done. We take the term Combined Operations very seriously. We couldn't do our job without your help. We have been saved on more than one occasion by sailors; isn't that right Chief?"

He grinned, "You will find, Lieutenant Williamson, that life with these chaps on board is never dull!"

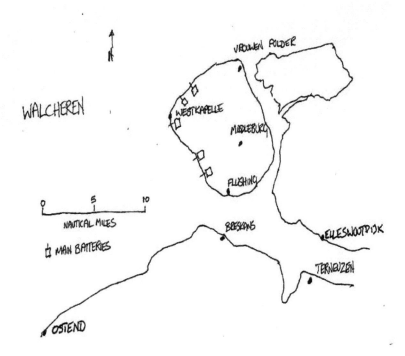

WALCHEREN

VROUWEN POLDER

WESTKAPELLE

MIDDLEBURG

FLUSHING

ELLESWOJTPIJK

BRESKANS

TERNEUZEN

0   5   10
NAUTICAL MILES

⊡ MAIN BATTERIES

OSTEND

Chapter 8

There were two large locks at the mouth of the canal. We were given priority and we were soon moored in the West Buitenhaven. We were the only naval vessel there and we managed to get a good berth. When the landing craft came through then it would be a little crowded.

I waved over Sergeant Poulson, "I will go ashore with Sergeant Barker and see if we can get somewhere to store our gear. I am guessing that Major Foster has somewhere planned as a headquarters but as he isn't here we will improvise. If you could, have the non-essential gear taken off the Motor Launch. I am sure that Navy does not want it overcrowded."

We stepped ashore and there was not a great deal to be seen. The Germans had fled quickly and we could see the damage the Canadians had caused when they had taken the canal. There were half damaged buildings and others which looked positively dangerous. Bomb craters and shell holes showed the intensity of the fighting as did the bullet holes in the walls.

"Not a lot to choose from, sir."

"How about that one?" I spied one which looked less damaged than the rest. From the look of the outside and the tables I guessed that it had been a café of some sort. It probably served the bargemen who would have used the canal. The windows were blown out but it looked as though there was just damage from bullets rather than bombs, grenades or shells. Barker went upstairs and I examined the kitchen. It still looked functional. I flicked a light switch and there was still power. The cooker looked to be a wood burner.

Gordy shouted, "Three rooms up here, sir. One has a bed in it and the other two look like they were used for storage."

"The kitchen is fine. Get the lads ashore. We will make this our new base until the major gets here."

I strolled back to the launch. With buffers to prevent damage next to the fragile hull the launch was tied tightly to the land. I went back aboard and climbed up to the bridge. Pointing north I said to Lieutenant Williamson, "That is Elleswoutdijk. It is the first place we are to land to assess the shore. Have you enough fuel for that trip?"

"I should think so. When are we going?"

"It will have to be tonight although if Major Foster sends us a message it may be a different time."

"Is it mined sir?"

"My guess would be yes. You will need sharp eyes watching from the bow."

"Isn't it dangerous?"

Bill Leslie took his pipe from his mouth and pointed with it. "So long as you use a wooden boat hook and don't touch the prongs it is a fairly simple task to keep them from the hull, sir. Once you know the pattern you can avoid them."

"The chief is right. A single boat can navigate them but the rogues are the ones to watch out for."

"Rogues?"

"The ones which have become loose. It sometimes happens."

"Who would you recommend, Chief?"

"I am as new to the crew as you are sir. I'll have a word. Some of the young ones seem bright enough. You need sharp young eyes."

"I will get my chaps to get some food on the go." I pointed to the building. We have a kitchen there. It is a little larger than your mess. We might as well indulge ourselves."

"I'll send over the leading hand from the mess with some food, sir. Share and share alike eh?"

I smiled, "Well we are almost in the Netherlands; let's go Dutch eh?"

We had a good meal. It was hot and there was plenty of, as Gordy said, 'proper tea'. I was anticipating an easy afternoon when a pair of lorries arrived and Major Foster and some Canadian Engineers disembarked. Gordy said, quietly, "There goes the neighbourhood eh sir?"

"Now Gordy, play nicely!"

Major Foster strode over, "I see you have sorted yourselves out. Good. The Engineers are here to put up some temporary buildings and a fuel dump. Until we open the Scheldt we will need to bring all the fuel by road. The intention is to do it at night. I have the first four tankers coming behind us. You can fuel directly from them until the storage tanks are installed. They are coming on a couple of landing craft."

I smiled, "This seems a little more organized than we are used to."

"I think Monty has woken up to the fact that this is important. We can have whatever we want or, rather, whatever we can find."

"That is good news, sir. We had planned on sailing tonight as the first target is just across the bay."

"We would like you to do that one tonight and then further along this coast tomorrow night."

"Sir, that is a waste of my men and of the boat."

"I don't understand."

"We don't need to land all my men in one place to scout out one beach. I can split into two different groups. I trust my men and we can cover more ground in a shorter time. I will only need four men with me and the rest can scout out the landing zones further down the coast."

"That would certainly expedite matters. If you think you can do it then go ahead."

"I'll use the café as a briefing hall."

"I will sit in, if you don't mind."

"It is your mission, sir. Be my guest. We have no secrets!"

When the men were gathered, I said, "There has been a slight change of plans. Sergeant Poulson and Sergeant Barker, I want you to take a patrol behind enemy lines to the west of us, and scout out the landing beaches for the next ten miles. The Canadians will be launching an attack there some time in the next seven days. We need to know what sort of obstacles they have and what the beaches are like. If you can get a prisoner or two then so much the better."

They both nodded. I could trust them to make the right decisions without me looking over their shoulder.

"I will take Beaumont, Hewitt, Wilkinson and Hay. We will carry out the original mission and sail across to Elleswoutdijk. Any questions?"

As I expected there were none.

"My team, I will meet you at the boat."

As they hurried off to gather their equipment Major Foster said, "That seemed a little easy."

"We were expecting to do this. They don't need an officer holding their hands. Don't forget sir that I was a sergeant and I had responsibility like this too. They will do a good job with or without me."

"Well I will let you get on with it. I am no engineer but I guess I will have to become one if this job is going to be done quickly."

My men were on the aft deck. We would not need Bergens and they were laying out their equipment. Bill Hay had a silenced Colt which he would be taking. The others all had Colts and they would be of more use than a rifle or a Tommy gun. Their saps, wire cutters and toggle ropes were all vital. I saw Hewitt coiling a rope. We might not need it but if we did not have it then I could guarantee that we would. The others were festooning their battle jerkins with grenades and other equipment. Hay had brought mine on deck and I did the same as they did. The difference was that I would have two pistols. I would take my Colt and my Luger. As well as the dagger in my boot I had a second one in a scabbard on the battle vest. I put my sap in my left trouser pocket.

When they were all ready and equipped, I said, "We will eat first. I want to leave just after dusk. I know they will have observers watching us so I will have the skipper sail east as though we are going to Antwerp. Once we are through the minefield we will take the dinghy and row ashore. Shepherd you will watch the boat. Hay, you will take Wilkinson and examine the beach. Beaumont and I will head inland. I want a maximum of two hours ashore and then we return."

"And what if we are spotted sir?"

"Try to get back to the boat without making too much noise but this isn't like Normandy. There we had to keep them guessing where we would land. Jerry knows we are coming." I was satisfied with my equipment. "Bill do a check on the equipment and I will go and see the Lieutenant."

Lieutenant Williamson and Bill Leslie had been watching us work. "We go tonight then?"

"We leave at dusk. I would suggest you head east until darkness falls in case Jerry is watching. If we can see them then they can see us. There will be glasses on us you can be sure of that. When we are at sea then head due north. We will take the rubber dinghy."

Bill Leslie said, "I will get it inflated, sir. If there are just five of you then there will be plenty of room." He hurried off.

"Have you decent charts, Lieutenant?"

"I think so sir. There is a narrow channel between two sandy areas. Luckily we are shallow draughted but I would like to avoid the shoals if possible."

"Your boat, Lieutenant, and it won't be a problem heading north but if we are pursued coming south we may not have much of a choice."

Right sir. I'll have Chief Petty Officer Leslie on the helm. I have heard he has a sixth sense about such things."

"We will be ashore for a maximum of two hours. You don't need to hang around but I wouldn't go too far. And I would stay closed up. The Chief has done this before; he will offer you good advice. I would take it."

He nodded, "He said you came through the ranks sir, is that true?"

"I enlisted as a private in the Loyal Lancashires. I never thought I would be an officer."

"But your background sir, your father was a senior officer, you were going to university…"

"All true, Lieutenant, but what I learned coming through the ranks was the best education I ever had. My father did the same. I am not saying that there is anything wrong with Officer Training but I like the way I earned my pips."

I went ashore to speak with my two sergeants. "Are you both happy with your instructions?"

"Yes sir. Safer this way, if you ask me. No minefield to cross and we can run back in three hours if we have to." Sergeant Poulson was confident. He was a fit man and he knew the strengths and weaknesses of the men he led. If he did stay in the service after the war, then he would be a good leader.

"Good. Bring them all back eh?"

"And you too, sir."

We left the berth with engines which were barely turning over. Lieutenant Williamson did as I had asked. His course took us east but away from the shore. After twenty minutes, when the light had faded, he said, "North by west Chief," and we turned to head through the shoals. Bill Leslie had identified two lookouts and they leaned over the front of the launch looking for signs of shallowing water. Others lined the sides looking for mines. We only had eight miles to go but we took it steadily and slowly. I blacked myself up as I waited. Until we reached the surf I would be a passenger.

The engines slowed perceptibly and a hand came along, "Sir, skipper says we are sixty yards from shore."

"Mines?"

"Either we were lucky sir or there were none."

"Good. Right lads, get the boat over the side."

With neither bags nor rifles to hamper us we quickly boarded the rubber boat. We had two men on each side and using powerful strokes we were soon ashore. As soon as we ground on to the sand we leapt into the shallows. Pulling the boat on to the damp sand of the high water mark I pointed left and right. My men nodded. I took out my dagger and began to walk up the beach. After three steps I stopped and picked up a handful of sand. It was fine sand. It would not be an obstacle to the landing craft. While Beaumont watched, I dug down a little. The sand below the surface was firm. Rising to my feet I head across the beach. I took nothing for granted and I looked for the signs that it had been mined.

We must have been lucky and chosen a path left through the centre for we saw none. When we reached the dunes, I took a grenade from my battle jerkin and laid it in the top of the dune. When we came back it would act as a marker for the safe path. I did not know if the beach was mined but I did know that the path we had taken was not. We would be able to follow our footsteps back to the boat. I looked around and saw that there was wire but it was not on the beach itself. It lay in the dunes. Any infantry running through the dunes would not see it until they were on it. As with all wire there was always a way through it. The men who laid it had to be able to service it. In the heat of battle, you would not find it quickly but we saw it and moved through the double wall of wire. Twenty yards behind the dunes I saw the pillboxes. I froze. Were there men inside?

I lay flat and Beaumont emulated me. I crawled towards them. What type of weapons did they have? I heard the Germans. They were not in the pillboxes but behind them. The smell of their cigarettes drifted over to me. Their talk was of the duty sergeant and a debate about the ending of the war. Translated into English and it would have been the same for Americans, British or Canadians. It was tempting to try to take the men prisoner but I had no idea how many others were there. Instead I risked rising to peer into the pillbox. As I rose I saw the barrel of a heavy machine gun. I did not detect any occupants. That meant the pill boxes just had sentries at night, they were not manned. Where were the men who would man them?

Tapping Beaumont on the shoulder, I crawled to the end of the pill box. I took out my silenced Colt. There was a trench five yards away. Like the pill boxes it was empty. I made the sign for Beaumont to wait and to cover me and then I crouched and headed between the pill box and the trench. I needed to find where the men were. As I emerged at the back of the pillbox I saw the glow of the cigarettes from the two Germans who were twenty yards from me. I kept moving slowly and I heard a noise. It was the sound of men and music. It sounded to me like a radio. I might not have seen it had a German not opened a door from the bunker which had been built into the dunes. The noise became louder and I knew where the Germans were. The had a concrete bunker buried into the sand dunes. I retraced my steps.

I was just approaching Beaumont; I saw his shape when a German stepped from the shadows. I think he had been relieving himself. He saw Beaumont and shouted, "Who are you?"

He only had a field cap on and I ran behind him and smacked him on the back of the head with the sap I had pulled from my pocket. I said quietly, "No time for niceties, Beaumont, run!"

"Sir!"

He stood and leapt like a hare for the dunes. We used our own footsteps to retrace our path. We quickly negotiated the barbed wire but, behind us, I heard the clamour as the German shouted for help. I had not hit him to kill, merely to stun. Lights came on behind us. They had large lights on the top of the pillboxes. I saw them dancing across the beach. It would only be a matter of time before they spotted the dinghy and Shepherd. I turned and aimed the Colt at the nearest. I fired once and it went out. Four more bullets and the other two were eliminated. The beach was once again plunged into darkness. I rose and ran. A spatter of rifle fire filled the air. They were firing blind but a lucky shot could kill just as easily as a sniper's bullet.

Beaumont had reached the grenade and he waited. "You lead, Beaumont. I will see if I can trick them away from here." As he ran for the dinghy I pulled the pin and hurled it as far to my left, along the beach, as I could. I ran after Beaumont. I hoped that I would make them think I had stepped on to a mine. I was lucky. The grenade exploded and one of the fragments set off a hidden mine. The double explosion lit up the sky and I saw that the other two had reached the dinghy and Shepherd had it held in the shallows. Even as I neared them Beaumont threw himself into the dinghy. I waded out to them. They were already pulling away from shore. I grabbed the trailing rope and pulled myself on board. The machine gun in the pillbox began to chatter. They were spraying the beach area. As I pulled myself on board the rubber dinghy I heard the Lieutenant shout, "Open fire!" and the guns on the Motor launch began to fire from the dark. I cursed. They were giving away the position of the boat. As I tumbled aboard the dinghy began to move quicker. It was not quick enough for the German machine gunner tracked bullets across the Motor Launch.

I heard Bill Leslie's voice shout, from the dark, "Check! Check! Check!"

The Motor Launch's guns stopped firing. The German machine gunner kept firing but he was now off target. As I saw the bow loom up I shouted, "Throw a line." The surf would take my voice away. The rope was thrown and snaked out towards me. I caught it and began to pull. We bumped against The Motor Launch. The scrambling net was lowered and many hands helped us aboard. As I flopped on to the deck I said, "Lieutenant, I would get home as quickly as possible. They may have E-Boats and, trust me, you do not want to tangle with them."

"Right sir. Full speed Chief."

"Everyone okay?"

"Yes sir. We thought you hadcopped one when the lights came on."

"It was close. What did you discover, Hay?"

"The beach is mined. You must have managed to find the only path through it sir."

"They only have machine guns but the bunkers are hidden and they have wire. Good job chaps." They nodded and then Bill Hay gave a pointed look at the bridge.

I took off my battle jerkin. I handed it to Roger Beaumont, "You lads get below decks. I will join you."

I climbed up to the bridge. "Thanks Lieutenant."

"When they started firing I thought you were a goner!"

"Next time, Lieutenant, it would be better if you didn't fire. You gave away your position."

"But the machine gun...."

"Was firing blind. The gun was in a pill box. It would take a lucky shot to hit it." I saw that he had not realised that. I smiled, "Thank you for your efforts though. It was appreciated. I shall join my men below decks. I will see if I can make some decent cocoa!"

We reached the berth just before dawn. I had taken the oral report from Bill Hay and written mine. We had come close to disaster but we had just stayed on the right side of successful. Now I would have to see if the rest of my section had been as successful.

When I stepped ashore I was greeted by Major Foster, "Well?"

"If you still have flail tanks then there should be no problem. There are no mines at sea but there are on land. They are using machine guns to defend the beach. I saw no concrete tank obstacles."

"That is a relief. Your other men are not back yet."

"There is time. I hope your engineers have breakfast on! I could eat a horse with the skin on!"

Major Foster looked nonplussed, "Sorry, I didn't think!"

"I am teasing sir. Staff officers never worry about food. We will sort something out." Major Foster had forgotten how to be a soldier in the field. "If you come to the café I will give you the details of the beach and my lads can get some food on the go."

We sat at the table and I used the crude map I had drawn to identify the features we had found. "We landed to the east of the houses. I thought we could take The Motor Launch and look at the defences there during daylight. Williamson has some good glasses."

He shook his head, "That won't be necessary Tom. Aerial Reconnaissance has shown that they have it heavily defended. The Canadians are leery about attacking a town ever since Dieppe."

Shepherd had the frying pan out and Beaumont had the kettle on. Food came first. We were the first back and would have food ready for the others when they arrived. Sergeant Poulson and my men tramped in at eight o'clock. I counted them in. None had been lost. No matter what they reported that was good news.

The two sergeants came directly to the Major and myself. "They have some concrete obstacles sir. There are three waves of wire and they have mortars mixed in with the machine guns."

"Is the beach mined?"

"No sir."

Major Foster stood. "Thanks for that Tom, I have to get back to Ghent! That is great news. I will bring back new orders. Until then rest, you have earned it."

Shepherd said, "Doesn't he want his bacon then?"

"I guess not!"

The crew of the Motor Launch spent the day repairing the bullet holes in their launch. They had been lucky. Nothing vital had been struck. Lieutenant Williamson's lesson could have been worse. Had not Bill Leslie ordered the men to cease fire then the mission might have ended in disaster although, as Bill Hay had pointed out, "We were close enough to paddle home in the dinghy."

That was true but the next two operations would be more dangerous and we would have further to travel. While my men cleaned their weapons and got some rest I watched the rest of the landing craft arrive. There were also truckloads of Canadian troops. They headed west to the camps which were being erected there. The Engineers building the fuelling depot, barracks and headquarters building had worked through the night. The captain in charge joined me when we ate lunch. "We should be out of your hair by tomorrow morning."

"There's no rush you know. We are happy in the café. The roof is sound. We are used to roughing it."

He shook his head, "We have more work to do. Our general has more work planned for us."

I could work out what that was. Breskans was a short way from Flushing. Once the mainland was captured then the Canadians would be able to launch an amphibious assault. Our next visit behind the lines would be to Flushing and I knew from aerial photography that we would have to negotiate a minefield to reach it.

Chapter 9

Major Foster and his headquarters staff arrived the next morning, The Canadians had finished the headquarters hut and the barracks. Both were temporary structures. We knew they would be cold in the winter and that was rapidly approaching. I had decided that we would stay in our café. The two storage tanks were the last to be finished and the Canadians were working on them when Major Foster sent a runner for me.

He now had an office. It was bare save for a map pinned to the wall, "Tom, we have more information. It looks like the start of October is the start date for the Canadians to cross the isthmus and to take the rest of the enemy held land to the west of us."

"That gives us a little more leeway then. I think they need more time to repair the Motor Launch." There had been some problems with the engine and the last thing we needed was a boat which could not get us home.

In the end we did not go until the 12th. The launch developed a problem with the engines. Emerson's experience on the E-boat came to the rescue of the leading hand who ran the engine room. We finally left in the late afternoon. We had two rubber dinghies this time. We would take eight men ashore. We hugged the southern shore of the Scheldt as we headed west. Once again, we headed slowly through the river. There were shoals as well as floating obstacles immediately off the port of Flushing. As darkness fell we headed closer to Flushing and, once again, the crew fended off the obstacles that we encountered. They were not mines but logs attached to the sea bed by ropes. They would not explode but any landing craft would become fouled.

Once we had passed them then we had to run the gauntlet of the searchlights. They were not looking specifically for us; our engines were barely turning over, but they appeared to be working to a pattern. The beaches and the defences we were examining were to the west of Flushing and it was as we were passing the entrance to the port that a lucky light found us. Lieutenant Williamson had his wits about him. He ordered full speed and the crawling launch became a greyhound as it roared and leapt forward. We lost the light but they knew we were out there. A fusillade of Oerlikon, machine guns and 40 mm cannon tore through the air. They were firing blind. The searchlights danced across the water as they sought us. The young commander had learned his lesson and our guns remained silent. We headed due west, away from the coast. When we saw the lights were well astern of us he turned to head north and he resumed his slow approach. We could see the surf when we aground on the Roan Bank. Had we been going quickly then we would have become stuck but Chief Petty Officer Leslie stopped the engines and began to back us off them.

I saw the dilemma on the Lieutenant's face. "Done worry Lieutenant, we will paddle from here. If you sail up and down the edge of the shoal, we will find you."

"But the Germans will be alerted!"

"They don't know we intend to land though. We will need two hours again." I turned, "Right lads, in the water. Sergeant Poulson you take charge of the rest of the men." I clambered into my boat. I had Bill Hay, Joe Wilkinson and Ken Shepherd with me. Gordy was in command of the other boat. We would separate to cover as much of the beach as we could.

I took my paddle and we began to stroke towards the shore. We had only gone sixty yards when I saw the deadly spikes of a mine ahead. We were in a minefield. Had the launch brought us closer then who knew what damage might have been done. As it was we were able to avoid them by paddling slowly. It was nerve-wracking but, unless we were careless, we would not be in any great danger. We had lost sight of the other dinghy. That was a good thing. If we couldn't see them then any sentries would struggle to see us. Then we saw the deadly stakes sticking up out of the water. They were there to rip the bottom out of any landing craft. At high tide, they would be invisible and could tear through a wooden landing craft. I made a mental note of their position. It meant we would have to attack at low tide.

As we neared the beach Hay and I stopped paddling. I saw wire on the beach. The aerial photographs had shown that too. As the front of the boat rose on a wave Hay and I leapt out and, grabbing the painter, we began to pull the dinghy ashore. As soon as Wilkinson and Shepherd jumped out it became easier. We pulled it away from the water. The German wire was beyond the high water mark and we left the dingy there. I had not seen any sign of sentries. That didn't mean there were none. Once the dinghy was safe I led my men through the wire. I checked the sand. It was smooth. There were no indentations showing that something lay beneath the surface. It would not impede a landing craft.

Having passed through the wire we paused at the low dunes. They were little more than windblown sand slightly higher than the beach. Behind them lay the real defences. I saw the concrete emplacements and the barrels of guns. This time there were 20 mm cannon as well as machine guns. There were far more than we had seen down the coast. We crawled towards them. Once again, the German sentries appeared to have a lax attitude towards their duty. They were not looking seaward. We lay below the barrels and heard the conversation. It soon became apparent why their attention was landward.

"Dieter was killed yesterday."

"I know. The resistance has become active since the Canadians started pushing from Antwerp."

"They say that four others were killed in Walcheren."

"And I heard that Commandos landed down the coast. I think we will soon be in the firing line."

A voice suddenly barked out, "You two ladies! Watch the sea! If I see you looking to the land again you will be peeling potatoes for the rest of the war."

I heard one mumble, "That is safer than waiting to have your throat cut!"

I crawled along the front of the emplacements below the apertures. The first block was forty yards long. At the end was a gap and I crawled through it. There was a road and behind it I saw the barrels of the naval pieces. After checking that the coast was clear of sentries I rose and waved my men towards the guns. There were four of them and they looked to be 150mm. These were the ones which would wreak havoc on the landing craft. I led my men to the concrete embrasures. It was thick concrete. I estimated it to be ten feet thick at least. Bombers would not do much damage to it. Major Foster was correct; this would need naval guns. The front would be their only weak spot.

Satisfied that we had seen enough we headed back to the beach. Having been away from the launch for an hour it was time to return. Just then I heard a rifle from the far end of the beach. That was where Gordy and his men were. I heard no fire in return and that was a good thing but I did hear, just feet away from where we sheltered, the non-commissioned officer who had berated the sentries shout, "Hans, Heinrich, get down to the beach and check the wire. Post number eight has reported Commandos ashore. I will rouse the guard."

I drew my silenced Colt and, standing with feet apart, shot him. I hit him in the chest and he was thrown back. The guard would not be roused. Turning I ran down towards the beach. With our rubber soled shoes, we were silent. The two Germans had obeyed orders and were running towards the sea. I heard one of them shout, "A boat!"

As they turned, one said, "Kommando!"

I levelled my Colt and said, "Lower your weapons or you will die." I knew that Hay had his Colt out too. They both dropped their weapons. "Turn around!" As they did so I said, in English, "Wilkinson, Shepherd, sleepy time!"

"Sir."

They walked up to the two men and smacked the saps against the back of their heads. They flopped to the sand. When they woke, they would think themselves lucky that they had crossed Commandos and lived. Further up the beach I heard the sound of small arms fire.

"Into the boat."

"But Gordy!"

"Gordy is a big boy and he knows what to do. Let's do our duty eh, Shepherd?"

"Sir."

We refloated the boat and began to paddle out beyond the stakes. We kept paddling until we reached the rough position we had left the launch. There was no one there. We were alone.

"Just hold this position, eh lads. Navy will be back."

I saw the flashes further up the beach as the firefight continued. It was hard not to panic. This time we were too far from home to paddle. We would have to wait and hope that the young lieutenant was in command of the situation and would return for us. The flashes and the firing stopped. Bill Hay looked at me and shrugged. We both knew that our men could have been captured or killed. We were not invincible.

We bobbed around for almost thirty minutes. I used the fixed point of the light at the end of the quay in Flushing to keep us roughly on station. We did not have to be precise. If I heard the launch, then I would use my torch to signal it. Wilkinson said, "Sir, I can hear something. It sounds like a boat."

"Have your guns ready. It might be German."

Despite the fact there were just four of us in a rubber boat, the thought of surrender never entered our minds. So long as we were alive and had weapons then we had a chance. I heard the noise of the engines too. It was coming from the west. I aimed the Colt in the direction of the approaching vessel. I could make out the white foam from the bows. Suddenly the white disappeared and the boat stopped. There was an eerie silence.

Then I heard a whistle. It was Sergeant Poulson. I took the torch from my battle jerkin and, keeping my body to shield it from the land, flashed three times. The engine started and the motor launch loomed up out of the dark.

"Am I glad to see you, sir." Sergeant Poulson dropped a rope for Bill Hay and a scrambling net for us. When we were secured we clambered up the side.

"Gordy?"

"They were surprised. They got caught up on the barbed wire. Hewitt is seeing to them. I think it is just Gordy's pride which is hurt."

"Any casualties on the Motor Launch?"

"No, sir. The Lieutenant did everything the right way. He is a quick learner."

"That is the trouble in this war, Sergeant, you are either the quick or the dead."

"We did notice the harbour when we passed. It does not look well defended. I think they are relying on the heavy gun emplacements we saw, sir. There is a little beach just next to the breakwater. The main harbour has heavy guns but not the two breakwaters."

"Well spotted, Sergeant. You could be right. The guns which fired on us did not seem to be numerous. I shall mention it when we get back."

I joined the Lieutenant on the bridge, "Thanks for picking my men up, Lieutenant, and for coming for us."

"It's our job sir. I think I am getting better at this. There was a great temptation to open fire. I am glad we didn't."

"I would keep well to the south of the bank. I know there is high tide but Jerry has planted stakes in the channel."

"And there are mines sir. We found them as we turned to pick up Sergeant Barker."

"Then we could have a tricky little trip the next time we go out. We have to scout Westkapelle."

"And we will need fuel before then. By the time we get home we will be on fumes."

I looked at Chief Petty Officer Leslie who grinned, "Don't worry, sir. We always have a jerrycan for emergencies!"

We reached home just after dawn. The petrol tankers were already waiting at the side of the canal. They were a welcome sight. Gordy came up to me as we approached the berth. "Sorry sir; I must be losing it. I shouldn't have let them spot us. And we got caught in the wire. That was stupid! If a recruit had done that I would have torn them off a strip."

"These things happen, Sergeant, and no one was lost."

"But sir, they know there are Commandos in the area!"

"They knew that already Gordy. I heard two Germans talking. Between us and the Dutch resistance they are worried sick."

As I stepped ashore I said, "See to the men, Sergeant Poulson. I will go and report."

Major Foster was now organised. He had sentries, clerks, maps and furniture. He even had a sergeant major who grinned and said, "I'll get you a brew sir. Looks like you need it."

"Thanks, Sarn't Major...?"

"Murphy sir, forty one Commando. Seconded to the major for this little jaunt."

I tapped on the Major's door and let myself in. "How did it go Tom?"

I sat down and gave him an oral report. He would expect a written one but it was always as well to give the spoken version first. The tea arrived and I drank it, gratefully. Major Foster had been busy making notes as I spoke. He went to the map. "The stakes and the logs, where were they?"

I stood and tapped the section, "About here."

The Major shaded it in red. "We'll call this the contaminated area. That information about the harbour confirms what the aerial reconnaissance showed us. I wondered if it would be made of sterner stuff close to the sea but obviously not. We have not yet set the plans in stone. It is a good thing we sent you chaps in. Useful stuff Tom. Well done. That patch of sand which Sergeant Poulson spotted will be quite useful." I sat down again. "The minefield and stakes will make your next trip a little tricky."

"Yes sir. The Lieutenant has his charts marked. We should manage."

"Well I would like you to hold for a day or two. The RAF are going to try and knock out a few more dykes. If they can do so then the land behind the coast might be flooded and stop the Germans reinforcing when our chaps go in."

"And the Canadians?"

"It will be closer to the end of the month before they are ready to go in."

"Slow and steady eh sir?"

"That is Eisenhower's way. Monty and Bradley want a surgical strike into the heart of the Ruhr. They argue that stopping German war production will bring the war to a quicker conclusion."

"Possibly."

He leaned forward, "The trouble is I have heard that the Germans are planning something. If we do it Monty's way there is a chance that a sudden counterattack might undo all our good work. We need a port. We have one but can't use it."

As I left to return to my men I saw now how vital our job was. The wounded looked worse than they actually were. The wire had cut their hands and faces. We were subdued that night. My men strove for perfection and making mistakes did not sit well with them.

The next day I took out the maps and aerial photographs. "This one will be our trickiest yet. I take full responsibility for the fact that the Germans almost caught us yesterday. We had enough men and we should have used them. This time we will take six in each boat and that way two can guard them. We also need two drops. I shall see the Lieutenant when I have finished here but one party will land south of Westkapelle and the other north. They are the two landing beaches which we might be able to use. It makes for a trickier pick up I know but it can't be helped. Familiarise yourselves with what we know. The RAF are going in to bomb the dykes. Hopefully much of the island will be flooded. Most of it is below sea level."

"Sir?"

"Yes?"

"What is the purpose of this mission? I don't mean our recce, I mean the amphibious landing."

"That is a good question, Beaumont. We just need the batteries silencing. The Navy needs to clear the mines in the Scheldt so that the ships can reach Antwerp. To do that we need the batteries eliminating. We don't need to capture Walcheren island. There is little of strategic value here but the guns stop us from clearing the minefields and using the Scheldt."

Gordy said, "If you ask me a better use of the Commandos would be to let our battalion go ashore at night and just blow up the guns. That would do it."

"And I agree with you, Gordy, but the powers that be want it done this way. We are not going in until the RAF has done some more damage. It will give us the chance to see the aerial photographs. That way we can gauge what to do. And for that reason we head further inland this time. Jerry has added a great deal of concrete to the perimeter. We are hoping that the middle is a softer target. That way when our lads break through it will be a decisive victory."

They nodded.

"One more thing; when the amphibious landings take place we will be going in with the battalion. The better job we do now then the more chance we have of surviving the real attack."

Leaving them to study the plans I went to the Motor Launch. Now that the fuel tanks were up and running Chief Petty Officer Leslie had made sure that we

85

had full tanks and some spare jerrycans. I noticed that Lieutenant Williamson was less formal now. He no longer bothered with a shirt and tie but wore a sweater and duffle coat as did most of the crew. He had adopted the comforter which we wore. It was cooler and now that September was almost gone the nights were much chillier. He still appeared to shave each day although most of his crew did not. As Bill Leslie often said, they were more like pirates than anything else. It was a good analogy.

"So, sir, when do we go again?"

"Eager eh Lieutenant? Not for a couple of days. The RAF are going to try to destroy the dykes and flood the island. We have to assess their effect but this trip will be the hardest." I opened the chart and laid it out on the bridge. "We have to land two parties, here and here. There is a shoal, Burkil Bank. They may even have stakes there. Added to that we know that there are large calibre gun emplacements. Our job is to discover the defences. The last thing we need is for the evidence to be a sunken Motor Launch."

Bill studied the map and said, "It would make sense, sir if we dropped south of Westkapelle first. The channel between the shoal and the island is narrow. If we made the second drop and headed out to sea we could sail in a circle and pick up south first and then north."

"It is three fathoms, Chief. We have plenty of room."

"Depends on the tides, sir and we grounded the other night. It isn't worth taking the chance is it, sir? Besides this way we don't need to hang around like an expectant father."

I agreed with Bill but I wanted the Lieutenant to make the decision himself. It would not affect us but Bill's plan was the right one. Eventually the Lieutenant nodded, "Right, Chief, that is what we will do. It does mean, Captain Harsker, that we will have to give you a specific time to be picked up and we won't be able to hang around."

"My lads know that. Well I will leave you to study your maps. As soon as I know when we go I will let you know,"

The Major sent for me two days later. He had a sheaf of photographs. "The bombers have done a marvellous job. Look at these Tom. Most of the island is under water. It is only the towns and the coastal strip which are intact. The water isn't that deep but it will make movement difficult. You and your chaps will need to see how hard it will be for Jerry to move troops around."

"We go tonight then sir?"

"You go tonight. And, between you and I, the day after tomorrow is when Operation Market Garden begins. With any luck Monty will be successful and it will make life easier for our lads when they go in."

"Do we know when that will be?"

"D-Day is still the 1st of November. The Canadians are set to begin their advance the first week in October."

As I went to tell my men and the boat's crews the news I could not help but reflect that there seemed to be too much optimism. D-Day had almost been a disaster. Had the Utah landings been typical then we would have lost the beachhead. I never liked counted chickens! They seemed to be putting great faith in this attempt to capture bridges in such a dramatic fashion.

Breskans had by now been captured and we could sail even closer to the southern bank of the Scheldt. It made life easier for us. Then we headed due north. Lieutenant Williamson had marked the minefield on his map. His crew had worked out that it was a line rather than a field. For a small boat like us that made life easier. Once we had passed two mines we would be safe from any other underwater obstruction. It was still an unpleasant experience as we slowly sailed between the prongs of the deadly mines. The two hands with the wooden boat hooks had practised in the canal and they were quite adept at fending away the mines. We then sailed north west with the black shadow of the land to the left. We were further north than the searchlights which had probed the water or perhaps they had been destroyed in the bombing raids. The bombers would do little damage to the concrete emplacements but the searchlights had to be out in the open and I hoped that they had been damaged. I had seen the guns in the emplacements. One shell would blow us out of the water.

The weather had been deteriorating for the last few days. The sea was choppier although we were so close to the land that it was bearable. When the launch went out to sea, however, having dropped us off, I feared that the crew would have a difficult time. A rogue mine, freed from its mooring could spell disaster.

All of that went from my mind as we neared the coast. My team would be dropped off first. I had Hay, Fletcher, Beaumont, Hewitt and Crowe with me. Sergeant Poulson would lead the others north of Westkapelle. I watched the surf and the darkened dunes as we closed with the shore. I put from my mind the hidden stakes; the crew would watch for them. At the forefront of my mind was the worry that our last two incursions would have alerted the Germans. I knew that we had left a gap of a few days but, even so, this was the third time we had visited the well.

The boat was lowered and we climbed aboard. We only had thirty yards to paddle. The Lieutenant now had more confidence and had brought us in as close as he had dared. I doubted that he would be able to manage the same feat on the pick-up. I checked my watch just before I descended. I saw Lieutenant Williamson doing the same. We had exactly three hours to perform our task. That was probably longer than was safe for we would have to risk daylight as we sailed back to our base.

The rubber dinghy was overcrowded but the wind, tide and luck were all with us. We ground ashore. I saw that here the beach was cleared of obstacles. We dragged the boat to the base of the steep dunes. I saw now why the Germans had adopted this strategy. The top of the dunes had a solid line of wire. It was a fence. Any infantry who made the beach would struggle up the dunes and then have to battle the wire.

Hewitt and Crowe were going to act as our guards. When the dinghy was secured they came with the rest of us up the slope. I reached the top and peered over. More by good luck than anything else I saw that we had arrived at a part where there were no sentries. I saw, in the distance, the glow of a glowing cigarette but where we had reached was quiet save for the sound of the sea and the wind which moaned as it blew. I took out my wire cutters and held them up. The others did the same. With six wire snips we made short work of the wire. I wanted a gap large enough for us to get through quickly.

The four of us who were going to make the reconnaissance slipped through and Hewitt and Crowe put the ends back together. It would easily be seen in daylight but, at night, it looked as though the wire was whole. This was our last mission. It would not matter if the Germans knew we had been here.

Once over the dunes we moved towards the emplacements which we could see. Above us loomed the first of the 150mm naval guns in their emplacements. I could see marks where bombs had struck but there was no damage. I saw the barrels of anti-aircraft guns too. There were 88 mm as well as 75 mm. Beyond them I saw the barrels of another three of these huge guns. We moved forward and I heard the bark of dogs to our right. As I looked I saw that here they had built individual pill boxes. I saw the shadows of machine gun barrels. If there were dogs then they had more patrols. It would be hard but we had a job to do. I waved the men forward. Hay took the rear.

As we descended the rear of the embrasures it was into darkness. From our left there was the faintest whiff of wood smoke. That would be the small hamlet of Westkapelle. My feet splashed in water. We were now in the inundation caused by the breaching of the dykes. We stepped into the water. At first ankle deep it became deeper the further inland we went. It reached my knees but no deeper. We had walked half a mile inland. The water had caused problems but it was not deep enough to trouble vehicles. The Germans could reinforce the beaches.

I turned us around and headed towards Westkapelle. I would return to our rendezvous point from that direction. The water became shallower. Reaching the base of the dunes I checked my watch. We had just over an hour until our pick up. I heard voices to our right. My gun was out in an instant and the four of us crouched and waited. Above us, on the crest of the dunes I saw a German patrol. They had no dogs with them. If they had then we would have had a problem. There were five men in the patrol. They had field caps and their rifles were slung over their shoulders. They walked in silence.

I waited until they had disappeared to our left and then we scrambled up the dunes. I looked to my right. The hamlet was less than half a mile away. The darkness meant we could not see any detail but I recognised that they had double banks of wire and there was another of the huge guns. I risked walking the same route as the German patrol. I held up my gun. The others nodded and took out their weapons too.

We were just a hundred yards from the first gun we had seen when I heard a dog bark and then the sound of a German gun. It was obvious that they had either found my two men or the boat. We ran. The sound of gunfire increased. I heard the distinctive sound of a Colt. Neither Crowe nor Hewitt had silencers for their weapons. I saw the German patrol ahead. They were sheltered beneath the huge gun and firing at the wire. They were sixty yards from me and it was in the dark but we were merely shadows. Further down the beach I heard the sound of a klaxon. The alarm had been given. I knelt and aimed my gun. I emptied the magazine at the five Germans. Hay used his silenced Colt. The Germans had no idea the direction from which the bullets were fires. Rising I holstered my Colt and took out a grenade. The Germans had pulled back thinking that the bullets which had hit four of them were from my men on the beach. Hay had not emptied his gun and, as we neared them, he put two into the one soldier who had not been hit.

"Get to the boat!"

The three of them ran towards the wire. I heard the sound of voices coming towards me. I also heard the bark of a dog. I had just pulled the pin when the Doberman leapt from the dark. My hand was already drawn back and I smashed my fist with the grenade in it into the side of the dog's head. It fell stunned. A fusillade of bullets zipped around me. I pulled back my hand, released the handle and threw the grenade as far as I could. My men had parted the wire and I ran and dived through the gap. As I did a forward roll towards the beach the sky was lit by the grenade. There were shouts and screams as the Germans were showered with shrapnel. I reached the beach and heard Hay shout, "Sir, in the water."

I ran towards the sea as machine guns belatedly opened fire at the wire. I waded out to where the dinghy bobbed. The bullets from the shore continued to fire blindly into the darkened sea. I was pulled on board and we paddled out. We paddled hard until I could not see the wire. Then we stopped.

"Anyone hurt?"

"No sir."

I looked at my watch. We had just fifteen minutes to wait. Would the Germans give us that time?

"Better get a little further out."

As we paddled out further the sea became choppier. We were overcrowded. "Crowe and Beaumont, stop paddling and start bailing."

The sky above the beach was suddenly illuminated by a star shell. Had we stayed where we were then we would have been seen and been within range of the beach guns. As it was the machine guns fired. At that range a hit would have been lucky. Their first shots were short and, as the shell slowly dropped, their second was too high. The sea was plunged into darkness.

"Sir! The launch!"

I saw the launch's bow as she powered towards us. The star shell had done us a favour. It had shown the boat where we were.

As the second star shell lit the sky we grabbed the scrambling net. This time the machine gunners were using tracer and I saw the bullets snake their way towards us. All six of us were on the net and I shouted, "Go! Go! Go!"

The rubber dinghy would have to be sacrificed. The launch turned and roared north in one move. We had to cling on for dear life. The helmsman turned us away from danger. As we came on to a straighter course hands reached down to lift us aboard.

I rolled and flopped on the deck like a cod fish. I looked up at Abel Seaman Spalding, "Thanks sailor!"

He grinned, "You lads lead exciting lives sir! A bit too exciting for me!"

I stood and made my way up to the bridge. I saw that it was Bill on the wheel, "Thanks. That was damned close."

The Lieutenant said, "Was it worth it sir?"

"It certainly was. The dykes have been breached but the flooding is not deep enough to cause problems. I just hope that Sergeant Poulson has had more luck than us."

We sailed north. I saw lights appearing to our right as the alarm rippled up the coast. I took out my glasses as we neared the northern dunes. These were not as steep as those we had had to negotiate but I saw the barrels of the big guns. The RAF had not even dented them.

The lookout whistled and I peered over the Perspex of the bridge. I saw the dinghy bobbing in the water. With no fire from the shore we were able to recover both the men and the dinghy.

"I think we can go home, Lieutenant."

He pointed west. "We will have to take a detour, sir. When we were heading to pick you up one of the lookouts spotted a rogue mine. We will have to travel in daylight."

"Can't be helped Lieutenant. You did a good job. Thanks." I gathered my men below decks. "It looks like we will have to travel in daylight. This launch isn't heavily armed so we will have to do what we have done before and use our Tommy guns."

Gordy said, "A shame we haven't got a grenade launcher. They are handy."

Sergeant Poulson shook his head, "If it is an E-boat which comes after us then that wouldn't help much."

"Speculation gets us nowhere. Hewitt, sort out some food. The crew have too much to do. Emerson get the kettle on. It will be a long way home."

When dawn broke we had passed the minefield but we were still on the wrong side of the German lines. The Lieutenant had increased the speed and was using the channel which was close to the coast. There were small batteries to our right on the southern bank of the Scheldt. We were stood to from before dawn's first light.

Bill Hay shaded his eyes and looked upwards. "Low cloud cover sir. They might not get any aircraft up."

I was not so certain. I was a pilot and knew that some pilots would fly in these conditions. "There are guns on the shore and there are small craft the Germans could use. Until we pass Breskans we are in danger."

Ironically we could see Breskans when all hell broke loose. Although the coast was half a mile away 88 mm guns began to fire at us from the southern shore of the Scheldt.

"Full speed chief! We will have to risk the shoals!"

"Aircraft at three o'clock!"

The sharp eyed lookout had spotted the two 109s as they swung around. Lieutenant Williamson said, "Gun crews fire when you have a target."

Water spouts told us that the shore guns had our range. Chief Petty Officer Leslie shouted, "I am going to weave! Hang onto something!"

My men all had their Thompsons and I braced myself with my back against the bridge and feet against the hatch. I did not need to tell my men when to fire. This would not be our first time under fire from attacking aircraft. I saw that the two aeroplanes were heading towards us from line astern. The pom poms at the front would only be able to fire when the two aeroplanes soared over the bridge. They would target the 40mm at the stern. With just a guard around the barrel the two gunners would be exposed to the machine guns mounted in the wings of the two Messerschmitts. The pilot in me noticed that they were flying one above the other to allow them both to fire at the same time. These were old hands. My only hope was that they did not realise that they would have to face twelve Thompsons as well.

The 40 mm began to fire. They were using tracer and I saw the arc of the shells. The two Germans opened fire at the same time. The cone of fire from the two aeroplanes destroyed the gun and the two gunners in a five second burst. Blood spattered the bridge. We could not fire yet. We would be wasting bullets. They fired a second burst but Bill Leslie threw their aim off with a manoeuvre to the left. When they were a hundred yards away we began to fire. We did not aim; we just threw up a wall of metal through which the aeroplanes would have to fly. My gun clicked empty and as I reached for another magazine the leading aircraft exploded just astern of us. I do not know what we hit but it was effective. I was pushed against the bridge by the blast while others were thrown to the deck. I saw that the explosion send debris towards the second 109. Something must have done some damage for smoke began to come from the engine of the second aeroplane and the pilot wheeled away. Those of my men who had reloaded and regained their feet opened fire but did no further damage.

"Captain Harsker! The skipper! He has been hit!"

Chapter 10

"Hewitt!"

I ran to the Lieutenant. He had been hit in the upper right arm. It was a bloody wound and the Lieutenant looked pale. He gave Chief Petty Officer Leslie a wan smile, "Take charge, Chief I may…"

He passed out.

Hewitt had his medical kit with him. The launch did not warrant an SBA but Hewitt was the best medic I had ever met. He said, "Sir, get his jacket off."

One of the crew, white faced, came up to the bridge, He pointed to the wrecked gun and crew, "Chief Petty Officer, Hughes and Hook, what do we do with them?"

Bill did not take his eyes from the sea, "Just cover their bodies with blankets for now. I will sort them out when we get back. Go on son, you can do nowt for them now. They are past caring." His voice was very gentle. The young rating looked to be barely eighteen.

"Here, sir, press this dressing against the wound."

Blood was pouring from the wound and I held the dressing as tightly as I could. Hewitt quickly applied a tourniquet and tightened it. He took a hypodermic from his kit and injected the Lieutenant's arm. "Wilkinson, Crowe, carry the Lieutenant down to the mess. Sir, keep the pressure on. I'll go and get the table ready."

My two Commandos gently lifted the Lieutenant and we manoeuvred our way from the bridge. Getting him down the stairs was hard and I had to release the pressure briefly. The tourniquet was doing its job and little blood flowed. Hewitt had made the table into a makeshift operating able. He had already washed his hands and donned rubber gloves. He had two table lights ready. "On the table lads." The two men laid him gently on the table.

I saw the trickle of blood coming down his cheek. "Hewitt, he has a wound to his head too. That is why he passed out."

Hewitt got the lamp and held it close. He took a piece of lint and wiped away the blood. "He has been lucky, sir… it is just a graze. Alan, you take charge of the tourniquet. Release it when I say and then tighten it. Joe, you hang around in case I need you. Thanks for your help, sir. Bill might need you up top."

"Right."

It was a shock to step on to the deck. The blood from the gunners had spread over a large area. The buckled shield and bent barrel were testament to the firepower of the two fighters. I saw a young rating who had covered their bodies vomiting over the side. Bill shook his head, "They are young lads. This has come as a shock to them."

I saw that the side of Bill's head had some of the Lieutenant's blood on it and there were a couple of bullet holes close to the wheel. "You were lucky."

"Aye sir but how long can a man's luck last. That 88 took the lad next to me on the 523 and this one hit the skipper. Third time....?"

Sailors were always superstitious. "Hewitt is working on the Lieutenant. He was hit in the head too."

"Is he all right?"

"I don't know. Can't we move a little faster?"

"Sorry, sir, Jerry hit an oil line. Until the engineer repairs it we have to waddle along like a duck."

I shouted below, "Radio get in touch with base and say we have wounded on board. We need a doctor and an ambulance."

"Sir!"

It took an hour to repair the damaged line and that was the longest hour I could remember but no one else approached. We had long passed the batteries and were now approaching the Canadian lines. Hewitt came up as we neared the mouth of the canal. "The bullet went straight through, sir, but I am not certain if it nicked the bone. I gave him something for the pain. He has come to. He wanted to come back to the bridge but I told him that you had everything in hand."

"I have a doctor standing by."

I saw the army ambulance when we arrived. The Canadian advance had stalled a little and there was a hiatus which meant few casualties. Sam had been lucky. Hewitt had my men bring him on deck. His crew all cheered. I think that tiny gesture made up for the wound. He was no longer the young untried officer; he had battle scars and he had led them.

The medical orderlies took over once we had tied up. "You can leave him with us, sir. There is a doctor waiting for him."

As the Canadian orderlies loaded him into the ambulance he tried to say something. Whatever it was it was lost in the noise of the traffic coming down the canal. They were readying the landing craft. The amphibious assault on the north bank of the Scheldt would soon begin. Gordy brought up my gear, "Take the men ashore, Gordy. I will join you soon."

"Right sir." He walked over to Bill Leslie and clapped him about the shoulders. "Well done Bill! For a taxi driver you aren't half bad!"

"Aye well if I lived off your tips I'd starve! You watch out for yourself Gordy. I'd like a pint off you when all this is over."

Gordy waved a hand as he stepped ashore.

I looked at the bloody deck, "I hate to leave you to clear all this up, Bill."

"Second in command, sir, it's my job. We were lucky. If your lads hadn't been here then I think they would have got us on a second pass. It was just their bad luck to be on the gun. They were good lads."

I nodded, "I think the Lieutenant will need some helping writing to their relatives."

Bill's face fell, "I'd forgotten about that."

"I will inform Major Foster. He can arrange for the burial of them."

"I'll sew them in their hammocks, sir. It's an old navy tradition and it will make it easier for the young lads. We don't want them to have to look at their bodies. We have seen it all before but…"

I shook his hand, "We keep saying goodbye and then meet up again. But just in case this is… well it has been an honour to serve with you. And hopefully we can get together after the war."

"Aye sir, it has a nice ring to it that, '*end to the war*'. That's worth a drink."

Major Foster was waiting impatiently for me on the quayside. For him the dead men were an incidental. "Well?"

Shaking my head I said, "The dykes have been breached but it won't stop vehicles. They have wire and concrete waiting at Westkapelle. And the minefield… the bigger landing craft won't even get close."

"I know. We are going to use Buffaloes and DUKWs. They can be carried aboard the big boys and then launched when it gets too dangerous for the landing craft. It is another reason why we have not started yet."

"I see we have more landing craft."

"They are for the attack on South Beveland. Compared with Flushing and Westkapelle that should be relatively easy."

"Amphibious landings are never easy."

"If you would write your report. I will read it and then get back to you with any questions. Your transport to take you to Ostend will be here tomorrow."

"Right. I'll get on with it then." I turned, "The launch had two fatalities. Bill Leslie is on his own."

He nodded and picked up the newly installed field telephone, "I will get on to it straightaway. How is the Lieutenant?"

"I am not certain. It was just his arm but…"

"Quite. I hope he is all right. He has potential."

Would he live long enough to show just what he could achieve? I made my way back to the café. "Sergeant Poulson, nip back to the Motor Launch. Tell Bill that we are leaving tomorrow if he wants first dibs on the café."

"Right sir! I think that will please him."

It took an hour to write everything up. When Polly returned I added what he had told me. I guessed that the northern dunes would be marginally easier than the southern ones but neither would be a cake walk. By the time I returned I saw a lorry removing the two bodies from the launch and Bill had his crew hosing and scrubbing the deck. When the Lieutenant returned there would be no sign of the blood. The mangled gun had already been removed.

I handed the report to the Major. "What will happen to the launch now sir?"

"Oh it is still useful. It represents the most potent vessel we have in the river. The experience the crew gained with your chaps will be invaluable." He tapped the papers to straighten them. "You will want to get a little rest eh? I will see you in the morning before you leave. The journey south should be just a little easier than the one north." He was a little blasé about the whole thing. I suppose that came with the job. He dealt with the bigger picture and two dead ratings were a small price to pay for what we had learned.

Returning to the café I found it deserted save for my three sergeants. "Where is everybody?"

"Fletcher decided that we ought to give a party for the crew of the Motor Launch as this was going to be our last night here. He took the lads to get what they needed."

"Where from? There's nothing here!"

Gordy laughed, "This is Fletcher we are talking about, sir. With his guile and Beaumont's brains they are a frightening pair. The rest just go along with them. Don't worry it will turn out tickety boo!"

"That's what worries me. Thank God we will be sixty miles away by this time tomorrow! Do the crew know?"

"Not yet, sir. We thought you could invite them. Bill is your mate, isn't he sir?"

"You are right." I strolled back to the canal. Bill was sitting on a bollard smoking his pipe. "All squared away then?"

"Aye sir. It wouldn't do for the young Lieutenant to see the mess. This is better. Any idea how he is?"

"It is a bit early yet. If you pop over to the office in an hour or so and ask Major Foster to phone for you."

"Will do. Thanks sir."

"And you and your lads are invited to a party in the café tonight. Scouse Fletcher has decided we should part with a party."

Bill smiled, "That will stop them brooding. It would do them good to hear from your lads. You lost soldiers didn't you, sir?"

"Too many to count Chief, far too many."

"Well the veterans can help the young lads. A grand idea sir, a party! Good old Scouse. He might be a scallywag but thank God he is on our side."

As I headed back to the café I ran through some of their names: Fred Briggs, Jack Jackson, George Lowe, Peter Groves, Jimmy Smith, John Herbert, Harry Gowland, Reg Smythe and Grimsdale. I could not even remember Commando Grimsdale's first name. All had fought alongside me and all were now dead. They were spread from North Africa to Normandy and everywhere in between.

I reached the café and as I opened the door said, "Bert Grimsdale!"

"What sir?"

"Nothing, Polly, I was just remembering a name." I smiled, "I feel all the better for it." The day that we forgot the dead was the day their sacrifice became a waste. I would not forget. I would never forget and I would make sure that for the rest of my days I helped others to remember what these brave men had done in the dark days of this war.

Fletcher and his crew came back laden. I stood with my arm across the door, "Before you take one more step I want to know if the Military Police, or even worse the Belgian police, will be hot on your tails."

He affected an innocent look, "Sir, I am. what's the word, Rog?"

"Much maligned!"

"That's it sir! What he said. None of this is nicked! We traded for some and some of the other stuff we was given."

"What did you trade?"

"You would be surprised what they want. You remember when we were in Boom and Antwerp, well we relieved some of the Jerries of stuff they wouldn't need: flags, bayonets, daggers, pistols."

"Pistols?"

"They had no ammo for them. And a jerrycan of petrol goes a long way here, sir. So there you are, sir. We have a feast for tonight. We even managed to get a piggy! Joe Wilkinson is butchering it now. Dead handy with a knife is Joe."

"And where did you get the pig?"

He held up fingers as he enumerated, "Petrol, two haversacks, two old Mauser pistols, one was knackered sir, some German money we had and a couple of Commando berets."

I glared at them but it was an act. I was trying to stop myself from laughing, "And who is short of berets now then?"

Scouse smiled, "We are going back to the battalion aren't we sir? I am pretty certain that Daddy Grant will have new uniforms for us."

I stood aside and let them pass. Beaumont had a sheepish look on his face. "I fear, Beaumont, that the Commandos have merely prepared you for a life of crime. If your parents hoped for a bright future then they will be disappointed. I hope they enjoy visiting Pentonville Jail!"

Ken Shepherd said cheerfully, "We're Commandos sir! There's no jail could keep us for long! We were trained by you, remember!"

Bill Leslie brought rum for the sergeants and me. It was a party to remember. Bill was happy that his young ratings were mixing with my men. They were of a similar age but my men had survived. They had seen good friends die. They spoke of the memories they would have of their friends. They told jokes about the dead and the way they had lived. In my experience the best cure was a bunch of warriors eating, drinking and talking.

Bill Leslie leaned over and topped up my mug, "Thank you for this sir. The lads needed it."

"Don't thank me, Bill, it was Scouse who did it all."

"But he would not have thought of it without you running the show. Thanks." He toasted me. He was drinking neaters; I had watered mine. "Oh and the Lieutenant is going to be fine. The major rang the hospital for us. John did a good job and the bullet missed the bone. He hasn't got concussion. By the time the boat is repaired then he will be back on duty."

"And that is good news."

"So you lads are off to Ostend then sir?"

"We are and you and the launch will be the Royal Navy in the Scheldt!"
He laughed, "Priceless!"

Part Three
Attack at Flushing

Chapter 11

It was a relatively short journey to Ostend but the roads were clogged with Canadian troops heading for the north. Even as we had left the canal we had seen more barges arriving. We went back via Ghent and it seemed to me as though it was totally back to normal. There were people going about their business and they had even repaired some of the buildings. I suppose the people of Belgium were resilient. They had only been born in 1815 and had had a turbulent time since then.

As we drove south I wondered who was in command of our battalion now. We had been away for a long time. Officers had been promoted. I was not even certain if Lord Lovat had returned after being wounded at the battle of Belleville. It would be hard for us to become part of a regular unit once more. We had enjoyed too much freedom and I knew that my men would resent the presence of others.

Ostend was heaving. Soldiers and tanks vied with the people returning to a recently liberated town. It took us forever to make our way through the port. The harassed Military Police were not in the best of moods. Had my men not had an officer in the cab then I do not think they would have helped us at all. Frayed nerves do not make for smooth journeys. Eventually we saw the crude wooden sign which told us that we were home. I did not recognise the sentry. As Gordy said later, 'His uniform was too clean for him to be an old hand, sir!'

He snapped a smart salute. "Sir, Lieutenant Colonel Dawson said would you report to his office when you arrive."

"And where would that be, Private?"

"Sorry sir, it is a large tent. Go down the main track and it is the first right."

"And where are the tents for my men?"

He looked at me blankly, "The Colonel said for you to report to him, sir."

Shaking my head I said, "Freddie, drive on."

Gordy said in a derisory tone, "Wet behind the ears!"

When we pulled up outside the tent the sentry shouted something. Sergeant Major Dean strode out. He grinned at me, "Good to see you sir! Mrs. Dean sends her regards."

"Good to see you too, Reg. Any idea where my lads are billeted?"

He nodded, "I'll take you in and then show the lads their new home." He gave a slight frown. "The new colonel is hot on smartness, sir."

"My decent uniform is still in Rouen."

"No sir, the from the camp the kit was sent here. Anyway, sir, too late now." He lifted the flap and said, "Captain Harsker sir. Just arrived from his mission."

"Send him in then, Sergeant Major Dean and have someone bring us a cup of tea eh?"

"Yes sir." He gestured with his arm and held the flap open for me.

It was a simple tent although they had put in a plywood floor. There was a small desk to the side with a chair and then a larger one with three chairs before it. A map of the area stood on an easel. It was functional. He was younger than I had expected and he did not look like the fearsome character Reg Dean had implied. However, I knew what Reg meant. I looked dirty and dishevelled. The Colonel had a pressed and cleaned uniform. I smelled dirty!

"Sorry about my appearance sir but…"

He waved an airy hand, "Good God man I have seen the reports Major Foster has sent and I am astounded. What you and your men have done is above and beyond. You can have a bath and get a clean uniform from Quarter Master Grant later. Right now I want to get to know the most decorated officer under my command."

"There's not much to tell, sir."

Reg came in with the tea. The Colonel smiled, "You were right Sergeant Major, he is incredibly modest."

"Always has been, sir. I met his dad once and he is exactly the same."

"Of course, I should have made the connection. The British Ace from the Great War! Right then, Harsker. You have my undivided attention. Tell me about yourself."

I was the worst person in the world to ask but I did as I was ordered. I gave him the bare bones of my missions and operations. He was like a kitten with a ball of string. He was not happy until they were completely unravelled.

After I had finished he stood, "I am afraid that your work is not finished yet, Captain." He went to a map on an easel. "We are going in at Flushing. We have to take out the batteries there. Now you have been ashore and know what we face. You can give us the vital first-hand knowledge that we will need to succeed."

"Yes sir. It is the mines and the underwater obstacles that will hurt us. They will slow down the landing craft and then they can use their cannon and machine guns to have a field day. At Normandy they cleared the landing area. If we are going in next month then they don't have time. I can see the difficulty. Those big guns can hit anything which comes close to the shore but it will not be easy, sir."

"Major Foster has suggested to Admiral Ramsay that we try to take the town. You were at Dieppe and St. Nazaire. What is your opinion?"

"I think it will be easier than either of those. They don't have a citadel on high ground which can fire and direct fire. That was the problem at Dieppe. I think we could do it but we would have to scale a sea wall."

"Commandos can do that."

"True sir, but how many have done so recently? We did it at Ouistreham but I know a lot of others who last did it when they were training. That is wholly different to doing it under fire."

"Then that will be your job, Captain. I want the Commandos who are going in the first wave to be able to scramble up a sea wall like a damned spider!"

"Very well sir. Is D-Day still the 1st of November?"

"It is, although I expect us to move north before then."

"Don't the Germans hold that area, sir? We had to detour through Ghent to avoid their positions."

"The Canadians are confident that they can shift them before too soon. Anyway take tomorrow to find somewhere to train and then we begin the day after."

"Sir."

Sergeant Major Dean was waiting for me outside. "We are still getting organised, sir, but we will get there." He pointed up one of the tracks which radiated from the Colonel's tent. "There is your lorry, sir. I took the liberty of billeting you all together. You have your own tent, of course. Your lorry will need to be taken to the lorry park. I told Emerson where it was. I am pleased to see you, sir, safe and sound."

"And you Reg."

"And Miss Tancraville?"

"I hope she is well but I haven't seen her since before Normandy and I have had no mail since Paris. I dare say it is still chasing me around."

He frowned, "I will check up on that, sir."

"Sergeant Major Dean, when you have a moment!" The Colonel's request was, in effect, a command.

"Have to go, sir."

Polly and Gordy had everything organized. Emerson was climbing back into the cab even as I arrived. "Fred's just taking the lorry to the lorry park. I have sent Fletcher and Beaumont to get our gear. This is your tent sir. Gordy and I are sharing as are Hewitt and Hay. The lads have a bigger tent. It will be cosy."

"Right. Well, let the chaps have today to find their feet and their way around camp. Tomorrow we have to find somewhere close to train the men in scaling a sea wall."

Sergeant Poulson was sharp, "It is Flushing then, sir?"

"It looks like that is what we have drawn."

"It could be worse, sir. It could be Westkapelle."

"Ever the optimist, sergeant."

I saw that Reg had found some plywood for my tent. It looked to be an old packing case which had been taken apart. It wobbled a little but was better than the bare earth. That would keep things a little cleaner. They had left my Bergen and gear on my cot. That was all the furniture I had. There was an oil lamp looking a little lost by the side of the bed. I emptied my bag and then laid everything out, neatly on the bed. The weapons would need cleaning. I looked at the magazines. They would need replenishing. A voice outside said, "Sir?"

"Come in Beaumont."

The young Commando entered with a kitbag. "Here's your gear sir. We saw a few familiar faces around. Quarter Master Grant is here. He asked if you would pop in to see him when you have a minute. His stores are four tents from the mess tent and officers' mess."

"Right, Beaumont. I will do."

The first thing I did, after I had unpacked my kit bag, was to change into a clean and decent uniform. It was slightly creased but it looked better than the dirty and faded one I wore. Sea water, rain and the detritus of all the raids had taken its toll. Had I been back in England then Mum would have made it into dusters! With all my kit on it my cot looked messy. I decided to visit with Daddy Grant. He wanted to see me and I had a few requests to make of him.

When I emerged Scouse Fletcher gave an exaggerated salute, "Very smart, sir!"

I shook my head, "It would not do you any harm to smarten up too, Fletcher."

"Oh, I intend to sir. We have a town full of Belgian girls who will be desperate to show their gratitude to heroes like us!"

"Sorry to disappoint you, Fletcher, but there will be no leave."

He shook his head, "Those poor women they don't know what they are missing!"

My right arm was in constant motion as I marched through the camp. I had got out of the habit of saluting. We didn't bother in our section but here things would be different. Two young privates were behind the trestle table in the Quarter Master's tent. "Sir!"

"Is Quarter Master Grant around?"

"Yes sir!"

Before they could find him, my old sergeant emerged from the flap at the rear. He had the inevitable pipe in his mouth. "Good to see you sir!" He turned to the two privates. "I want you two to go to the special tent. There is a packing case there with the Captain's name on it. Go and bring it here."

"Yes, Quartermaster."

"My name, Daddy?"

"Yes sir. As soon as I found out you were heading back here I started to collect the kind of things I know you need. I have some German weapons and bits of kit as well as much ammunition for your Thompsons and Colts. I even managed to get three more silencers."

"You are a hero. How are you keeping?"

"I feel that I am more use here than back in Blighty. At least here I am close to the sharp end again. I would like to be here at the finish of all this."

"Despite what they are all saying, Daddy, it is not even close to the end. Jerry is just regrouping. This is not over."

"Aye I know. But I can dream. And I have something here for you. I kept it safe." He went to a locked metal box which lay on the corner of the trestle table. He took out a key and opened it. He handed me a pair of letters as though they were the most valuable things in the world. "Your mum came down to the camp not long before we left. She said she and your young lady both had letters for you. I think they were worried that you hadn't replied to their letters. Your mum is sharp as a tack sir. A lovely lady. She stayed with Reg and his wife. She gave me these for you and made me promise that I would give them to you when I next saw you."

"Thanks Daddy. They are a pair! I bet Susan found out where I was! I can just imagine them conspiring."

"You are a lucky chap sir and that's no error." His two men lugged the heavy box out. "If you take that with the Captain…"

"One more thing Quarter Master, have you a grenade launcher, grenades and an empty packing case? I need it to keep my tent tidy."

"Of course sir. Hang on a jiffy." He went out of the back and brought a long wooden box out. He placed it on the one the two soldiers were carrying.

"Quarter Master! This is heavy!"

"And you call yourselves Commandos! When you get to the Captain's section take a look at those lads with him! They are real Commandos! Hang on." He opened the box and put the grenade launcher and adapted grenades into it.

"Now hurry up and don't drop it!"

They struggled all the way back to our tents. Daddy was right. These were soldiers wearing a Commando uniform. A real Commando was made through working as a team and fighting against impossible odds behind the lines.

"Just drop them here. Thanks."

I saw the relief on their faces as they laid the two boxes down. They saluted and scurried off back to the Quarter Master's tent.

I opened the box and took out the grenade launcher and grenades. "Sergeant Poulson."

"Sir."

"A present from the QM. German weapons and ammo. Share out the .45 ammo and then have the German weapons cleaned. We will use them when the lads are being trained."

"Live firing sir?"

"We have to get them up to speed. The last assault any of them made was Normandy. That is four months ago and half of them never saw action there. You saw the defences at Walcheren. They need to be battle ready and that is our job."

I lugged the now empty packing case into my tent. I lay it on its side so that I could open it and use it to store weapons and clothes. It took me half an hour to organize it and then I closed it and placed the clean clothes I would wear in the morning on the top. Being in the army had taught me how to organize myself. I then took off my battle dress and laid it on my packing case. The light was fading and so I lit the oil lamp. It smoked at first; it was new, but the warm glow was comforting. I opened Mum's letter first. It was like eating your Sunday dinner; you saved the best for last. I would save Susan's letter.

August 1944
My Dear Son
Susan and I have not heard from you for some time. I daresay our letters are somewhere in France. I know what you have been up to thanks to Susan. You are just like your father! You are never content to sit back! At least you will receive an uncensored letter. I hate the blue lines. It feels as though someone has been going through your things! Susan has told me that you will be re-joining your battalion soon and so I intend to give this to someone you trust.

Your father has been sent to the far east. My two boys are both far from me. I know the newspapers are full of headlines about the war ending but I remember how many died in the Great War after they said that. Keep your head down! Until they sign some sort of peace treaty then young men will continue to die.

Mary is still a ferry pilot and she seems to enjoy it. She has spoken of continuing flying after the war is over. I would rather she would do as you have done and find someone nice to spend the rest of her days with!

Susan and I meet up once a week for tea and a chat. We are making plans. Don't roll your eyes! I can't see you but I know that is what you are doing. Your dad was the same. You might as well resign yourself to the fact that we are going to organize your life from the moment this war ends and there is nothing you can do about it!

Life is not getting any easier at home. The rations we have are now spread even further. It will take some time for this great country of ours to get back on its feet but with men like you and your Commandos we can make it great again. I know I am wasting ink and breath but try to keep your head down. Survive this war! We need you.

All my love,
Your Mother xxx

I carefully folded the letter and replaced it in the envelope. When things looked hopeless I would open it and read it. Mum was like a rock. When Dad had been swanning off around the world and Mary and I had been growing up it had been Mum who held everything together. She was a reassuring certainty in a world of uncertainty.

I sniffed the envelope of Susan's letter before I opened it. There was still the faintest aroma of her perfume. I used my dagger to slit it open. When I opened the letter a lock of her hair fell from it. I carefully laid it on the bed.

London August 1944
My Dearest Tom,

Your mother and I are concerned that you have not replied to our letters. I know that they are probably still following you all over but, as I have discovered that you will be re-joining your unit your mother has said she will give the letters to someone called Daddy Grant. This feels deliciously naughty. I can write an uncensored letter. Your mother says that we can trust this Daddy as he served with you. I envy you the loyalty of your men. I like the girls I work with but I do not think they would rally round like your men do.

Your exploits have kept me awake at night. You are not named but when I read a report or hear a radio transmission about the special Commandos then I know it is you. Major Foster's reports are a big clue where you are. Do be careful!

Your mum is a force of nature. She is planning our wedding and where we will live! I visited your house for a weekend in June when I was given a leave after the landings. You have a lovely home and she has been redecorating your old bedroom. I am sorry, Tom, but you will not find the bedroom you grew up in when you return. It is now a grown up bedroom. Beattie says that we can live there until you decide what you want to do and where you want to live. She is so practical. You are lucky in both your parents.

I could write more but your mum is waiting to take the train down to your old camp.

I have put a lock of my hair in the letter. I hope it reminds you of me. I would hate for you to forget me. I don't want your head turned by these French girls you must be meeting.

Keep your head down and I love you, now and always, Susan xxx

Anna's kiss suddenly made me feel guilty. I read and reread that until I heard Sergeant Poulson shout, "Mess!"

I put the letter back in the envelope and smartened myself up. It would not do to meet my brother officers looking scruffy. I knew that I needed a haircut and a decent shave. They would have to wait until the morning.

My men were waiting for me outside my tent. "Thought we could go in together, sir. They have a Sergeants' Mess and Officers' Mess in one tent."

"Thank you, Sergeant Poulson."

We marched to the mess tents. The reading of the letters had made us late. Our appearance made conversation stop as we walked into the joint mess. The Colonel waved me over. The sergeants had to queue but we had orderlies to serve us.

"Here you are Captain, we saved a seat for you here between Major Boucher-Myers and Lieutenant Gregson. The young lieutenant is keen to talk to you." I nodded to the other officers as I sat down. I realised that I did not recognise a single face. The deaths, wounds, promotions and transfers had taken all the officers I knew away. I felt like the new boy at school. I had experienced that many times when growing up with a father who was moved from airfield to airfield. The colonel continued, "Captain Harsker has just returned from Flushing. The day after tomorrow he will be training officer and put you all through your paces. We may well have a sea wall to ascend under fire!"

Major Boucher-Myers said, "I have heard good things about you. I spent some time working with Major Foster in the planning for D-Day. He speaks highly of you."

"He's a good chap. He is up north working on this next operation. We are in good hands."

"And I hear you were in the 1st Loyal Lancashires?"

"I was."

"I was in the East Lancashires. Small world eh?"

"It certainly is, Major."

The Major smiled, "The name is Bill. Can't be bothered with titles here in the mess. I dare say we will get the chance to chat but young Gregson there is about to burst out of his battle dress."

I turned to the eager young man. The thin pencil moustache told me that he was desperately trying to look older. "Pleased to meet you, Lieutenant, but don't believe all the stories you hear. My life has been duller than you think."

"It's John sir, and you are wrong. You have a V.C. and an M.C. I heard you are in for a bar too!"

"Winning medals is a lottery, John. I know many men who deserved those honours more than I. So tell me, have you been in the Commandos long?"

"I qualified in January, sir. I just missed you when you went to Normandy. I was at Ringway doing parachute training. You have jumped haven't you?"

"Yes, a couple of times. The Dakotas are better than the old Whitleys we used to use. You just dropped out of the bomb doors in those! We had more Roman candles than I care to remember."

"I thought about joining the paratroopers but my uncle is in the Commandos and I followed him. I was named after him. John Marsden."

"John? How is he? We served together before St. Nazaire."

"I know sir. He is a Major now and in the far east with Number One Commando."

"Did you not want a transfer to his unit?"

"I wanted to be in action as soon as possible sir. It takes weeks to get to the Far East. I don't want to miss out on the next battle. I hoped to be in on D-Day but I just missed it. I hear that Bréville was a hard fought battle."

"It was." The food had arrived and I leaned back to allow the orderlies to serve us. There was beer or wine and I chose the wine. I turned to Lieutenant Gregson. "Every battle is hard fought, John. The Germans are tough. When we go to Flushing they will hang on to what they have. You to have to be clever, fitter and deadlier than the men you fight."

"I know sir."

"How are the men you lead?"

"All good chaps."

"Your sergeant?"

"Young and keen sir, like all of them."

"Your job, John, is to use that keenness and not abuse it. Weigh up the value of your men's lives against the objective. Sometimes there are ways around problems. Commandos are thinkers. Use your mind more often than you use your gun and you will go far. More importantly you will have more chance of surviving this war."

I was questioned about Flushing by the Major and the other officers. I pulled no punches and told them of the difficulties we might encounter.

My men enjoyed their meal in the mess and as I lay in my cot, reading the letters again I heard them coming back to their tents. They had not been drinking but had been in high spirits having been talking to the other Commandos. They were singing.

Bless 'em all,
Bless 'em all.
The long and the short and the tall,
Bless all those Sergeants and WO1's,
Bless all those Corporals and their bleedin' sons,
Cos' we're saying goodbye to 'em all.
And back to their Billets they crawl,
You'll get no promotion this side of the ocean,
So cheer up my lads bless 'em all

Suddenly Reg Dean's voice rent the night, "And if you don't shut up now the lot of you will be on Jankers from now until hell freezes over!"

There was silence. Reg Dean had spoken.

Chapter 12

Ostend and the surrounding land were fairly flat and I despaired of finding a sea wall that we could use. I was lucky. The Germans were still holding out in Dunkirk and the coast road south was closed. On the Zee Dijk, not far from the bombed out airfield, I found a high dyke which would suit perfectly. It matched the one at Flushing. Although not as steep it would allow the men to land from the sea and try to scale the steep wall. The beach we would be using in Flushing, code named Uncle Beach, was close to the breakwater. This was as close as we could find. We would be able to use the dunes above the road and the abandoned German defences. It was perfect. I left my men to prepare the defences and then Emerson and I went back to the camp.

The Colonel was not in his tent. "He has gone to Ghent, sir, for a meeting." Reg waved me over, "And to hear news, sir. I had it from one of the radio operators that the paras have gone in. It happened a few days ago apparently. Eindhoven, Nijmegen and Arnhem are all being attacked! The bloke I spoke to said that the war could be over by Christmas. If they take those bridges then we are across the Rhine and we will soon be in Berlin."

He sounded so excited and I hated to prick his bubble but I had to, "Reg can you think of any operation which has gone smoothly enough for us to reach all of our objectives? We were supposed to be in Caen a day after we landed; it took weeks. I think it a bold strategy and it might work but I am sceptical."

He nodded, "You might well be right. I think I just wanted it to be over."

"And I think that is true of all of us. Tell the Colonel, when he returns, that we have a suitable wall for them to train." I stood and went to the map. I tapped the beach. "It is here. I would suggest using two landing craft at a time. We can have two in the morning and two in the afternoon. If we have four days we might get through them all."

"Right sir."

"Oh and tell him we are using live rounds."

"Live rounds, sir?"

"He wanted real. We will give him real."

"But remember Slapton Sands sir!"

Smiling I said, "The difference, Sergeant Major, is that it wasn't Commandos firing at Slapton Sands. No one will get hurt. You have my word on that."

After I left the tent I went to the lorry. "Head back to the lads and bring them back when they are finished making the defences."

I headed for the Quartermaster's stores. I had some more things to pick up. There was little point in training and being soft on the men. The Germans would not.

That evening the conversation was thankfully not, as on the previous night, about me, but the ambitious parachute drop by American, British and Polish paratroopers. The news had filtered through. Many were already talking about the attack as though it had been successful. All that we knew was that it had taken place in the third week of September. The news we had was three or four days old. The young officers like John Gregson were envious. The landings on D-Day had been small scale compared with this. I remained silent. Major Boucher-Myers said, "You are quiet Tom. Do you envy the paratroopers?"

Shaking my head I said, "I fought with them at Bréville and a finer force of soldiers I have yet to meet but when we chased the Germans from Falaise they saved a lot of their good armour. A great deal escaped from the pocket. They have Waffen SS and they are still in good shape. The paratroopers go in with even less heavy weapons than we do. Do you think they can stop a Mark IV let alone a Tiger or a Panther with a six pounder? That is assuming they land enough of them. Remember the Americans at St. Mere Église? They were spread over a huge area. Many of them landed in the town and were massacred. This sounds like an ambitious drop. I am no general but I might have tried just one bridge or perhaps two but a whole line of bridges is asking for trouble."

John Gregson had been listening, "I thought you would have been all for this. I hear they have the Guards Armoured Division too."

"When we went into Antwerp we were held up by Panzerschrecks and 88s. We met very few tanks. We were lucky when we managed to take one bridge but our luck ran out when we got close to a defended town."

The Major said, shrewdly, "But you lost no men."

"We had wounds but we were just the scouts. The Rifles and the 11th Armoured took casualties sir. A rocket makes a mess of a scout car sir and that is what the Guards will be using to check the road. Tanks need open country where they are not restricted. That is why we beat Jerry at Falaise. He had open country tanks and the bocage hemmed him in. The land they are crossing is covered in bridges. You block a bridge or you barricade a bridge and the advance stalls. Sometimes a quick fix doesn't work."

John Gregson had obviously done his homework, "Yes sir but this is precisely what the Germans did in 1940! They used the paratroopers to take the main centres."

"German Paratroopers are the equal of ours. They were successful at Crete and in Holland. Those two actions wiped them out as a force. They have never been used since. The remnants are still in the Netherlands fighting as line troops. Is it really worth gambling the Red Devils in the hope of a quick victory?"

The Major laughed, "Well thank you for that bucket of cold water Captain!"

"With respect sir, I have been fighting the Germans since 1940. I would rather take it slower and guarantee winning than waste men's lives as they did in the Great War in the hope of a win on the football pools! It might come off but the odds are stacked against it."

I did not enjoy being so negative but I did not want my battalion to go into battle thinking that the war was almost over. We only won when we thought we were going to lose. The British are stubborn that way.

After we had messed I gathered my men in the back of the lorry and explained what we would do. When I had finished they seemed happy enough. "I have spoken with the Colonel before dinner and he said he would like it to be as realistic as possible. He is happy for us to use live ammunition. I have told him that we will be careful. Do not make a liar out of me. You are all good enough shots to miss just as you are to hit when we fire at Germans. The first two sections who attack tomorrow have been given carte blanche to choose their time and method of attack. We will be up at three and in position by three thirty."

"You think they will try a sneak attack before dawn?"

"I do indeed. It is what I would do. They will try to catch us napping. There are two big boxes at the back of my tent. Put them on the lorry."

"What are they sir?"

"Searchlights!"

The men were eager and we were in position by three fifteen. I had a German sub machine gun and my sniper rifle. I had plans to scare them just a little. Major Boucher-Myers and his sections would be the first to attack. Lieutenant Gregson was part of that force. I knew they were keen to outwit me. I hoped I was ready for the challenge.

I had my binoculars and was scanning the dark sea. The German defences had not needed much cleaning up. We would present a good target for the Commandos who would be landing. Shepherd and Beaumont had rigged up the thunder flashes which I hoped would replicate the shells and mortars the Germans would be using. Emerson and Fletcher were ready with the searchlights while Sergeants Poulson and Barker had the two flare pistols ready to light the night.

Alan Crowe said, "I can hear them sir."

I used my glasses and scanned the sea again. I spotted them. They were two dark shapes and they were about a hundred yards from shore. They were using the Landing Craft Infantry (small) which held a hundred men each. I knew they only had eighty in each one. They did not use a ramp but had gangplanks which were launched by rollers over the deck. They were vulnerable on the beach. The beach itself was shallow. It was no more than thirty yards deep and then they had fifty feet of seawall over which they would have to scramble.

"Wait for it, wait for it! Emerson and Fletcher, now! Flares, now!"

The effect was spectacular. The pre-dawn light turned day as the two flares fell, lighting the sky, and the searchlights struck the boats. Three Commandos, standing on the bows ready to land, were so shaken that they fell into the water.

"Open fire!"

My men were looking forward to this and their bullets zipped over the heads of the two boats. I heard the officers shouting for their men to get off the boats as quickly as they could. Using the telescopic sight I aimed to the right of a stanchion on the right hand boat. Major Boucher-Myers was next to it. As the bullet pinged close to his head I saw him turn in shock. I fired four more bullets at the metal parts of the landing craft. As the men jumped in the water and prepared to race across the beach I shouted, "Now, Shepherd!"

My two explosive experts had set the thunder flashes in irregular lines up the beach. They now exploded them as the Commandos staggered across the sand. Most threw themselves to the ground as the charges exploded. It was like daylight as the two searchlights lit up the beach. By the time they managed to reach the sea wall the one hundred and fifty men were well spread out. I saw Lieutenant Gregson exhorting his men to climb the sea wall. We had covered it in the grease the cooks had collected from their cooking. The men who reached the sea wall were taking three steps forward and two steps back. Daylight had broken by the time the first exhausted Commandos pulled themselves over the wall and reached the road. My men all stood and emptied their guns ten feet above their heads.

Major Boucher-Myers was amongst them. He was breathing so heavily that he could barely speak. He walked over to me with his hand held out, "Well done Captain, you have made your point."

"Your men did well and they never gave up."

"You are right and we would have been firing back at you too had this been the real thing."

I pointed to the searchlights. "They would have been all that you would have seen. A night time attack is for a small group of men. A large number will attract attention and if the enemy knows you are coming then you are in trouble. We had flares and search lights when we did our recce. If they had been in force then we would not be here today."

He nodded, "And that bullet, the one that nearly took my moustache?"

"Yes sir that was me. I aimed at the side away from you so that any ricochet would miss."

"And for that I am grateful. Now would you and your men tell us how we should have done things?"

We spent an hour giving them tips and then half of my men went with them in the landing craft to land again. We had no more thunder flashes but we did fire over their heads.

Lieutenant Gregson said, "The grease, that wasn't realistic sir was it?"

"There is weed on the sea wall at Flushing, Lieutenant. It might not be greasy but it is slippery."

"And do you get around it?"

"You don't. You just have to go slowly with Germans firing at you. You will need two hands to hold on and so you need half of your men keeping down a covering fire. Try the light infantry method; one man cover his partner; they move and switch."

They headed back at eleven to allow the next sections to train. It gave us the chance to set our thunder flashes. The flares and the searchlights would be unnecessary. The exercise proved just as useful. No one fell into the sea because of the lights but other than that it went the same. There was no happier set of Commandos than my men as we headed back to camp. We now knew that we had more skill than most of the men with whom we served. We had always suspected it but now we knew. None would make anything of it. They were not that type, but inside each man felt a little better about himself.

Over the next few days we repeated the exercise. Of course, as Commandos spoke of what they could expect, the attackers became better on their first attempt. I did not mind. It meant that our men would be better prepared for the assault and fewer, hopefully, would die. Our satisfaction at the results of our efforts was offset by the bad news from the north east. I took no satisfaction in the news that the airborne offensive had failed. As I had dreaded, the Germans had found Panzers to stop the advance and the last bridge, Arnhem, had not been taken. Although bridges and land had been taken the vital bridge had not and, with winter approaching, it looked like stalemate there.

As usual we only heard the full story in the second week of October. The lack of news and the rumours seemed to confirm that it had not gone well. The Colonel and the Major were summoned to Ghent on the 15th of October. We had finished our training and, after cleaning up our training area and returning the excess equipment to Quartermaster Grant, we began our own preparations for the assault which was still scheduled for the 1st. The day after the colonel had returned all the officers were summoned to the mess tent for a briefing.

"Gentlemen Operation Market Garden did not succeed as well as it might have done. The final objective was not reached."

A buzz of chatter rippled through the tent. John Gregson looked at me as though I was some sort of clairvoyant. I shrugged.

Major Boucher-Myers stood, "Gentlemen, quiet, if you please."

The colonel continued, "Field Marshal Montgomery has now made our attack a priority. We will be travelling north to the south bank of the Scheldt where we will embark on the night of the 31st. We are to take the town of Flushing. We will be part of the 155th Infantry Brigade. We will be attached to the King's Own Scottish Borderers and the Royal Scots. Brigadier Maclaren will be in command. Attached to us will be Commandant Kieffer. He will command number five and six troops of the French Commandos who will be accompanying us." He looked at me, "Some of you know the Commandant I believe."

Eyes swivelled towards me and I nodded.

"We have a few days to get the men as fit as we can and to make sure that we have all that we need. Thanks to Captain Harsker and his men I am sure we are better prepared but in light of the Airborne operation, even more is riding on this. We have to succeed and open Antwerp before winter sets in. Now Major Boucher-Myers will go through the individual dispositions."

It took the rest of the morning for the plan to be explained in full. We were to go in first at 05.30 with Major Boucher. Our target was one of the two breakwaters. If that was successful then we were to clear the guns which covered Uncle Beach and the main landing area. They would land at 06.40. I thought it was an ambitious time frame. It assumed, as with all army plans conceived far from the battle field, that the Germans would cooperate fully and nothing would go wrong. Tarbrush was the code name for the assault party which would take the other breakwater. They were from the Kings Own Scottish Borderers.

Many of the officers had questions and it was one o'clock before we were dismissed. The cooks had been waiting to set up the mess for lunch and we were hurried out. The colonel and the major waved me to their side. "Captain Harsker, if you would come with us to the office."

"Sir."

Reg Dean and a corporal were waiting for us.

"Tea, Sergeant Major."

"Sir, Mackenzie, you heard the colonel; chop, chop."

"Commandant Kieffer spoke very highly of you Tom."

"They are good soldiers. We went in with them on D-Day."

"They will be leading the assault on the main beaches. However aerial photographs show that they have placed a 40 mm gun at the end of the eastern breakwater. That is our target. Major Foster wants you to go to Breskans and then cross the river to eliminate the gun. We are aware of the vulnerability of the LCA to cannon fire."

"That is what we will be using in the actual attack, sir?"

Major Boucher-Myers nodded, "Yes, Captain. The Buffaloes will launch from the LCTs and will be further out when they begin their attack. It is vital that we clear the breakwater quickly so that we can attack the guns covering Uncle Beach, if we do not then a lot of men will die."

"Why not use bombers to destroy it?"

"They have tried and missed. The main target still remains the dykes and the concrete emplacements."

"What about the big guns, sir? Will the battleship and monitors be engaging them?"

The colonel and the major exchanged glances, "When they have supported the marines on Westkapelle then, yes. But, initially, we will have to endure their fire. It is thought that the Westkapelle batteries pose the greatest threat. The Canadians are making great strides in the advance from the mainland. It is hoped that they will exert pressure from the east by the time we go in from the river."

I bit back my retort. Once again the planners were making assumptions which I knew to be false. Little would be gained from a complaint. I would sound as though I was whining. "Right sir, so we leave when?"

"Today, as soon as your men have eaten. But watch out Tom. The Canadians say that the road north is clear but Major Foster said that there might be some isolated units. Go as though you are travelling through hostile territory. We are giving you a Kangaroo. It will be a little slower than a Bedford but you will have all day to get there."

"Right sir. Liaison?"

"The Motor Launch you used will be in Breskans and Major Foster will be waiting there. He is travelling from the canal on the launch. He will brief you."

"Sir, I'll be off."

As I headed back to the section I knew that the plans had been changed as a result of the failed landing. The gun had not been there when we had scouted out the port. I had no doubt that they would place a second on the other breakwater. The defeat of the paratroopers would have made the Germans even more determined to hold on to their islands which defended the river.

"Right lads, time to pack up." I heard the sound of an armoured vehicle. The Kangaroo lumbered towards us.

Fred Emerson's face broke into a grin, "Is that ours sir?"

"It is indeed. Do you think you can handle it?"

"Does a duck quack sir? No bother!"

"Where to sir?"

"We are heading, Sergeant Poulson, for Breskans. They want us to go to Flushing and knock out a 40mm. And before you ask, they have tried using bombers and failed."

"Righto sir. Are we coming back here?"

"I doubt it. Better take everything with us. It will be a little crowded but we can strap my packing case to the rear and use that for the ammo and guns. We can sit up top. Apparently, we may run into Germans on the way north. The Canadians have supposedly cleared the road but there are still bands of Germans trying to get home."

I was pleased now that we had been so careful about replacing equipment, guns and ammunition. We would be many miles from the nearest QM stores!

Chapter 13

It was the middle of the afternoon by the time we finally got going. Grey scudding clouds threatened rain and, as I sat up top, I donned my oilskin. Heedful of the warning I had Bill Hay on the Browning machine gun just in case we found any Germans and I had my Thompson close to hand. We had fifty miles to go. We could have made it a shorter journey but that would have risked taking us closer to the fighting.

We passed Bruges and continued to head east. The converted tanks did not go as quickly as the Bedford we had used before but it was safer and we would reach our new home in three or four hours at the most. We had just passed Aalter and were heading for the bridge over the canal, the Brug-Noord, when we heard the firing ahead.

"Stop, Freddie, let's see what is ahead."

I took out the binoculars. The Low Countries were well named and I could see all the way to the canal. I saw grey figures firing. I moved the glasses to the right and saw Canadian soldiers who were defending the canal bridge.

"Okay Emerson, full speed. German soldiers to the west of the canal. I think they are trying to get home!"

I cocked my Thompson and then looked again with the glasses. It was just a handful of Canadians. They were behind sandbags but they appeared to have no machine guns. The Germans were in force. I heard the chatter of an MG 42. Numbers were harder to estimate for many were taking cover and I just saw the flash from their muzzles.

"Crowe, get the grenade launcher. Let's see if we can discourage them. Lance Sergeant Hay open fire as soon as you are in range."

"Sir."

I looked again through the glasses and saw an explosion in front of the sandbags. We were four hundred yards away. It was too far for the grenade launcher but Bill Hay saw his chance and he fired a burst. The gun had tracer rounds and we saw the bullets arc towards the Germans. They missed but it switched their attention to us. They began to fire at us but at that range their sub machine guns were inaccurate. Emerson was racing along at more than twenty miles an hour and soon we were all in range. Alan Crowe was a master with the grenade launcher. He had the eye for it. He had been a good cricketer at school and it showed. His first grenade soared high. He knew how to handle the weapon and it exploded just short of the Germans. The effect was spectacular. The shrapnel forced them down and they could no longer fire at us. We, in contrast, were able to pour fire at their position. As we were a tracked vehicle

Emerson was able to leave the road and he did so, heading directly for their position.

Suddenly I saw a white flag being waved and the sound of Germans shouting, "We surrender!"

"Cease Fire! Hewitt go and see if the Canadians need any help. Gordy take two men and disarm the Germans. See if they have any papers." I turned to Alan Crowe, "Spectacular shot, Alan, well done.

"When all this is over sir I might take up cricket again! You never know sir, I might get to play for Surrey or Essex."

We had learned long ago that German papers were often the most valuable item we could take. When we were behind the lines they were often the difference between success and failure.

"Emerson, take us across the canal. When we have finished here I want to push on to the Motor Launch."

"Sir."

When we reached the other side I jumped down and walked back to the Canadian position. Hewitt was bandaging a Canadian Sergeant's arm. Another lay with his cape draped over his body. The other four looked to be unscathed.

The Canadian Sergeant saluted, "Sergeant Matthews, Calgary Highlanders. Good job you came sir. We were almost dead meat."

"Glad to be of help. Have you a radio?"

He shook his head, "No sir but the Lieutenant will be along with our relief in an hour."

I pointed to the eight Germans who had survived our attack and were shuffling towards us. "Can you watch these until then?" I handed him a couple of German submachine guns. "These should keep them quiet."

"It will be a pleasure." He gestured to the body, "Hank was a good guy. If they get antsy I will use this."

I nodded, "We will take the grenades. We quite like them. Hewitt, have you fixed up the Jerries?"

"Just finishing, sir."

The most senior officer was a sergeant. I spoke to him in German. "You are now the prisoners of these men. If you behave then nothing will happen. Do not try to escape. They are angry that they lost a man."

The sergeant was surly, "And we lost men too. What if we get angry?"

"Then you will die! You invaded this land and we have beaten you. You lost! Be a man and deal with it!" I turned to the Canadians and said loudly and slowly, "It they give you any trouble, shoot them! Those are my orders." I saw that the Germans spoke enough English to understand my words. Their shoulders sagged in resignation. "They should behave now sergeant. Good luck."

"And to you, sir."

The delay meant that we did not get to Breskans until after dark. Knowing that the Motor Launch would be there we headed for the sea. We had seen Breskans when we had raided and knew that there was a harbour. As we passed through the ruined buildings I kept an eye open for the harbour we had seen. When I spied it my heart sank. There were signs, in English, telling us to stay clear as the Germans had mined the whole quayside.

Then Beaumont shouted. "There sir, I can see a wooden jetty and the Motor Launch."

"Good. Head for it, Emerson, but keep clear of the area with the mines eh?"

I saw that there were some ruined houses nearby; I had no idea where the civilians would be. A soldier waved us towards one of them.

He was a staff officer, "Lieutenant Wilford- Smith sir; Major Foster asked me to wait for you. This house is your billet sir. There is a field kitchen half a mile along the road."

"Where is the Major?"

"He will be along shortly sir. He is speaking with the Brigadier on the field telephone."

"Right, Sergeant, take the Kangaroo and go and get the men fed. Save some for me. I will have a word with the Lieutenant."

"Sir."

I climbed on to the Motor Launch. Leading Seaman Giggs knuckled his head, "Evening sir. Back again eh?"

"I am indeed, and the lieutenant?"

"In the mess with the Chief."

I descended below deck and saw that the Lieutenant still had his arm in a sling. Then I remembered that it had only been a few days since he had been wounded.

"Evening sir! Reunited again."

"We are Chief. How are you Sam?"

"They needed me, apparently. As the senior naval officer in the Scheldt I was returned to duty." He laughed, "Mind you all we have done for three days is to ferry officers from the canal to here. But I suspect your presence indicates something else."

"It does and I am afraid it will put you in harm's way again. They want us to go to Flushing and destroy a gun. There is no way we can do that quietly. It will be a hot one."

"The Chief made some improvements while I was in the hospital. He rigged a shield around the forward gun and until we get a new Oerlikon he has a double Browning with an oil drum for protection where the aft gun was destroyed."

"Oil drum chief?"

"Double oil drums really. One inside the other and the gap is filled with kapok. We found some German life belts and used them. It is better than nothing, sir and the gunner can duck down if it gets too dangerous."

"Very inventive."

"I remembered the sort of thing Lieutenant Jorgenson did."

"Well I just thought I would check in. I am off for a bite to eat. We have been given a billet in the buildings opposite."

"Not as nice as the café sir."

"No Bill. That was something to savour all right."

The mobile field kitchen served hot food. It all tasted the same but there was plenty of it. My men waved me to a table. Sergeant Poulson handed me my mess tin and Gordy my mug of tea.

"Everyone fit in the launch, sir?"

"Yes the young Lieutenant is back on duty. Still wounded but he is a game 'un."

The men chatted amongst themselves. The war was not a subject for discussion. When they had finished criticising the food they moved on to food they would have at home when the war was over. Once again beer was a popular topic of discussion. Then they began to talk of their plans after the war. That worried me. As Market Garden had shown the war was far from over.

"Tom! You made it. A word eh?"

I turned and saw Major Foster and his young lieutenant. The staff officer had a leather attaché case attached to his wrist.

I swallowed the last of my tea. "See you later, Sergeant."

They led me to a caravan which was attached to a Bedford lorry. "This is the general's own caravan. He said we could use it."

Inside it was furnished as a mobile office. There were four chairs and we sat on three of them. The lieutenant took out an aerial photograph of Flushing. Major Foster jabbed a finger at the eastern breakwater. "They erected this two nights' ago. The RAF have tried to bomb it but without success."

"I can see why." There was a low concrete wall surrounding it. I guessed they had cemented concrete blocks together. It was the quickest way to build a concrete gun position. Around those were sandbags and there was a metal roof. A tank busting Typhoon would have done some damage but little else.

"And we think they are building one on the western breakwater." I could see the concrete blocks which were already in place.

"And what do you want us to do, sir? If we don't go until the 1st then they have time to build and rebuild these over and over again."

"I know. We would like you to take them out on the 28th. That is under a week from now. That should prevent them from rebuilding but if you could make the breakwater unstable then that might help."

"You don't ask for much do you sir?"

"Beaumont and yourself are both good engineers."

"We will figure something out. And how about D-Day? What do we do then? Are we to go in on the LCA and LCPs with the rest of the troop?"

"No, Tom. You will go in half an hour before the advance party. Williamson will drop you off. We want you to take the breakwater on the east side. It will be close to Uncle Beach and that is where our men will be landing. Major Boucher-Myers and the rest of his troop will land at 05.40. Their job is to support you and, if possible, occupy the west breakwater. Then the troop will attack the guns which overlook Uncle Beach. The supporting troops will land at 06.40. The Commandos have to hold until daylight."

117

"You mean we take the breakwaters and then leave them?"

"Major Boucher-Myers has enough men to leave a guard there. And you will be leading the attack on the guns. It is your area of expertise."

"Right sir." After studying the maps for a little longer and asking more questions about the logistics of the attack I left to brief my men. At least we had seven days to prepare and study maps. I was more confident about the rest of the Commandos. I had seen them training and they would be ready. I just feared that we were being spread a little thin.

The next day we began to analyse the new information. It was not just the guns that they had added. They now had wire in the breakwater and on the beaches. They knew we were coming. I realised it would not be a surprise to them as the Canadians had been moving from Antwerp, across the isthmus, to close with the island. Canadian and British guns were also lining the shore behind the ruined houses. We would have our own barrage. This time the artillery would be firing in both directions.

I sat with my sergeants and Lieutenant Williamson while the men went for a ten mile run. We had a plan to devise.

"We will be using a dinghy. If we are taking explosives then that means we can only take eight men sir."

"Then we use three dinghies. A rubber dinghy is cheaper than a man's life. I think we need all of our men ashore this time, Sergeant Poulson."

"Right sir."

"You and Gordy can take the western breakwater. You can use Ken Shepherd as your explosives expert. You will have to hold the breakwater for up to an hour. I will be dropped off at the eastern breakwater. There will only be four of us. Beaumont can set the charges and we will take a couple of Bren guns."

"We are just going in to blow up the guns then sir?"

I nodded, "We go in, set the charges, blow the guns and get out before they can react."

"When we go in on the main attack, sir, will we be landing at the same places?"

"No Sergeant Poulson. We will all land at one breakwater. There will be a landing craft which will secure the other."

"I can stay close sir, and give covering fire."

"I don't want the Motor Launch risking, Sam. You might be needed to evacuate us off if things go wrong."

"Wrong, sir?"

"It was MLs and MTBs that saved men at Dieppe and St. Nazaire."

"We will be careful, sir, but we are part of Combined Operations. We wear the same badge as your chaps."

"Very well but if I give the order to pull out then you do so."

"Sir!"

"Good."

"The guns we are taking out sir, they aren't the big naval guns are they sir? That would take more explosive than we could carry."

"No, Gordy. The King's Own will deal with those. We are to make the beach safe for them. If we can flank the German guns and use the heights to get above them we can make it impossible for them to fire at our lads. Or so difficult that they don't hurt them too much."

Sergeant Poulson had been studying the map and he frowned as he looked at me. "Sir they seem to have made the town into a veritable fortress. There are new pillboxes and barbed wire at all the intersections."

"The brass have waited too long. We should have gone in yesterday. Every day will see the defences beefed up even more. And now we have to wait until a couple of days before the attack to do so."

"We'll do it sir. The lads are as well trained a bunch as I can remember."

"You are right Sergeant Poulson but we have to hold for an hour before Major Boucher-Myers and the rest of the Commandos arrive."

With that sobering thought we went through the timetable of the attacks and the problems we might encounter. We had learned this was the best way to succeed: you imagined that you would fail. We ironed all the problems that were likely to occur in the two attacks before heading back to our men.

Every day more and more troops and landing craft arrived. The German batteries across the river began to make life difficult for us. A couple of landing craft were sunk and the rest had to be moved to a place of safety. Sam took the Motor Launch back to Terneuzen too. It was not worth the risk of being moored where the Germans could fire at will. We knew we would not need it for a couple of days.

Life in the ruined houses was not easy. Already damaged, the shelling from the north of the river just made them dirtier and less stable. My men were resilient. The rest of the troop began to arrive in dribs and drabs. Ostend seemed like a luxury hotel in comparison with the war zone that was Breskans.

The night before the operation we sailed the Motor Launch across the river. We were going to eliminate the searchlights which they used to deter us. Peter Davis had been our other sniper but he was still in Rouen recovering. I was the only Commando on the Motor Launch which headed across the river. The two searchlights played across the water between the east and west breakwaters. We were half a mile away and Lieutenant Williamson had positioned his boat to one side. I could still see the searchlights. I used the bridge as a rest and aimed at the one on the right. I fired four bullets. Two were enough and the light was snuffed out. They quickly turned off the other but I knew where it was. The German tracer and the shells from the 40mm marked its place as clearly as a sign. I emptied the rest of the bullets into the searchlight. I did not see them strike but I would discover, the next day, if I had been successful. The Lieutenant spun the Motor Launch around and sailed back to Breskans without firing a shot. The Germans fired blindly into the sea.

The next day I used the powerful glasses on the Motor Launch to spy out Flushing. I saw the damage to the searchlights. They would not spot us. The island was cut off from its supply base. They would have to use what they had and searchlights were in short supply. Satisfied that we could now approach unseen I briefed the men for one last time and then we had an afternoon snooze. We would be busy over the next twelve hours.

We left Breskans after dark. We were fast enough to be able to cross the river in minutes but we wanted to avoid detection. We went under engines which were throttled back. This was not the same crew we had first met. The deaths of their two comrades and the success they had enjoyed had made them veterans almost overnight. The phrase '*the quick and the dead*' sprang to mind.

We had used our glasses to spy out the target. The second 40mm was in place and on the eastern breakwater they had added a third gun. As yet it was unprotected but we knew that it was likely they would be working, even while we attacked. It would not change our plans. We knew that there were mines in the water but it was not an obstacle which could stop us. The RAF's bombing had interfered with the pattern and they had no ships to replace the ones they had laid. They would not stop us; we would just avoid them.

We were blacked up and ready to go. With battle jerkins festooned with grenades and Tommy guns in hand we would be able to defend our demolition experts. Beaumont just had his Colt as did Ken Shepherd. If they had to fire a gun, then we had failed. With no searchlights to pick us out we were invisible. There was just two hundred yards between the two breakwaters and Lieutenant Williamson stopped a hundred yards from them. We launched all four dinghies at the same time. The Motor Launch had its engines cut and would drift with the tide.

The four of us paddled hard. I knew that there would be sentries. My Tommy gun was slung over my shoulder and I had my Colt in my belt. Speed was of the essence. Even if we were seen we would not back down. We were Commandos and we knew what we were doing. The boat bumped into the rocks at the base of the breakwater. We had a short length of rope and a grapnel hook. Fletcher leapt ashore and rammed the hook between the rocks. It would hold the dinghy. If it did not, then we would swim.

Beaumont was the most laden. He had the charges in his Bergen and therefore Fletcher, Hay and myself scrambled up the seawall until we came to the breakwater. Made of huge concrete blocks it was not difficult to climb. The three of us were like spiders as we ascended to the wire at the top of the breakwater. We knew the obstacle was there but it would not stop us. I slipped the silenced Colt from my belt. Lance Sergeant Hay now had one, too. Fletcher had a throwing knife. He would be the back-up.

As I peered over the top I saw, just ten feet from me, a German sentry. He saw me the instant I saw him. He was pulling his rifle around as I levelled my Colt. I fired two shots and then grabbed the wooden support for the barbed wire to pull myself up. He fell to the ground, dead. I rolled over the wire. The battle jerkin saved me from too much damage. Bill Hay's gun ended the life of a second sentry and then I was on my feet and racing to the brazier and gun emplacement. As a head emerged from the sentry box I fired two more shots. I looked around. The sentries were all dead. I waved Bill and we moved down the breakwater.

We had secured the breakwater; now we needed to destroy the two guns. I had three German grenades on my battle jerkin. We hurried to the end where we could see the building called the Oranje Mill. The breakwater was littered with bollards, boxes and coiled ropes. At the end of the breakwater was a guard post. There were guards there but their backs were towards us for their job was to watch the road which headed to the main harbour. The boxes and ropes which lay along the breakwater were perfect both for cover and to enable us to neutralise them. They would channel the guards when they ran towards us. Bill set out our grenades as booby traps using parachute cords while I kept watch on the guard post. The sentries were forty feet away and I could hear them as they talked but they were busy keeping warm. They would not leave the brazier unless they had to. Then we hurried back to the end of the breakwater where Fletcher and Beaumont were busy finishing off the demolitions. Both guns had been wired with explosives. The one in the concrete emplacement needed more. Beaumont was well aware of the need to make sure that the breakwater could not be easily repaired and the guns replaced before our attack.

It had all gone well, too well. We had just reached the gun when there was the bark of gunfire from the other breakwater. I saw the muzzle flashes. "It's time, Roger!"

Beaumont stood. "All done sir. The timer is set for five minutes. We should leave now, eh sir?"

"Then move," I changed my magazine. The sentries at the end of the breakwater began to run towards the end of our position. I levelled my gun. It was not needed. They tripped the first of the parachute cords. The grenades wreaked carnage. As I ran to the dinghy I heard the sound of Thompsons coming from the other breakwater. The Germans had rifles and my men would outgun them. I scrambled down the slippery sea wall. I came down like a downhill skier using my rubber soled shoes as skis! I was the last one in the dinghy and we paddled out, furiously, to the Motor Launch. We could just see its shadow. The demolitions at the east breakwater went off. When our explosives lit up the night sky then we saw it even more clearly. Pieces of metal and concrete flew over our heads. My men knew explosives and the guns would be completely destroyed. With scrambling nets hung over the side the Motor Launch was a welcome sight. We hauled ourselves aboard and I heard Lieutenant Williamson say, "Hang on we'll go to the other boats."

I ran to the bridge and saw the two dinghies just twenty feet away. The Germans on the breakwater were firing at them. In the dark water they were hard to spot. We saw them because we knew what we were looking for.

The Lieutenant shouted, "Open fire!"

The fore and aft guns opened up and cleared the west breakwater. I fired my gun as did my other men. We did not aim for there was smoke and darkness but a badly aimed bullet can still kill. In the town I heard the klaxons and the sirens as the Germans reacted to our attack. The west breakwater exploded and lit the night sky just as the two dinghies were hauled aboard. The flying debris cleared the surviving Germans at the end of the breakwater.

"Right Chief Petty Officer Leslie! Let's go home."

As we headed into the darkness we could see the fires burning and hear the ammunition as it exploded. The Germans in the town opened fire too but they were firing blind and hampered by the fact that the breakwaters were on fire. "That went well sir."

"It did indeed, Lieutenant. Any casualties Sergeant?"

"None sir. Sorry, the guards at the guard post decided to bring some coffee for those on the end of the breakwater."

"No harm done! Let us hope that they don't replace the guns before the attack."

Roger Beaumont shouted up from the aft deck, "I doubt it sir. Shepherd and I packed explosives between the stones. They will need to replace the larger stones and repoint them. Cement takes time to set. There will be no guns when we go in. Not there at any rate."

"Good. Back in time for breakfast. I hope the field kitchen is open."

"Doesn't matter sir."

"Why not Fletcher?"

"Beaumont and I found a couple of dozen eggs and a side of bacon sir after we had had our little nap today. We can have a fry up; it won't be the Full English but…"

"Fletcher I am not going to ask. Just don't ask for me to be a character reference at your court martial!"

"Of course not sir."

Chapter 14

The rest of the battalion arrived over the next few days. Headquarters and supplies would not be coming. For that I was grateful. I did not want Reg and Daddy to be in the front line. The German shells made life on the Scheldt even more hazardous! Lieutenant Gregson arrived on the 30th. He and his men were billeted in the same block of ruined houses as my men.

"We stay here, sir?"

"It will just be for a couple of nights." I pointed across the river, "It isn't as though we have far to go is it?"

Just then two of the German guns opened fire. I knew that they were aimed to our right but Lieutenant Gregson threw himself to the ground. He looked sheepish as he rose. "Sorry sir."

"That was the right thing to do. We are used to the guns and know where they are going to hit from the sound. Believe me I would have hit the deck sooner than you had they been heading in our direction." I pointed to the east. "There is a field kitchen over there. Take your men and get them fed. Until the Colonel gets here there is not a great deal for you to do."

We took the opportunity to get as much rest as we could and to prepare our equipment. When we crossed the river we knew we would not receive supplies. We would be on our own. It was possible we might be cut off. We would carry too much rather than too little.

We had not seen Major Foster since before our raid and he returned on the 31st. He looked worried. "Problem sir?"

"We haven't been able to destroy as many of the dykes and the defences as we would have liked. It is going to be a hot landing. And the weather is going to be marginal. It will make it tricky launching the Buffaloes. Not only that, the RAF cannot promise air cover."

"And how is the Canadian advance going?" I decided to ask for all the bad news at once.

"Not as fast as either we or they would have liked. The Isthmus held us up." He smiled, but it was a wan smile, "We will get there."

"The plan is still the same then sir?"

"The commandos will embark at 03.15. Yes you and the launch go in before the others. You land at Uncle Beach, close to the east breakwater. You need to secure the landing there for Major Boucher-Myers and his men. They will be right behind you." He paused, "The artillery will lift their barrage at 5.40 just when the Major and his men land."

I gave him a sharp look. "You mean we have to avoid German fire and friendly fire?"

"Sorry, Tom. But the guns will be targeting the ordnance and not the beach. You don't need to go far inland. Just clear a way through the wire. The shelling will keep the Germans in their bunkers and dugouts." He smiled, "You do this sort of thing so well!"

"Don't try the soft soap sir, it doesn't suit. You know we will obey orders but I am keenly aware that my men only have so much luck."

"Surely you, of all people, don't believe in luck!"

"In our line of work you have to, sir. You know that your skills can only take you so far. We'll hold on but it isn't because of orders it is because if we do then more of our comrades will survive and that is worth fighting for. We are all brothers in arms. I think Shakespeare had it right in Henry V[th], sir."

When I told the men they were remarkably philosophical about it all. Nor did it change Lieutenant Williamson's decision to wait around in case he was needed. I came to the conclusion that I was leading a bunch of madmen.

We loaded the launch on the afternoon. The German shells were annoying but our forces had begun to lay smoke and the Germans did not waste their ammunition. We had proper wire cutters and heavy duty gloves. There was little point in trying to use our home made ones. We had our Bergens for we knew not how long we might be ashore. We had rations, ropes, camouflage netting as well as the usual ammunition and equipment. I made sure that we had grenade launchers and their grenades. We had needed them in Antwerp and I knew that they would come in handy once more. We also took enough rations for three days. We had been promised that we would be resupplied within the day. I did not believe the prediction.

The whole of the troop had arrived and I knew that I would be needed at Headquarters. Leaving Sergeant Poulson to organize the last of the details I went ashore to speak with the Colonel and the Major.

"I understand that you are going in ahead of us, Captain?"

"Yes Major. Major Foster was concerned about the wire. You need to be up and moving towards those guns before the French Commandos and the rest of the brigade land. We will make three paths for you. There will be neither mines nor wire and you should be able to get up the beach quickly. It will be easier than the training at Ostend sir."

"We will try to be as quick as we can."

I shook my head, "Keep to the timetable, sir. The last thing we want is for you to rush and hit the wrong place. In the dark it would be too easy to go to the wrong place and Uncle Beach is the only beach in Flushing. We know how long we have to hold on for. We will be there when you arrive."

"But the gunners will still be firing our artillery until we land."

"We know Colonel. Major Foster has assured me that they are not aiming at the beach."

"You seem to have a great deal of confidence in our gunners."

"It is confidence in my men to adapt and survive." I turned as the first of the landing craft arrived. "I think we are luckier than the marines who will be going in at Westkapelle; they have to use Buffaloes." It had been decided to use Landing Craft as we had now taken out the guns. The mines and shallows near to Westkapelle made Buffaloes a priority for them. "Just remember, Major, to tell your lads to keep their heads down and as soon as they beach run like Jesse Owens! We will be waiting by the Oranje Mill."

The Major shook my hand, "Good luck Tom."

"And you too, sir."

We left our mooring soon after I returned. The landing craft needed it to begin loading the Commandos. Sam took us half a mile offshore. The river was just four or five miles across at this point. We threw out a sea anchor and waited on deck. We had the three dinghies inflated and they were close to the newly repaired aft gun. We would only have fifty feet or so to paddle when we were embarked.

I stayed on the bridge with Bill and the Lieutenant. The Lieutenant was chain smoking and Bill had his inevitable pipe filled with the rum soaked tobacco. It gave off a pleasant aroma. Before battles warriors talk of the most inconsequential things and so it was with us.

"Have you never smoked, sir?"

"No Sam. Never got the habit. If I had I think I would be like the Chief here and smoke a pipe. My grandfather smoked a pipe and I always associated the smell with him and their home. It was comforting."

"I find it helps to calm my nerves!"

Bill and I exchanged a glance, "Nerves are a way of keeping you on your toes." I nodded to Bill, "You don't smoke for that reason do you Chief Petty Officer?"

"No sir. It's not so much a habit as a ritual. You have to clean out the pipe with your penknife, pull a cleaner through it and then pack the baccy. There's a knack to it. Not too tight and not too loose. Then you light it and draw. Sometimes I can get away with one match but if not then no matter. If I fill it right I can keep one going for an hour. It rarely happens at sea, sir, but when I am at home in the Griffin Inn enjoying a pint of dark mild it feels very soothing. I think the pipe relaxes me, it reminds me of safer times at home."

"I never really got in the habit of going into a pub." I wondered if the young Lieutenant had been old enough to go into a pub before he joined up.

Bill shook his head, "You don't know what you are missing. No women nattering on. Just blokes around a table. You can play dominoes or darts or, more often than not, you put the world to rights. The world would be a safer place if folks like Hitler, Stalin and Old Winnie sat around a table and drank a few pints."

I laughed, "I think Churchill would win. He can drink from what I have heard."

"You met him, didn't you sir?"

"Yes Bill, back in the early days."

"You have met Churchill?"

"Yes Sam, it was only briefly but he impressed me. Chamberlain might have been a nice chap but you can't have a pacifist running the country; not when you have others hell bent on your destruction."

Bill tapped his pipe out in his hand and scattered the glowing ashes to the wind. "I'll just take a turn around the boat sir, make sure it's all ship shape and Bristol fashion."

After he had gone I said, "You are lucky to have Bill. He is the most level headed man I have ever met."

"I know sir. I think I have begun to become an officer now. I knew nothing when I came here."

"I know what you mean. I was lucky. Coming up through the ranks I had many people helping to make me the officer I am."

We raised anchor at 03.00 and, with our war faces on, we headed north across the river. We had the luxury of silence. The guns would begin in forty minutes at about the same time that the flotilla of landing craft left Breskans. The shore was in darkness. We intended to be dropped off just outside the breakwater and then paddle into the beach. The last mile was the most tortuous. The engines were cut so much that we were barely making way. The incoming tide was doing most of the work for us. I knew that Sam was desperate for a cigarette but he knew that the glowing end would be seen and he just gripped the bridge rail tightly. The Scheldt had mist most early mornings and this one was no exception. It would soon dissipate but, as we neared our target, it was both a blessing and curse. A blessing, in that it hid us a little more, and a curse in that the shore was more difficult to see. The crew of the Motor launch had improved dramatically over the last few weeks and the lookout at the bow hurried to the bridge, waving his arms. We had arrived.

"Stop engines. Right sir, your stop I believe. We will go back a little way and act as a marker for the Major when he comes."

"Thanks Lieutenant." Nodding to Bill I went aft and climbed down the scrambling net to the dinghy.

We pulled together hard as we paddled away from our launch. The mist made us a sort of shroud so that just our heads could be seen. It was vaguely surreal. I saw, to our right, the breakwater we had attacked. The Lieutenant's navigation had been perfect. It was now up to us to be as good.

The sand scraping along our bottom told us that we had arrived. Hay and I leapt from the boat and took out our Colts. We scanned the beach. We saw the wire but we neither heard dogs nor saw sentries. A tap on my shoulder told me that the boats had been secured. With three of us watching the Oranje Mill for any sign of Germans, the others began cutting through the wire. We had cleared just one roll when the shells began to fall. Although we had been expecting it the sudden cracks from the south made us jump. Alan Crowe glanced up at me. I pointed to the wire and made the 'hurry up' sign. We had to trust that our gunners would not land short. There was no reason why they should. Their targets were the guns which lay further back from the beach.

I heard, far to the west, the sound of the enormous guns of the three warships as they fired at the defences on Westkapelle. They heralded the beginning of the battle. The '*Warspite*' had fought in the Great War and she was still ready to fight twenty one years later. The monitors' fire soon joined their larger consort. By comparison the artillery across the river sounded like pop guns.

When the first shells fell they lit up the houses. Even though they landed a hundred and more yards from us the wave of concussion felt like being out in a force nine gale. It added urgency to my men's work. The quicker they did their job the sooner we could find shelter closer to the sea wall. It took another ten minutes to clear paths through the wire. My men moved the wire, using thick gloves, to one side so that the three paths could be clearly seen by Major Boucher-Myers and his men. I tied pieces of red cloth to the wire at the entrance to each of the channels. Even now the flotilla of landing craft would be heading through the dark to make their own landing. The difference would be that the Germans would know that they were coming.

I waved my men forward. We reached the sea wall which was a mere ten feet high. I kept my Colt in my hand as I made my way up. The shelling was still continuing but the spotters on the southern shore must have been able to see fall of shot for they appeared to be finding their targets. I heard an explosion which told me that ammunition had been hit.

I peered over the top of the sea wall. I could see the mill to my right and beyond it a fire. The shells had set alight part of Flushing. Directly ahead of us was a German dugout. It was a concrete shelter and I had no doubt that it contained German soldiers. They were the sentries who had taken shelter when the shelling started. I waved my men up. It took courage to do so for, as we did, one shell fell a little short and exploded just a hundred yards from where we stood. When we reached the dugout I saw that they had, not a door, but a blast curtain. It prevented soldiers being hit while not burying them if it buckled.

I made the sign for Hay and Fletcher to cover me and then, stepping through the blast curtain entered the dimly lit dugout. It was filled with Germans. I estimated more than twenty. None had a weapon in their hands. There were candles burning and they were hunkered down in two rows, seated on benches.

"Hands up gentlemen!"

I saw an officer reach to his holster. I fired a bullet into the wooden beam above his head.

"Next time, Lieutenant, it will be between your eyes."

The officer saw, for the first time, the flash on my shoulder, "Kommando!" His hands leapt into the air.

I spoke without turning, "Crowe, come and collect the weapons." Alan moved amongst them efficiently. Bill and I watched every German as they had their guns and grenades taken from them. Until Crowe collected them all in we would be watchful for tricks.

Bill said, "If the rest of the assault goes as well as this sir it will all be over today."

"We were lucky, Lance Sergeant Hay. These were sheltering. When the shelling stops then the others will emerge from their bunkers. I want you and Crowe to stay in here and watch them until the Major arrives."

"Sir."

I left the dugout. "Beaumont, take Fletcher and see if there are Germans at the Oranje Mill."

"Sir."

"Gordy take Emerson and Shepherd, set up the Bren gun to cover the east. The rest of you come with me. We will head to the Merchant's Dock."

"Sir."

The fire in the centre of the town had now taken hold. Flames were leaping into the sky and still the shells fell. The Germans were firing in reply but it was an erratic fire. I checked my watch. The landing craft would be just off the shore. I headed towards the western breakwater. Suddenly an Oerlikon began firing. I saw the tracer rounds. As I looked left I saw a landing craft. It was early! The artillery was still firing. The Oerlikon was at the Merchant's Dock; it had not been there when we had raided. Further from the harbour it only had a narrow field of fire. Tragically the LCT was in it. The crew had taken the wrong line on their approach. Now they would pay dearly for it. We could not reach the Oerlikon quickly. There were obstacles in the way and we would have to cross a bridge over the canal.

Joe Wilkinson said, "Sir, that is Lieutenant Gregson's boat! He is heading for the wrong breakwater." I glanced to my left and saw the cannon shells tear into the hull of the landing craft. They were not as well protected as they might have been.

If I had had my sniper rifle I might have been able to help but I did not. "Sergeant Poulson, you and Wilkinson stay here. Set up a defensive position; use your Thompson and the grenade launcher. Keep them occupied. Those lads will need help when they get ashore."

"Where are you off to sir?"

"Hewitt and I will try to take down the gun. Give us covering fire. Come on Hewitt. Stay close."

There were anti-tank blocks and wire barricades between us and the dock gates. It was too late to clear them. Luckily for us all attention was on the landing craft. If there was one then there would be others. One of the shells had destroyed a house and the door was hanging forlornly from one hinge. I tore it off and hurled it over the wire. Using it as a bridge the two of us ran over it towards the bascule bridge. Suddenly the shelling stopped. It was 05.40. In the distance we could still hear the sound of the naval guns but there appeared to be a longer gap between shells. I wondered if they had suffered any damage. Soon the all clear would sound and the Germans would emerge, like moles, from their holes.

The Oerlikon was still firing and now the Germans had set up a mortar and a heavy machine gun. They were a hundred yards from us but were protected by sand bags. As we hurtled over the bridge I fired a hopeful burst from my

Thompson. One of the bullets must have hit the gun for the gunners turned and I saw them point at us.

Having crossed the bridge I looked for some cover. Once again the early shells which had fallen slightly short had damaged a building and there were large pieces of masonry and rubble. As the Germans turned to fire at us we threw ourselves into the shelter of the largest pieces. The bullets zipped over our head. I heard the sound of Thompsons as Sergeant Poulson and his men sent hopeful bullets towards the Germans. The range was too great but the hail of lead was intimidating. I heard the crack of the grenade launcher. It exploded short but the shrapnel flew over the top of the sandbags. The Germans ducked.

"Next time the grenade launcher fires, you go left and I will go right."

"Right sir!"

Once again the Germans rose and fired at the rubble before us. Splinters of brick, stone and mortar flew into the air but we had no intention of showing our heads. The distinctive crack of the grenade launcher being fired had us both ready to run. As soon as it exploded we broke cover. This time the grenade had fallen closer to the Germans but, even so, shrapnel still flew towards us too. We bore charmed lives. I saw a half demolished house and I ran to it. The Germans recovered quickly and they began to fire. The smoke, my speed and the darkness meant they missed me and I ran inside the building. I saw a half damaged staircase and, throwing caution to the wind, ran up it. Pieces of wood clattered to the ground for it was badly damaged but it held. I reached the upper floor. I was forty yards from the enemy and I could see the Oerlikon. I aimed the Thompson and, spraying it from side to side, emptied the magazine. The whole crew were hit. The other soldiers who were nearby turned and fired at me and I ducked back. As I did so I saw, to my horror, that the landing craft was drifting. It had been badly shot up.

I reloaded and then took out two German grenades. They were the best weapon to throw long distances. I smashed the porcelain cap of one and pulled the cord. I counted to two and then hurled it high, through the shattered window. I ducked again and heard it explode. There were screams and shouts for it had exploded in the air. I stood and threw the second grenade directly at the emplacement. I heard Hewitt's Thompson as he kept firing at the Germans. I watched the grenade scythe through the Oerlikon emplacement. The ammunition began to explode. In the harbour I saw the Motor Launch. Sam had managed to reach the stricken Landing Craft and was towing it out of the line of fire.

I took my Thompson and sprayed the emplacement. I saw hands raised.

"Hewitt, cover them while I come down!"

"Sir."

I waited until Hewitt had stood and was covering them with his gun and then I descended. As I reached the door I shouted, "Sergeant Poulson!"

"Sir!"

"Get over here."

The emplacement was like an abattoir. There were just eight survivors and some of those were wounded. The exploding ammunition made life hazardous and I moved the Germans away from the danger. The Oerlikon was destroyed as were the mortars but the German heavy machine gun looked to be functional. The last of the ammunition exploded and the emplacement was safe to enter.

When my men arrived I said, "Get the machine gun set up to cover the hotel."

Even as I gave orders bullets flew from the hotel. I said to the Germans, in German, "Drop your weapons and lie face down! I don't want you being shot by your own men!" Only the officers had weapons and they complied immediately.

I took out my glasses and scanned the hotel. I could see that the Germans were rushing men into the area. Heavy machine guns were being set up. Now we needed the rest of the Commandos. My twelve men had done all that was humanly possible. I wondered if Major Boucher-Myers had suffered the same fate as Lieutenant Gregson and drifted off course.

Beaumont suddenly appeared. "Sir, the Germans have a fortified position at the Oranje Mill."

"Sergeant Poulson, are you all right here?"

"Aye sir. We have ammo and we have sandbags. So long as the lads have our backs then we can hold out."

"Good man." I pointed to the Germans, "You come with us and no tricks. Come on Roger, let's go and find the Major." We led the prisoners back to the dugout.

By the time we reached the captured dugout the first of the Commandos led by Major Boucher-Myers appeared. "Well done Captain. Bit of a cock up. I don't know where Captain Johnson and Lieutenant Gregson are."

"They hit the wrong breakwater, sir. Their landing craft was pretty badly shot up. Lieutenant Williamson has towed the survivors out. Your men are it until the second wave comes in. Sergeant Poulson has captured a gun emplacement at the Merchant's Dock and we have thirty four prisoners here."

The major was decisive. "Lieutenant Shelly, take two men and escort the prisoners to the landing craft. Captain Harsker's men are too valuable to waste as guards!"

"Sir!"

As they were taken away Hay and Crowe rejoined us. I pointed to the heights to the east of us. "Those guns are still causing problems sir."

"Then let's get into action. The rest of the brigade are just half an hour away. We had it bad enough but if they get hit then the operation will be a failure."

I had eight of my men and they would have to do. "Gordy, pack up your gun. We are heading for the guns to the east of the town."

"Right sir!"

Our first obstacle was the Oranje Mill. The Germans had fortified it. Major Boucher-Myers said, "Heavy weapons company! I want every mortar you can drop landing on that strongpoint. Captain Wetherspoon. Take your men and be ready to assault them when they are weakened."

I took the opportunity to reload my weapon. My men stood expectantly around me. "The Het Dock is just north of us. They have 75 mm guns there. They will do serious damage to the landing craft coming into the main harbour." I turned to Major Boucher-Myers. "I will take my men to the Het Dock, sir, and try to silence those guns."

"You only have eight men and you will have to get past the Oranje Mill."

"Don't worry, sir. We will manage." I turned. "Beaumont, on my shoulder. Then Gordy. Bill, you are Tail End Charlie."

"Sir!"

"Sir!"

I walked to the end of the position that the major's men had occupied. The Germans in the Oranje Mill had now poked their weapons from the windows. Soon the major's men would make life difficult for them. I waited for the first mortar shells to drop. The second they did I shouted, "Now!"

We ran low and kept jinking from side to side. The effect of the mortars was to make the defenders hide and we made it past the end of their building unscathed. We found ourselves in a dark part of the docks. The flashes from the German guns some two hundred yards from us marked their position. It would have been easy to charge them and heroically capture them but I did not think that they would be so careless as to leave them undefended. I halted my men a hundred yards from the sandbagged positions. We sheltered in the lee of a half ruined building. The fires behind them illuminated the gunners and the guns. I took out my glasses and checked the area before them. I saw three heavy machine guns behind sandbags. If I had had my Mauser then I could have picked them off. I did not and so I had to improvise.

"Bill, Gordy, you have silenced Colts. I want us to crawl close to the sandbags and pick off the gunners. We will use the cover of the fallen bricks and stones. Hewitt, you are in charge. If they return fire then lay down a fusillade from the Thompsons." I handed him mine, "Here, you don't need to reload."

I lay down and began to snake towards the enemy. I wanted to be as close as I could. When my gun was empty then I would use my grenades. The three of us had the potential to shoot twenty seven men. A third of that would be acceptable. I reached a small half demolished wall just forty yards from the Germans. We remained unseen for they thought their flank was protected by those in the Oranje Mill. I raised my gun and, using the two handed grip, I squeezed a bullet off. It hit a German sergeant in the neck and he fell dead. Those around him looked confused. Bill and Gordy both took advantage and two more men fell wounded or dead. I shifted my target to the left and fired three bullets. I hit two men.

Suddenly every head disappeared below the sandbags and I crawled quickly covering another thirty feet. I saw the barrel of one of the machine guns move to target our flank. I lay on my back and pulled out two grenades. I was close enough to throw them into the position and I pulled the pins on them both and threw them in rapid succession. My two sergeants were of the same mind and all six grenades exploded like a ripple behind the sandbags. We were, ironically, protected from the blast by the sandbags and I rose and ran to the smoke filled German lines. There were dead and there were dying. As I vaulted the sandbags I had my pistol in my hand and I fired at every German who looked as though he was a threat. When my gun emptied I took out my Luger and I aimed at the gunners around the nearest 75 mm. It was just fifty feet from me. Three bullets found flesh and the others took cover. Bill and Gordy fired at the other guns and soon the battery ceased firing.

The rest of my men raced after us and we took shelter in the German defences. As I was handed my machine gun I said, "Take cover and pour fire on the gunners. If they are hiding then they can't fire!"

"Sir."

I reloaded the Thompson. I heard the sounds of men moaning. We had hit them hard. If the Major could get here quickly then one objective would have been secured. Private Crowe said, "Sir, I have the grenade launcher!"

"Good man! Let's put the wind up Fritz eh!"

"Sir!"

"The rest of you keep up a covering fire. Right Crowe, do your worst!"

He was an artist with the grenade launcher. His first grenade landed at the closest 75 mm. The crew were slaughtered and the gun knocked to the side.

"Well done, Alan! Fletcher, Beaumont, move closer and use your grenades!"

I sprayed my Thompson blindly. It did not matter that I did not hit anyone. It forced them to keep their heads down. Crowe's next grenade fell a little short but Beaumont and Fletcher had reached the first destroyed gun and they waved us forward. I stood and ran. Fletcher and Beaumont threw two grenades which kept the Germans hunkered down and we reached the bloodbath of the German gun. Crowe's grenade had killed them all.

Fletcher had found an undamaged German heavy machine gun and he began to fire it. "Here Rog, load for me eh?"

The gun had a greater range than our Thompsons and the crews of the last two German guns began to fall.

"Stop! We surrender!"

"Throw down your weapons then!"

When the survivors of the three batteries raised their hand we had achieved our main objective and the main landings were taking place. We had collected the prisoners and disarmed them by the time Major Boucher-Myers and his men arrived having cleared the Oranje Mill. We now had our corner of Flushing. We could move on.

Chapter 15

We saw the landing craft beach safely. Bullets still struck the vessels but they were not 75 mm shells. Commandant Kieffer himself led his men ashore. Although the batteries were silenced there were still German soldiers in dugouts and behind sandbags. We poured fire on their flanks. When they began to surrender we knew that the eastern side of the harbour front was in our hands.

Commandant Kieffer grinned when he saw us, "Captain Harsker, once more you are there when we need you." He pointed to the guns. "I knew that you would silence them."

"It was our pleasure."

Major Boucher-Myers turned, "And now we had better make sure that Uncle Beach is open, Captain."

"Take care Captain!" He waved his arm and led his French Commandos to their target. The guns at the harbour.

"And you Commandant."

We made our way back to the beach the same path the major had used. As we neared it he set his men to clearing the wire back further to enable the King's Own Scottish Borderers to land. "I will go and rejoin my men." I could still hear gunfire from the Merchant's Dock.

"As soon as the beach is clear and the landing craft are here then we will join you."

We headed along the docks, over the bascule bridge and reached Sergeant Poulson and his men. They had built a sandbagged barrier. "Best keep your head down, sir. The Germans are in that hotel yonder."

I peered over the top of the sandbags. Now that the sun had risen the dark shapes of night became buildings. I saw that the hotel was a three storied affair. It had a sandbagged entrance and the Germans had made it a strong point. It barred the way into the old town. We would have to clear it but it would be suicide for my twelve men to try it.

"Fletcher, go with Beaumont and Emerson, see if you can find any heavy German weapons."

"Sir."

Of course we had destroyed the best German weapon, the Oerlikon. I hoped that they might find something useful. Sergeant Poulson had not had time to do much other than make his defences stronger.

He pointed to the sea, "The Motor Launch finally took the landing craft to safety. I think he was going to take her into Uncle Beach with the other landing craft. It was a good piece of seamanship sir. He had to endure a lot of small arms fire from the hotel and naval barracks."

"Naval barracks?"

"Yes sir. Do you remember we saw it on the aerial photographs? I couldn't identify it in the dark but you can just make it out now sir. It is in the same block as the hotel. It is just a hundred yards further west."

Just then I heard movement behind me as Lieutenant Mulgrave brought his section along. "Major's compliments sir. He thought you could use us. He wants me to become familiar with how you work and this part of the town sir."

"Thanks, Lieutenant. Just spread your men out. We are trying to work out how to eliminate the defences at the hotel."

"We could always rush them, sir!" Lieutenant Mulgrave was very enthusiastic. A friend of John Gregson's, he had the same attitude towards the job. He was keen to do his part for King and Country.

"And that would get a lot of good Commandos killed. Don't be in such a hurry. Our job was to secure the beaches. We have done that. Getting here is just a bonus."

"Right sir. Sergeant, you heard the Captain, spread the men out."

My three men returned carrying a pair of Panzerschrecks and some ammunition. "Well done."

"Aye sir they were close by the dugout we first took. Beaumont here reckoned that as there were no anti-tank blocks around the quay Jerry would need something to destroy the tanks. Clever little bugger aren't you Beaumont."

"I try!"

"Good, then you two take them and get yourself a loader each. Wait for my order. Crowe, Sergeant Barker. On my command I want you to use grenade launchers to make life difficult for those in the hotel."

"Sir!"

"Lieutenant, as soon as we have made the front of the building untenable we go in. Have your men move in pairs. One fires the other runs. Use whatever cover you can get and watch out for the large building further west. It is the naval barracks and is fortified. And remember Jerry can be sneaky. Look out for booby traps!"

"Sir!"

I checked that my Thompson was loaded as well as my Colt. I removed the silencer and put it in my Bergen. I replaced the grenades I had used from the spares in my bag.

"Ready sir!"

"Rockets and grenades, fire!" I raised my head over the sandbags so that I could see the effect and judge the moment to attack. As I did so a bullet smacked into the sandbags next to me. It was a warning. The rockets flew straight and true. They both exploded on either side of the door. Then the grenades landed on the sandbags themselves.

"Open fire!"

Now that the sandbags were damaged then our guns could begin to take their toll. They tore into the sandbags and beyond. Some would find bodies. Others would make the Germans take cover. Just then I heard the sound of aero engines. I looked to my left and saw a tank busting Typhoon screaming in. It sent rockets to slam into the naval barracks. As two more antitank rockets slammed into the hotel I shouted, "Now Lieutenant, now Sergeant Poulson!" I rolled over the sandbags as two more grenades hit the entrance to the hotel. I did not fire my gun. There were no targets. The front of the hotel was wreathed in smoke and flames. Some of the Lieutenant's men were firing. They might regret that when they reached the hotel and found they had no bullets left.

I was the first to reach the entrance and the sandbags had been cleared by the grenades. Fletcher and Beaumont were sending rockets into the upper floors of the hotel. Even as I ran through the body littered entrance small pieces of masonry crashed down around me. As I burst into the lobby I caught a glimpse of a white face and, pulling the trigger on the Thompson, I fired four shots. The face disappeared and I ran through the lobby. I had hit the German in the head and all four bullets had found their mark. At such close range the Thompson was a deadly weapon. From ten to a hundred yards it was almost the perfect weapon. As I glanced to my left I saw some of Lieutenant Mulgrave's men reloading their magazines. One fell to a bullet fired from the hotel. I still had sixteen left to fire.

Bullets rattled from the corridor ahead. I put my back against the wall and took out a Mills bomb. Bill Hay and more of my men appeared in the doorway. I waved them to cover and, pulling the pin, threw the grenade down the corridor. As soon as it exploded I raced down, firing my Tommy gun as I went. I saw that it had exploded in the kitchen. It had set the gas alight and the kitchen was burning. I turned and shouted, "Clear the upstairs. The rear is on fire."

"Sir!"

I saw Lieutenant Mulgrave, "Lieutenant, have your men clear the ground floor."

I took the opportunity to reload and then headed up the stairs. I still had ten bullets but I wanted a full magazine in case I met larger numbers. There was a rattle of gunfire above me. I recognised the sound of a Colt and something indistinct in German. Then I heard Bill Hay shout in German, "Come out with your hands up Fritz!"

A line of dispirited Germans appeared from the floor above me. They descended with their hands on their heads.

"We have these Sergeant, check that no one is hiding out."

"Sir."

The Lieutenant was waiting in the lobby along with Beaumont, Fletcher, Emerson and Shepherd. "All clear sir."

"Good. Then have three of your men escort these prisoners to Uncle Beach. I am guessing that the headquarters will be there."

"Yes sir, Captain Dawson has set up the command centre at the Oranje Mill."

"Let's clear out of this building. That fire will soon be out of control."

"Hotel is clear sir."

"Thanks, Bill. Let's get out before it comes crashing down on us." Bill Hay and I were the last ones out of the smoking hotel. Until it burned itself out then progress along the front would be difficult. "Back to our sandbagged position and let's find out our new orders."

When we reached our original position we replenished our ammunition, drank some water and reloaded our guns. Shepherd said, "Sir, the King's Own are landing."

"Good then we might be able to hand this sector over to them."

Lieutenant Mulgrave asked, "Why don't we head off to the west, sir?"

"Because the hotel is on fire Lieutenant and there are large numbers of German troops there. Our job was to secure the landing area. Don't worry, Lieutenant, this is far from over."

There was a crash from our front as part of the hotel collapsed on itself. A column of smoke billowed up and began to drift west. When the three Commandos returned, having delivered the prisoners to the beaches, the corporal said, "Sir, we have orders to hand this position over to the King's Own Scottish Borderers sir and pull back to the Oranje Mill."

I smiled at the Lieutenant, "There you are Lieutenant. We have another job to do!"

The Captain of the King's Own Scottish Borderers who arrived said, "It is a bit hairy at the beach. The Germans have machine guns and they are dropping shells on it. This is a little more peaceful here."

"There is a large naval barracks just down the road. We need some heavy ordnance really, or tanks if we are going to attack it."

"And we haven't got them yet. Jerry is making is hard to embark at Breskans. Now that it is daylight they have line of sight. They sank two landing Craft which were being loaded. The attack is going slower than they expected."

Just then we heard the roar of a pair of Typhoons as they raced in and blasted the two barracks to the west of us with rockets. I peered through the glasses and saw that they had done little damage. The Germans had built bomb proof bunkers.

"Well good luck. Come on chaps, back to the Oranje Mill."

"When we reached the Mill we had to run the gauntlet of enemy fire. When we had been there last we had had the protection of the night. Now it was daylight and the higher buildings to the north of us afforded the enemy not only cover but also the ability to direct fire and they were making good use of it. The troops who were landing had to run for their lives. Had the wire not been cleared then it would have been a bloodbath.

"Sergeant, have the men take cover. They had better eat some rations. I am not certain when we will get the opportunity later on."

"Right sir."

Inside the Mill Captain Rewcastle sat with a radio operator. He had headphones on and he waved as I entered. Major Boucher-Myers emerged from a small room. He gave me a sheepish grin, "Must have eaten something 'off'. Good job there is a toilet here. How are things going?"

"Now that the hotel is eliminated then that flank is stable but I can't see us making progress west; not for a while at any rate."

"And things are pretty bad here. Look, Tom, could you take your chaps and Lieutenant Mulgrave's section and try to get to Het Dock? Commandant Kieffer and his men are trying to clear the mole to the main harbour but they are under fire. They have snipers on the cranes and heavy machine guns. He has lost eight men already."

"Right sir." I went to the map which Captain Rewcastle had pinned to the wall. I think he had intended to mark our successes and progress. I saw the Het Dock. There would be cranes there and they would have a good field of fire to the mole and the main harbour. The French would be enfiladed. I used my finger to trace a route through the streets to the dock. I looked at my watch. It was 10.30. "Things are behind schedule already. Any idea how the Westkapelle landings are going?"

"Believe it or not, worse! They have lost half a dozen landing craft. At least we lost just the one."

"Lieutenant Gregson?"

"Bought it, I am afraid. Your Lieutenant Williamson did a sterling job and saved half of the section but not John. A shame, the boy had potential."

"He did indeed." I shook my head as though to clear the image of the fresh faced officer who would never see the end of the war. "Right sir. I'll be off. I'll send a runner back with messages."

"Good luck Tom."

Once outside I was back in the maelstrom of explosions and gunfire. The south side of the building was protected but I knew that as soon as we left its safety we would have to endure gun fire and snipers. "Sergeants and officers to me!" As they came I hung my binoculars around my neck and tucked them in my battledress.

Lieutenant Mulgrave and the sergeants hurried to my side. "We have to winkle out the machine guns and snipers from the Het Dock area."

"But we were supposed to be in the Old Town by now, sir!"

"I know Lieutenant but these things rarely go to plan. We are Commandos and we adapt. We do this job. We have to take pressure off the French Commandos. There are three roads and they run south west to north east. If we take three of those roads and use the buildings to our left for shelter we should reach Grave Street. We will then be just a hundred yards from their position. However, there will be little shelter from there on in. Lieutenant you and your men use the two roads to the right and I will take my men up the one to the left. We will see you there."

"Right sir!"

"And Lieutenant, take it steadily. Check before you move. Look high and check low. If Jerry surrenders then search them and make sure they have no weapons. We are already behind schedule, another hour or two will not hurt."

"Yes sir!"

We rejoined our men and I gathered them around me. "Lance Sergeant Hay make sure we have plenty of ammunition for the Bren. That will be our heaviest weapon. Sergeant Barker, you and Private Crowe will use the grenade launchers. Wilkinson and Emerson. Bring the rocket launcher. How many rockets do we have left?"

"Just four sir."

"Then they will have to do. You two stick with Sergeant Poulson."

"Sir."

"Beaumont and Fletcher, you two will be with me and we will lead. Sergeant Poulson, tail end Charlie in case I cop one."

"Right sir."

"Let's go!"

A mortar shell exploded in the road we were going to take just thirty seconds before we reached it. "Right lads! We need to shift!" We ran. I knew that the mortar would be reloading. We had to be across the street and as far down the road before it did. The three of us at the head of the section ran across the road to the shelter of the buildings and then sprinted the fifty yards to Grave Street. We crossed the street just as the mortar shell exploded in the middle of the street we had just vacated. I saw that Lieutenant Mulgrave and his section had not arrived yet.

I went to the corner of the warehouse and peered around. This was Wilhelmina Street. There was a post office at the end, not far from the dock, and they had fortified it. I saw sandbags at the end of the street and machine guns. I took out my binoculars and risked another peek. I saw men on the roofs of the buildings at the end. They were low warehouses and perfect for defence. The houses had a small wall at the top. A decorative feature, it was better protection than a sandbag. Behind them I saw the cranes. They afforded an even better view. I used the binoculars. There were grey uniforms. I had just put my glasses away and stepped back when a bullet hit the wall where I had just stood. They had snipers.

Lieutenant Mulgrave came over to me. "What now sir?"

"Nothing easy I am afraid. They have the ends of the roads blocked and men on the roofs. We will take this street. You and your men the one to the right. Move and fire. Use the buildings for cover. Do you have grenade launchers?"

"The Captain didn't think they were of much use."

"Mortars?"

"Yes sir, we have one."

"Then use that to keep their heads down. Good luck, Lieutenant."

I went to Bill Hay, "Set the Bren up here. The Germans are just over a hundred yards away. They have a wall behind which they can hide. Use the ammo sparingly but keep their heads down. Gordy, I want you and Crowe to lob three or four grenades. It will give Bill time to set up the Bren."

"Sir!"

"The rest of you as soon as the Bren opens fire then we move. Sergeant Poulson, save the rockets for a decent target. We can't afford to waste them."

"Sir."

The two grenade launchers cracked. They reloaded and as the first ones exploded they sent a second in the same direction. Bill took the opportunity to move the Bren into position. Hewitt lay next to him as loader and in case anything happened to him. As soon as the .303 bullets spat out I ran. The street was wreathed in smoke. One of the grenades had hit part of the building and ignited something. The Germans fired blindly. I saw, through the smoke, a doorway and I hurled myself through it. Fletcher and Beaumont followed me.

"See if there is a way upstairs, Beaumont. Fletcher keep a watch on the street."

As Roger hurried away I heard the sound of the Bren. Bill was firing short bursts. I examined the room we were in. It looked to be an office of some description. There were half destroyed desks, filing cabinets and the floor was littered with half burned paper.

"Sir, there is a way up to the roof."

"Good. Let's go Fletcher."

We climbed a rickety and dilapidated staircase. There was no one in the building which looked a little unsafe. Shells had damaged it. There was a hatch which led to the roof. I peered out and saw that the roof was empty. I rolled out and had my Thompson ready to fire. The door opened on to a flat walkway close to a gently sloping roof. The roof would be slippery but, more importantly, noisy. I saw that we could make our way down to the Germans who were on the roof of the last two buildings along the terrace. Their attention was on Lieutenant Mulgrave, Sergeant Poulson and the rest of the Commandos as they made their way along the street. We would have to creep along and then clamber over the small walls which gave stability to the structure. However, we could keep low and we would not be seen until we actually climbed over the walls.

I began to crawl. My two men followed me. I could see nothing as I crawled but I could hear gunfire. The two grenade launchers were firing but my two men were conserving ammunition. Bill Hay's Bren chattered. I reached the first low wall and peered over. I saw the Germans. They were fifty yards away. I could have shot at them but there was a chance that I might have missed. We needed to be closer. I turned and said, "We roll over the wall one at a time. Jerry is just fifty yards away."

"Sir!"

I crouched. Waiting until the grenade launcher sent another grenade I rolled over when the Germans ducked. I crawled and, once more, I could not see them. When I reached the final wall I lifted my head slowly. I was just fifteen yards away from the sandbagged German strongpoint; I was close enough. I sat with my back to the wall and took out two grenades. I had no German ones left. I would have to use Mills bombs. My two men joined me and sat with their backs to the low wall. I made the sign for the two of them to rise on my command and fire. They nodded. I mouthed, 'One, two, three.'

On 'three' I rose. Pulling the pin on one grenade I hurled it high into the air. The two Thompsons on either side opened fire and I threw the second grenade. I used a flatter trajectory for the second one.

"Grenade!"

The three of us dropped like stones as the two grenades exploded. Pieces of brick and mortar whizzed over our heads. I heard moans. Standing I rolled over the wall and ran the fifteen yards to the next wall. I saw a German head rise and I fired. The bullets tore into him. There were two more strongpoints but they were thirty yards from us. I climbed into the carnage of the sandbagged position we had just destroyed. The grenades had cleared the position but the German machine gun was undamaged. It had just been knocked over. I fired my Thompson at the next position and said, "Get the German machine gun turned around."

"Sir!"

I fired another burst at the Germans who were trying to turn their gun around to face us. Below me, in the street, I heard Sergeant Poulson roar, "At them, Commandos!" I heard the cheer rise from the street. I fired another burst and my gun clicked empty. I dropped it and drew my Colt. I saw a German pull his arm back. He was going to throw a grenade. Using the two handed grip I squeezed off four bullets. The grenade fell from the man's dying hands.

"Grenade!"

I dropped down behind the sandbags as the German grenade scythed through the German position. Beaumont had the German gun cocked and ready as I peered through the smoke and debris. Traversing the gun my men looked for any sign of a threat from the Germans. They fired at the last machine gun as the gunners tried to turn and fire their gun at us. The four men were cut down and two others raised their hands. We had done it!

A bullet suddenly plucked at the sleeve of my battle dress. I realised it did not come from the German position but from the snipers on top of the cranes. We had snuffed out the roof top opposition and now the men on the cranes were trying to eliminate us.

"Best get your head down sir." Beaumont turned the gun to fire at the four cranes. They were more than a hundred yards from our position and the metal struts and cabs gave good protection to the snipers. The glass of the cab helped to refract the light and they would be hard to kill. Until we destroyed them then the French and ourselves would continue to take casualties.

"Keep them under fire. I know it will be hard to hit them but your bullets will stop them firing back at us. I am going to find a rifle."

I crawled away and searched for an undamaged German rifle. I found one close to where the Germans had surrendered and took the three clips of bullets from the dead man's bandolier. The rifle had no sight but it was more accurate than the machine gun. I crawled back to the sandbags.

"We will have to change belts soon sir."

"Just use short bursts, Fletcher." I rested the rifle on the sandbags. I saw the first sniper. He was two hundred feet away. He wore a helmet. That, in itself, told me that he was not a specialist. Specialists preferred to have the sides of their head clear. The machine gun stopped firing and I saw his head rise as he prepared to fire. I fired three bullets. None of them hit him but his head jerked back down. A bullet struck the sandbag close to my head and I switched targets to the next crane. This one was closer to two hundred and thirty feet from me. This sniper also wore a helmet. Fletcher was having trouble with the belt. I saw the head rise and I squeezed two bullets off. I was lucky. One of them struck the side of the cab close to the sniper's head and the bullet ricocheted into him. I saw the rifle tumble to the streets. Beaumont opened fire again.

"Got, you, you bugger!"

I saw the first sniper fall from the cab. That left two but they were two hundred and fifty feet from us. I had just turned to seek a new target when I heard the roar of a rocket and our rocket launcher hit one of the two cranes. It struck just below the cab. There was a crack, a creak and a groan and then the leg fell into the dock followed by the cab itself.

"Pour fire on the last crane!"

Throwing caution to the wind I emptied my clip and put a new one in. I heard the Bren and the heavy German gun as bullets smashed into the cab of the last crane. The metal had been damaged by shells and the structure could take no more punishment.

When Beaumont and I had finished firing I took out my glasses. There was no sign of life. "You two go to the last emplacement. It should overlook the dock. Secure the two Germans who surrendered. I will go and join the others. I will get you relieved."

"Sir."

I peered into the street. The post office had been attacked by rockets and grenades. It explained why the Germans had surrendered so quickly. I saw them being herded together on the opposite side of the street, as I walked to the hatch which led downstairs. I glanced at my watch. It was the middle of the afternoon. Once again the plan had not gone as the planners had intended.

Chapter 16

I went down through the rooms which had been recently vacated by the Germans. I saw evidence that my men and those of Lieutenant Mulgrave had cleared the buildings using grenades. Bodies littered the rooms. When I emerged into Wilhelmina Street I saw the German survivors being lined up against a wall. Sergeant Poulson came up to me, "Well done, Sergeant. That was a good use for the rockets."

"Yes sir." He poked his finger through the hole in my battledress. "I see you were lucky again, sir."

"So it would appear. Did we lose any?"

He shook his head, "Our section was fine but Lieutenant Mulgrave lost two men dead and five wounded. It was those snipers."

"Right. If you take our section upstairs Beaumont and Fletcher are setting up a defensive position to watch the dock. I will head back with these prisoners and see what the major intends."

"And Lieutenant Mulgrave, sir?"

"He can set up a defensive position here along the dock. The Germans will have men in the shipyard too. We don't have enough here yet. We need reinforcements."

"Right sir."

He went to gather the section. "Lieutenant Mulgrave."

"Sir." He ran over.

"Give me a sergeant and four men. I will take these prisoners back to the Oranje Mill. I have my men setting up a CP on the roof. I want your men to build a barricade from the end of the street to the dock. Jerry might try a counterattack from the shipyard."

"Right sir. It went well!"

"We lost men, Lieutenant. When we don't lose men then we can say it went well."

"Yes sir, sorry sir. Sergeant Pendlebury, take four men and go with Captain Harsker."

"Sir."

"We will march these prisoners back to the Headquarters."

"Yes sir."

These German soldiers were just line infantry. All the fight looked to have gone from them but I knew that we needed to exercise our authority of they could cause trouble. Sergeant, search them. Look for hidden weapons. Check their boots for knives."

"Sir!"

Lieutenant Mulgrave said, "But they have surrendered sir!"

"And they might just decide that freedom sounds better. This way we have no surprises. Always search your prisoners!" He nodded. I shouted, in German to the prisoners after they had been searched, "You will move back down the road with my men. Do not try anything."

Their sagging shoulders and despondent look told me that they had had enough of war. When we reached the Oranje I saw that the numbers of captured men had increased. There were two platoons of the King's Own Scottish Borderers watching them. I saw more signs of organisation. There were a couple of fires and huge cauldrons of water being boiled. The British Army was good at improvising. Uncle Beach, however, was empty. There were ships neither landing nor leaving. It explained why the German prisoners were still here.

"Right Sergeant, you may rejoin the Lieutenant."

He pointed to the boiling kettles of water, "Sir, any chance of us taking some water back. The lads'll be gagging for a brew."

"Of course Sergeant." I remembered the dugout we had cleared twelve hours earlier. "If you go into that dugout you should find couple of dixies."

"Thanks sir, you are a gent!"

I went into the Oranje Mill. Major Boucher-Myers was there smoking and he was talking to Captain Rewcastle and a Major of the King's Own Scottish Borderers. "Well, Captain Harsker, how did it go?"

"We took the southern side of the Het Docks but the Germans still occupy the shipyard. We didn't have enough men to assault it."

"I know, Captain. Major Thompson here is the most senior officer to have landed from the King's Own Scottish Borderers. The German shells are making it too difficult for the landing craft. We are losing too many men before they even land. We are suspending operations until after dark. Then we can land more men. I will get reinforcements to you as soon as I can."

"Communications are a little difficult, sir. We can't ask for support in a hurry."

"I know. We are short of radios. We have more coming with the next landing craft. You will have a radio as soon as we get one. How are you off for ammunition and food?"

I smiled, "If you can't land men sir, then I think it highly unlikely that you have either ammunition of food. Don't worry. We will forage. We don't mind using German weapons."

"Good man. I want you to get some food and then be ready to go into action again. Keep Lieutenant Mulgrave with you. When you leave he can take over. Your part in all of this should have ended when we arrived. Sorry about this, Harsker!"

"We are part of the Brigade sir. We don't mind." I turned to Major Thompson, "And good luck to you, sir. The reinforcements you have brought are more than welcome."

"I feel like a spare part here. Those men guarding the prisoners are virtually the whole of my force at the moment!"

"Don't be in too much of a rush sir. The Germans are not giving up without a fight. There are more of them dying than surrendering."

I headed back to the new CP. I went first to inform Lieutenant Mulgrave of the new orders. "I would have one man in four on watch and let the rest sleep. We may be doing some night fighting. A tired man makes mistakes."

"Right sir. We are running low on ammo. Will it be replenished any time soon?"

"Don't count on it. Have your men find German weapons and ammo. There should be rations or food too. Always search the dead; they are past caring. If they had the post office as a command centre then there will be supplies there. Check it out."

"Thanks sir."

It was a pleasure to get back to my men. They had lit a fire in one of the fireplaces in the room below the roof and were already preparing food. They were organised. I saw Gordy, Hewitt, Shepherd and Crowe. They were already asleep. When I emerged on to the roof Sergeant Poulson said, "I thought we could all have a couple of hours' kip, sir. Things seemed quiet."

I told him what I had heard. He nodded, "Fletcher, you go and get your head down. If the radio comes you will needed to suss it out."

"Righto Sarge!"

Emerson handed me a mug, "Here y'are sir. A nice hot brew."

"I could do with this Fred. Cheers."

"I had a shufti at the shipyard, sir. That will be a tough nut to crack." Sergeant Poulson did not wait for orders. He anticipated them. Like me he knew the next target would be the shipyard. It made perfect sense.

"I think they are going to send us in at night. We had better make sure that everyone has the chance for a nap. We have German guns, grenades and ammo? I am not sure that we will have Mills bombs and .45 ammunition."

"Aye sir. We collected what they left on the roof and they had spare magazines and clips in the room below this one."

I walked to the end of the building which overlooked the shipyard. The Germans had used sandbags and shipbuilding machines to make a long defensive position. It looked a mess but I knew that it would be effective. There were machine guns as well as a couple of 88 mm anti-aircraft guns which could be used as anti-tank weapons. There was, however, a weakness in the defence. I saw that there was a building between us and the defence which had not been fortified. It looked to have been partly destroyed by artillery fire. The blackened roof bespoke a fire. It was just twenty yards from the western end of the German line. I could not see how we could use it but it was a start. I stood a three hour watch and then went into the room my men had commandeered as a bedroom. I was woken an hour later.

"Sir, they have brought the radio. Fletcher is setting it up. The runner said the Major wants to talk to you."

"Thanks, Alan. Any chance of a brew to wake me up?"

"Coming up sir. I still have a twist of tea."

I went downstairs to the outside toilet and then returned to the roof. Fletcher said, "Sir, they are sending up a company of the King's Own Scottish Borderers. They are going to take over the defence of the dock. At midnight there will be a barrage on the ship yard. We are to report fall of shot and when it lifts they want us and Lieutenant Mulgrave's men to try to breach their defences. They are going to use a rolling barrage. The Major and the rest of the troop will attack from the Merchant's Dock."

"Tell them we will be ready. Sergeant Poulson, as soon as the relief troops come, parade the men near the burned out post office."

"Sir."

"Gordy, better get the lads up and then do an equipment check. I will be off to see Lieutenant Mulgrave."

The Lieutenant had set a good watch. He now had eighteen men. It did not seem like a huge number but we were commandos and thirty commandos could do a great deal.

I waved him over. He stubbed his cigarette out., "Did you get some rest, Geoff?"

"Yes sir. I had a good couple of hours."

"Good. We are going in at midnight."

"Going in sir?"

I gave him our orders. "Now the way I want us to work it is for your men to be the second wave. I will take my men through the barricades when the shells are still firing. We can do so silently. When the firing begins or the alarm is given then you bring your men in fast and hard."

"We could go in with you, sir. My men are good."

"We need silence to get as far in as we can. I know my men can be silent. Besides this allows you to judge the weaknesses we find and exploit them."

"Sir."

"When the Borderers get here hand over the defences to them."

I returned as I heard the sound of boots coming up the street. It was the relief. "Captain Walker sir. We are your relief."

"Thank you." I pointed to the roof. "I have a command post on the roof but the main defences are there."

Nodding he said, "Lieutenant Daniels go with Sergeant Major O'Rourke and relieve the Commandos. Sergeant McIntyre, bring four men and come with us."

I led the six of them up to the roof. I pointed out the defences. Fletcher was still on the radio. "Do you have someone who can work the radio?"

Sergeant McIntyre said, "Aye sir, Private Jennings here is not too bad... for a Geordie!"

"Good then Fletcher rejoin the others. I will be down when the barrage begins." As the Borderers took up their position I explained my plan to the captain. "I need to make sure the barrage moves away from the edge before I order my men in."

"You will be going in before they finish firing?"

"If we want the Germans to be surprised then, yes. I am only taking thirty men. This needs to be a surgical strike. Shock them. We have been taking prisoners. Germans like order and organisation. They hate surprises."

We went to the roof which overlooked the shipyard. I saw that they had cranes there too. I knew that would mean snipers but, in the dark, we were relatively safe. I looked at my watch. It was 23.55. Private Jennings said, "Sir, it is Headquarters. They say they are ready to fire."

"I nodded and Captain Walker said, "You repeat our report eh?"

"Well aye sir."

We heard one shell at a minute to midnight. It landed in the Het Dock. "Long and right!"

There was the slightest of delay and then another shell was fired. This time it was to our left. "Short; fifty yards on line."

"Sir." He repeated it.

Five guns roared from the south of us, across the river the shells exploded in a line. One was dangerously close to our building. Being on the roof we were safe but if one shell was slightly off line then we could be hit. The other shells hit the barricade.

"Jennings tell them move fifty feet left."

"Sir!"

The correction worked. The shells began to destroy the defences. I watched as the guns moved north and east as they cleared the ground of obstacles and Germans.

"Right Captain. I shall be off."

"Good luck."

When I reached the street my men were all ready. I slung my Tommy gun over my back as Sergeant Poulson smeared my face and hands with blacking. I fitted my silencer. "Ready?"

"Yes sir."

I turned to Lieutenant Mulgrave. "Follow us in but give us twenty feet eh?"

"Sir."

We moved from the shelter of the building and into the rubble covered street. With Sergeant Poulson on the left of the line and Gordy Barker on the right we scurried across the street strewn with fallen masonry, bricks and pieces of metal. I saw the flash ahead as shells found something inflammable. We reached the barricade. The shells had blown a hole in it. I headed for it as one rogue shell exploded not fifty feet in front of me. The black night became daylight for an instant. I threw myself to the side. I hit something soft and found that I had struck the body of a dead German sentry. I rose and headed through the gap which one of the first shells had made.

Inside was chaos. There were fires and I saw German Medics helping the wounded. I crouched behind a wrecked 88. Levelling my Colt I aimed at a German Paratrooper officer who was by a field radio. I fired two shots. One hit him in the shoulder and he spun around. The other hit the radio which was being carried by another paratrooper. The Germans had no idea that we were inside their defences. I saw others fall as my men fired from hidden positions. Until the shells stopped then we were safe. I watched in horror as a shell plunged into the middle of the stretcher bearers and wounded. There were four men one moment and none the next. It had not been deliberate but it was tragic.

When the guns stopped the crack of artillery guns was replaced by the moans and cries of those seeking help. I spied a sandbagged command centre. I began to hurry across the shipyard. I heard the 'phut' as someone fired their silenced Colt. As a head appeared over the sandbags I fired. Inevitably we were spotted. There was a shout from our right and I heard the sound of rifles. Bullets pinged off the cobbles.

Behind me came the rattle of Tommy guns as Lieutenant Mulgrave and his section gave us the vital support we needed. To our left I heard the sound of Bren guns and grenades as the Major led the rest of the troop to attack from the south and west. I reached the sandbags of the Command Post and clambered up them. When I reached the top I saw that there was another radio inside and three men huddled around it. As I leaned over I said, "Surrender!"

I suddenly saw, in the flash of a grenade, that these were Waffen SS. Even as two of them pulled their guns around to fire at me I emptied my Colt. I was only saved from death by the sandbags of the command post and the fact that they were trying to level rifles at me. Even so my beret was plucked from my head. As I clicked on empty I realised that there was no firing from within. I rolled over the top and dropped in. They were all dead.

Bill Hay's head appeared from the side, "Should have used a grenade, sir." He handed me my beret. "That was bloody close."

"Thanks Bill." I knew why I had been so foolish. I had seen the shell kill the stretcher bearers and I had not wanted to kill without giving them a chance to surrender. It had been a mistake. Elite soldiers like the Waffen SS and Paratroopers did not surrender.

The Germans had recovered a little and were trying to organize a defence at the square known as Betje Wolf Plein. I holstered my Colt and swung around my Thompson. Stepping out of the bunker I saw my men moving in pairs. There was plenty of cover. I saw Lieutenant Mulgrave leading his men. They were running and in a line. The crack of bullets from the cranes told me they had snipers and three men fell.

"Sergeant Barker, take out the cranes!"

Although two cranes had been destroyed in the barrage there were still another three which had survived.

"Sir! You three bring your weapons and come with me." I saw him run towards some dead Germans.

Major Boucher-Myers appeared next to me. "Sorry we are a little late. They had a machine gun post which had survived. These are tougher troops than we have fought so far."

"Waffen SS and paratroopers sir. They are regrouping over there."

The major turned, "Captain Renwick, get your mortars set up here. Lay down a barrage."

"Sir!"

A bullet struck the runner next to the major. I pointed to the cranes. "They have snipers sir. I have sent some men to deal with them."

There was the whoosh of a rocket as Gordy used the Panzershreck he had found to hit one of the cranes.

The major nodded, "And I would guess they have started. As soon as the mortars start take your men from the right. I will bring the rest from the centre and the left."

"Sir. Sergeant Poulson get my section and bring them here." I took the opportunity to swig some water. "We are going in when the mortars fire. It should keep the German's heads down. Use grenades when we get close." The buildings at the side of the street had collapsed making a natural barrier across the street. In the dark it would be hard to pick targets. A grenade was more effective.

We heard the pop of the three mortars as they sent their bombs into the air. We crouched as we waited for the fall of shot. The first shells hit the masonry. I heard the sergeant behind me correct their aim and the next three fell behind the demolished building.

"Right lads! In." We had an easier task than the major for we were attacking obliquely from the side. I heard another crash from my right as Gordy took out another crane. Holding my Tommy gun in my left hand I took a Mills bomb from my battle jerkin. I pulled the pin with the thumb of my left hand and kept a tight grip on the grenade. From my left I heard the sound of firing as the Major and his men closed with the enemy. The muzzle flashes from behind the debris showed me where the Germans were. I was thirty feet away. I pulled back my arm and threw the grenade high, "Grenade!" As I threw myself to the ground I heard three more of my men give the same warning and my whole section fell to the ground.

The four grenades rippled as they exploded. As pieces of mortar and metal flew overhead I heard cries and screams. Even though I could hear little I rose and levelled my Thompson. I scrambled to the top of the fallen stones and sprayed in an arc before me. I used two short bursts. Fletcher and Beaumont crouched close by adding their fire.

I jumped down. I had fired half of my magazine. I took another grenade. The square was filled with retreating Germans who were falling back. There was a movement from my right and, as I dived to the ground, a muzzle flash. I dropped the grenade and pulled my trigger, emptying the magazine. The German fell. He was less than twelve feet from me. Bullets were fired from the square.

"Take cover!"

We had achieved our first objective. We had the shipyard. I picked up the fallen grenade and then reloaded my Thompson.

"Spread the men out Sergeant Poulson." In the prone position I saw the last of the cranes fall into the water as Gordy completed his mission. I finished reloading and, laying my grenade on the bricks in front of me, I half rose to peer towards the other side of the square. The Germans had fallen back to the other side. The square was empty and was a killing ground.

I heard Major Boucher-Myers shout, "Hold the line here! Are there any prisoners?"

I heard his sergeant shout, "No sir! These are the madmen! They are Waffen SS."

"Officers to me!"

"Take over sergeant!"

I crawled back towards the shipyard. When I was back at the German bunker I stood. The major smiled, "Textbook stuff, gentlemen. As soon as the sun comes up then the King's Own Scottish Borderers will take over. They have the job of taking the old town. We get to stand down until they have more orders for us. Supplies are now getting ashore. We should be getting some hot food."

"Sir, have you any idea how the Westkapelle landings are going? I have a brother in the Royal Marines."

"Not good, I am afraid. As Captain Harsker warned the brass, the beaches there are harder to attack. Hopefully we can get Flushing cleared and then put pressure to the south. I will go and have a word with the King's Own. Let's see if we can do this handover efficiently eh?"

Chapter 17

It was the middle of the morning by the time we were ready to hand over. More troops had arrived and we had to wait until they had marched up to the docks.

"Lieutenant Mulgrave."

"Yes, Major?"

"The Colonel wants an officer to act as liaison. You were with Captain Harsker at the Merchant's Dock. You know Flushing better than most. Would you care to volunteer?"

"Great sir! That's smashing!"

"You are liaison! No heroics. Let the King's Own take their turn with the bullets. Just advise!"

"Sir."

As he left I said, "I would have been the logical choice, sir."

"I know but Major Foster thinks you have done enough. I believe he has something else lined up for you. You are ordered back to the Oranje Mill to await orders. I will come back with you. We are regrouping. Our troop is to support the Royal Scots. Between us and the King's Own we hope to take Flushing by tomorrow morning."

We made our weary way back to the Headquarters and Uncle Beach. It had been a long time since we had landed and yet we had taken barely a mile or two of the town. I was reassured, as we headed towards the sea, by the sight of the reinforcements which were now landing by the boat load.

When we reached the mill I said, "Sergeant Poulson. Have the men make themselves comfortable. God knows when we will receive our orders. Just be ready to move at a moment's notice."

I joined the Major and Captain Rewcastle. The radio was on a table. A veritable mountain of cigarette butts littered the floor. It was testimony to the hours they had spent there. They were not using headphones but they had it with a speaker attached. It saved having to have an intermediary. I had not realised how tired I was until I sat in the chair a corporal brought to me. A private brought mugs of tea for us. We listened to messages coming from the troops as they advanced.

Major Boucher-Myers said, "It has not gone according to plan but, from what we are hearing, we are winning now. The Germans were a tougher nut to crack than we expected but we are getting there. The fresh troops have given us impetus and the Germans are now falling back. With the hinterland flooded it should soon be all over."

"With respect, sir, I never thought it would be an easy nut to crack. I just thought the planners were overly optimistic and we have still to takeW11 and W7. They lie between here and Westkapelle. We have passed them when we scouted. They are very impressive structures. Taking them will not be easy. If they have fought this hard for the two towns then imagine what they will do there."

"Not an optimist then Tom?"

"No sir, a realist."

Just then a naval messenger arrived with a letter. He went to the Major. "I have a message for a Captain Harsker, sir. It's from Major Foster."

The Major waved at me, "The chap with the hang dog expression is Captain Harsker."

He handed me the letter and I opened it. I recognised the major's scrawl. "Thanks. That will be all."

"Do you want me to wait for a reply, sir?"

I scanned it a second time, "No. They are sending a Motor Launch for us."

The rating saluted and left.

"Are these the orders, Tom?"

"They are, sir. The '*Erebus*' is having problems and the big ships are not managing to silence the batteries. It seems I was prescient when I mentioned the batteries. They are sending us in tonight with demolitions and 41 Commando will attack them in the morning. Our job is to do what we did for you; clear the beach and hold on until they get ashore. The Major seems to think the Motor Launch can get in and out without being seen."

The major looked at his watch. "You had better get your head down, Tom."

"No sir, I had better study the maps. I will let my lads sleep."

I began to pore over the maps. I knew the place. We had landed there before. The dunes were high but that might help us. I did not worry about our ability to blow up the guns; our problem would be landing and avoiding being seen. This would not be like our reconnaissance trip. They would be expecting us. The advantage we had was that they had been under fire for a couple of days. I doubted that they would have much food. If we landed in the dark then my men could make us seem a larger force than we actually were.

I stopped scanning the map after an hour. I had most of it in my head anyway. I was crossing the Mill to get another cup of tea when I heard Lieutenant Mulgrave's voice on the radio. I missed the first part but I heard the latter part. "…. *Twenty men surrendered to us. They are paratroopers! The 6th Parachute Regiment. They are hard looking men but they came like sheep! They look to have accepted captivity. The Captain is sending me back with four men. We'll bring them to you. Put the kettle on eh? We will have the rest of the town by dark if it carries on like this….*"

"Captain Harsker?"

I turned and saw Able Seaman Spalding in the doorway. He was one of the crew of the Motor Launch."

"Yes?"

"Skipper's compliments. He is tied up at the breakwater and he has your gear whenever you are ready."

"I'll be there as soon as I can."

I turned back, "Major Boucher-Myers you must warn the Lieutenant. Paras do not surrender and never like sheep! These are German elite; they will fight until the end! He cannot watch them with four men!"

"I am sure he knows what he is doing. You worry too much, Tom."

"No sir, I just know my enemies. The Paras are as bad as the Waffen SS. They are fanatics and they don't surrender."

"Captain don't worry about the Lieutenant. You have your own mission to worry about. I know that you are a good soldier but some of us are also good soldiers. Lieutenant Mulgrave knows what he is about. Now carry on with your mission eh? There's a good chap."

I was beaten. "Right sir." I went to find my men. They were all asleep. "Wakey, wakey, rise and shine, my lovely lads! The Motor Launch is waiting for us. You can finish off your kip there."

"Where to, sir?"

I lowered my voice, "Up the coast to help 41 Commando out."

"Fair enough, sir. Right lads. Someone get the Captain's gear too."

I went back to say goodbye and I heard Major Boucher-Myers say to the sergeant, "What? All of them?"

"Yes sir, apparently they turned a corner close to the Het Docks and pulled out knives. They slit the throats of Lieutenant Mulgrave and the four men and then headed north."

The Major looked at me. I had a sick feeling in my stomach. I knew the answer before I asked, "The German Paratroopers?"

He nodded, "Yes, you were right. Mulgrave and the four men ... Barbaric!"

"If we catch them then we will show them no mercy. We know who they are, sir. Twenty men from the 6th Parachute regiment. If they come into my sights they will not be leaving." I saluted. "We'll be off sir. Lieutenant Mulgrave was a good officer, as was John Gregson. The Germans will pay. I promise you that."

As I went down to the boat I was filled with a cold anger. I remembered back in 1940 a young Scouser who had been murdered by the Waffen SS. I had thought it an isolated incident but I now knew better.

As I boarded the launch my men saw my face and knew that something was amiss. "What's up sir?"

I told them.

"The bastards!" Their anger was universal. Even mild mannered John Hewitt adopted a murderous look.

"Where will they go sir? East?"

"That is a non-starter. The Canadians have the isthmus. My bet is that they will head for Westkapelle. The Germans are there in greater numbers. Anyway put it from your minds for the moment. Beaumont, Shepherd, go and find the demolitions."

"Right sir."

Chief Leslie took his pipe from his mouth and used it to point. "We left them in the mess. There's other stuff for you there, sir. There are ropes and pitons in case you have to climb and we have more ammo."

"Right lads, off you go."

When we were alone I said, "Where is the skipper?"

"He is talking to some of the Landing Craft captains. They wanted to thank him for towing off Lieutenant's Gregson's boat."

"How was it?"

"Grim sir. The boat was all wood and little bits of metal. The bullets tore through her. The young Lieutenant had a stomach wound. He lasted all the way across the Scheldt but died in the ambulance. All he kept talking about was how he had let you and his uncle down, sir. The skipper kept telling him it was nonsense." He tapped his pipe out on his hand and blew through it. "I have had enough of this game sir. I came in as a young lad and now it is the young lads who are dying."

"I know what you mean, Bill. We old hands just have to keep on doing what we have always done and try to keep the young 'uns alive. Tell Lieutenant Williamson I will be with my men in the mess."

Everything was organized by the time I got to the mess. Beaumont and Shepherd were busy examining the explosives and timers. Gordy was dividing up the rations while Sergeant Poulson and Bill Hay were divvying up the ammunition.

"We have made a separate pile for you, sir."

"Thanks. I haven't spoken to the Lieutenant yet but I had planned on sailing as soon as it is dark. 41 Commando are attacking at dawn."

"Are they coming in on Landing Craft sir?"

"Yes they are. Fletcher you will need the torch. As soon as we begin the ascent then you signal the launch who will signal the '*Warspite*' and '*Roberts*' to shift target from W7 to W11."

"Righto sir. It would be a bit of a bugger if we were blown up by our own side eh?"

"Quite."

I took my Bergen and emptied it. I then went through my ritual of refilling it. In theory we would only be ashore and alone for a short time but this operation had been dogged by disasters since we had arrived and it was better to plan for a long stay.

Able Seaman Spalding stuck his head around the door, "Skipper's aboard sir. He is waiting for you on the bridge. Cocoa, sir? I am getting one for the chief and the skipper."

"That would be perfect."

Sam was smoking again, "What time do you want to push off, sir?"

"Wait until dark. Jerry still has communication north and west of Flushing. It wouldn't do to warn the gun's crews that we are coming."

"It's worse than that, sir. When we were heading over we saw lorry loads of Germans heading up the coast. They are building strongpoints along the road to slow you down."

I worried about that. It was obvious that they could not win in Walcheren so why were they fighting so hard for it? The failure of Market Garden would have encouraged them but they had to have something planned. The lack of any armour north of the Scheldt showed that they were husbanding the tanks they still had. Why? My mind was too fuddled to make sense of it and I would need to be on top of my game if we were to succeed.

"I wondered why they suddenly called on us."

"And the guns themselves are a nightmare sir. It isn't just the big fifteen inch guns that are a problem. They have flak guns, 75s and 88s. "

"I know. These two gun emplacements, W11 and W7, control the whole of the west Scheldt. Listen, Sam, no heroics. You drop us, wait for the signal and then push off back to our side of the river." He stubbed his cigarette out. "I mean it, Sam, that is an order. I have lost two good young officers in the last few days. I don't want a third on my conscience."

"But sir, you put your life at risk."

"That is different. I am just obeying orders. Your orders are to drop us off and leave. Right?"

He sighed, "Right sir."

Just at that moment a flight of Typhoons screamed over. I heard three explosions which were so loud and the concussion so great that we felt it in the sheltered anchorage.

"That must have hurt someone, sir."

"Perhaps but more than likely it just made another obstacle for the infantry to get through." I wondered why they had not tried using the Typhoons on the gun emplacements. I answered myself straightaway. They were heavily protected by flak. A dive bomber has to dive into a target. It would be suicide. I could see why they had chosen us. We were small in number and stood a chance of slipping ashore unseen. We might not be able to destroy them on our own but we could cause enough trouble to allow 41 Commando to complete the mission. We were expendable.

"Here's the cocoa sir."

"Thanks Spalding."

The three of us stood in companionable silence drinking the rum infused cocoa. A Commando took pleasure when he could. In six hours' time I could be fighting for my life. The cocoa was a bit of home in my hand. Just the feel of the cup made me think of Mum. When we had been little she would bring Mary and me a cup at night. Grated Fry's chocolate on the top was a treat. That made me think of Susan. I tried not to think too much about the future for therein lay danger but when I did think of home I thought of Susan and our life together after the war. I knew that she and Mum would plan where we would live and the house. All I wanted was a little garden and an armchair. My Granddad had had an armchair. It was leather and old. It had high wings but when I had sat on his knee while he read me a story, before the fire, I had felt as safe as in the Tower of London. I would have such a chair and when I had a son I would sit and tell him stories in my armchair.

"You are quiet sir, is everything all right?"

"It is Bill. My mind is the one place to which I can retreat and find comfort. Then I can come back to this world and all the dangers. It is how I keep sane." I looked at my watch. It would be dark within the hour. "I had best get back to the lads. Thanks for the cocoa."

"I'll set sail as soon as I deem it appropriate, sir."

"We'll be ready. We will keep below decks just in case Jerry has watchers."

My men were all relaxed. Everything was bagged and they just had to put on their black faces. Sergeant Poulson pointed to a bowl. "Duty cook made corned beef hash sir. It's not half bad. He has some Piccalilli."

"That will do for me. Any bread and marge?

"It's a couple of days old but there are a couple of rounds sir."

By the time I had finished eating I felt the launch get underway. I applied the camouflage to my face and hands. I put my beret in my Bergen and put on my comforter. Although I had checked everything before I went through it all again: my two knives, pistols, Tommy gun. I patted each one as I thought of it. My sap, daggers, torch, binoculars, wire cutters and ammunition. Everything was ready.

"Right lads, we go in three dinghies. Beaumont and Shepherd, I want you in separate dinghies in case anything goes wrong. I will be the first ashore with Hay, Hewitt and Crowe. We will clear a path and secure the ropes. Gordy, tail end Charlie. The big guns are not the priority for us. It is the flak guns and smaller pieces. They are the ones that can hurt the marines."

"Do we have to be quiet, sir?"

"I am afraid so but I doubt that will last. That is another reason for the four of us to lead the way. We will use silenced Colts. I intend to approach the gun from the north. They have been sending troops to stop us attacking from the Flushing side. There is a long beach and sand dunes. Once we cross the road there is scrubland and then the high dyke. It is man-made and has stones and concrete. We may have to use ropes but I hope not."

"You say cross the road as though we just have to watch out for traffic but it will be more than that won't it sir?"

"Yes, Joe. There will be wire, strongpoints and machine guns. The sound of the naval bombardment should enable us to get close and to keep their heads down. At least that is the plan as outlined by Major Foster."

"He must read a lot of comics sir?"

"Why is that, Fletcher?"

"Because he thinks you are Superman sir! If he ever gives you a pair of red underpants to wear over your trousers then you know it!"

Everyone laughed and it made us all more relaxed. You could rely on Fletcher to lighten the mood.

Outside we heard the crack and crash of the naval guns as they pounded the shore. It was a stark reminder of what we were about to do.

"Right lads! Everyone on deck. Once more unto the breach and all that eh sir?"

"Right, Sergeant Poulson; we few, we happy few, we band of brothers."

Fletcher nodded, "Shakespeare! I remember sir!"

Chapter 18

Sam had learned well from Bill. He had the art of bringing us in almost silently. However it was unnecessary this time. We saw the muzzle flashes from the big guns as they pounded the beach positions. The sound of their fire seemed to roll as they monotonously fired. Sam's approach was necessary for we had to avoid a white bow wave which might be spotted by someone hardy enough to brave the shells. It was a dark and cloudy night which made finding the correct beach difficult. If we had not landed there before then we would not have managed it but the Chief recognised the patch of sand and we saw, above us, a pair of shadows which could only be one of the two gun emplacements. We had come inshore of the remaining mines and so we were close to the beach. I knew that, although the darkness would make the landing and assault difficult, it would also aid us for the Germans would find it hard to see us.

We slipped over the side into the dinghies. I idly reflected that we were getting through dinghies at a prodigious rate of knots! We paddled hard through the forty feet to the beach. The Lieutenant had brought us to within a foot of being grounded but he had, as the navy always did, done well. We were close to one of the groynes and I used it as a marker. As we paddled closer I saw fifteen inch shells hitting the concrete emplacements but they did not appear to be doing much damage. We pulled the dinghy ashore and laid it next to the groyne. Until daylight it would help to disguise it.

I looked over my shoulder and saw that the others were following in our wake. I led my team up the beach towards the sand dunes. 41 Commando would need daylight to land their craft. By then we had to have made sure that as many of the guns which would make their life hard were destroyed. The shells continued to rain down. I saw craters in the sand where they had struck. The incoming tide would wash them away. Up towards the guns, now illuminated when the shells struck and they fired back, I saw that they were having little effect. The concrete was ten feet thick. The '*Warspite's*' eight fifteen inch guns fired and then the two of the monitor. Even when they struck it did not seem to damage them over much.

The beach was littered with the obstacles intended to stop vehicles and vessels. Some had been destroyed but not enough to allow the vessels a safe landing. We could easily avoid them but they would remain a hazard for the Marines. I ran with Hewitt and, fifty feet up the beach we stopped and, with levelled Colts, I waved the other two forward. They ran past us and after another fifty feet they stopped. We were closer to the fall of shot now and we could feel the concussion from the blasts even though we were hundreds of feet from them. Bill Hay waved me on. We ran past them and reached the edge of the low dunes. More shells fell and tiny pieces of concrete zipped over our heads. The air was filled with the smell of cordite. I wondered if the message had been sent that Commandos were on the beach. Crouching I waved the others forward. Finally, the guns stopped. Fletcher's signal had reached the Motor Launch and they had passed it on. The silence was deafening. I felt like my breath sounded like a gale!

When they reached us they crouched next to us. We spread out in a line. I glanced up and saw wire. I pointed to Beaumont and Shepherd to remain in the dunes. They nodded and then the rest of us crawled up the dunes which were held together by tough marram grass. There was a temptation to use it to pull ourselves up but that would have been a mistake. I used my rubber soled shoes and knees for propulsion. With my Colt still held in my right hand I only had my left hand to push me up. When I reached the top I raised my head just a little. I could hear German voices as they began to talk. They would not emerge from their bunkers for a while. They would fear the guns firing again. Having been in such a tomb myself I knew the relief of getting out into the fresh air.

I rose and began to move towards the nearest dugout. I pointed to the flak position and at Crowe and Lance Sergeant Hay. They would destroy it and then the machine gun posts further down. My other two sergeants had led their men left and right. I had just reached the bunker when I saw a glint of light as the door was opened before the blast curtain had been replaced. I took out a grenade and laid it on the sand and then levelled my Colt.

The first German saw me and I was just eight feet from him. Standing on the dune I was above the bunker. I fired and he fell back. I pulled the pin on the grenade, leapt down and, flinging open the door rolled the grenade along the floor. I slammed the door shut to contain the blast. The sound was dampened by the concrete. I felt the concussion move it and heard the screams and shouts from within. I flung open the door and stepped inside. There had been twelve men; the crews of the flak gun and the machine gun. It was now a charnel house. Pausing only to grab a couple of grenades I emerged into the night and listened. There was just the sound of Germans in the huge gun emplacement. Someone was giving orders. They had obviously not heard the noise of the grenade exploding under eight feet of concrete.

I saw that my men had disabled both weapons and were laying a booby trap. When the Germans spotted the Marines and tried to use their guns they were in for a nasty surprise. I moved down to the next bunker. It was thirty yards further along. I saw the flak gun had been destroyed by the shelling. The door of the bunker opened and the light from inside spilled out. It was just twenty feet from where I crouched. They were emerging. I threw myself to the ground and levelled my Colt. The light from the bunker had ruined the night vision of the Germans but it would not last. Bill and my other two men threw themselves to the ground beside me. I risked looking at my watch. It was 03.00. We had three hours before the next boats would come in.

I was just wondering how the rest of my men were faring when I heard the chatter of German and British submachine guns. The Germans who had just come from the bunker looked around. I aimed at the sergeant who began shouting out orders. My bullet hit him in the head. It disappeared in blood, bone and brains. My three men also fired and hit their targets. I fired a second bullet and hit one in the shoulder. The survivors fired blindly into the dark and then ran for the safety of the gun emplacements some forty yards away.

I rose, "Quick, into their position. We will make it our own strongpoint."

We dived over the sandbags. Some had been damaged and others destroyed in the shelling. Bill Hay said, "Private Crowe, fetch some of those sandbags from the flak gun and rebuild the broken sections. Hewitt let's build up the rear."

I went to the German machine gun and, after checking that it had a belt of ammunition, cocked it. The gun fire further along the beach was sporadic. I saw the muzzle flashes. They were to the east and west of our position. I shouted, "Commandos!" I needed say no more. My men knew that was our rallying cry and they would make their way towards us. I resisted firing my newly acquired German machine gun. It would identify precisely where we were. My men knew roughly where I was and that would do. As soon as the survivors reached the emplacement then we could expect German fury.

As I waited I idly glanced at the bodies of the men we had shot. The privates were from the Marine-Artillerie-Abteilung 202. When I turned over the headless sergeant I saw that he was from the 6th Parachute Regiment. I had found at least one of Lieutenant Mulgrave's killers.

"That'll have to do sir. Alan, collect all the grenades and the weapons. We will need them."

"Aye Sarge. Do you want me to check out the bunker too?"

I said, "No. We take no risks. We have to hold for another three hours."

"Right sir."

"Lance Sergeant Hay have you seen this sergeant's uniform?"

He glanced down. "So they are here."

"It makes sense. They couldn't get any further north."

My men suddenly appeared and dived into the dugout. The exception was Ken Shepherd who was being supported by both Beaumont and Emerson. John Hewitt immediately took out his medical kit.

"It's his leg. The knee."

"Don't worry sir. I can still fight and I have the explosives!"

I saw Hewitt give the slightest shakes of his head. "Did you lay any charges?"

Both Shepherd and Beaumont nodded. Shepherd winced as Hewitt tore his trousers, "Sorry, Ken. I will give you something for the pain."

Beaumont pointed west. "We put them under the 75 mm and 88 mm flak guns. We were heading for the ones east when Jerry fired on Fletcher."

"Then don't worry about it. We have made a hole in the middle of their defences. When 41 Commando land they can come up the middle."

There was a fusillade from our front and Sergeant Poulson sprayed them with his Tommy gun. "Stand to lads."

As they went to the edge of the sandbags I said, "The German MG works."

Fletcher said, "Come on then Freddie! Let's give the Germans their bullets back."

Shepherd said, "Sir, what about those batteries. They can hit the landing craft as they come in."

"We'll worry about that later. Take care of him, John." Roger Beaumont was not standing to. "What are you doing Roger?"

He shrugged, "We brought these charges. Ken had this idea that we could use the charges and improvise a weapon. I am making satchel charges. If we can get close enough we can throw them into the emplacements themselves."

I patted Shepherd's shoulder, "Good lad! I can see we'll have to promote you. Hewitt join us when you are finished."

The Germans were now organized. I heard a German officer ordering one section to go to the left and the other to the right. Suddenly the sky was lit up as the demolitions under the guns exploded. They caught a squad which was trying to enfilade us. Pieces of metal and gun flew through the air. I saw the barrel of one gun smack into the huge concrete emplacement. It did little damage but I knew it would give those within a mighty shock.

"Well done lads, your explosives bought us a little time at any rate."

"That's one thing we know how to do sir, set a charge."

"You do indeed, Shepherd, you do indeed."

I had holstered my Colt and swung my Thompson around as the first wave of infantry came towards us. I recognised the distinctive headgear of the paratroopers. About four of the men advancing were the 6th Parachute regiment. It was petty, I know, but when I gave the order to fire I felt a great deal of satisfaction when two of the ones who fell to our bullets were paratroopers. Our superior firepower kept their heads down.

"Conserve your ammo and watch out for men trying to flank us."

We would stand no chance if they had mortars but it appeared they did not. Bill Hay said, "I can hear Germans to our left, sir. They are trying to flank us."

"Gordy, you and Private Crowe use the grenade launchers. I know you can't see your target; just lay down a pattern."

"Sir!"

The two of them fired as fast as they could reload. After six grenades I shouted, "Cease Fire." I waited and heard moans. "Bill?"

"There are still men moving but they are further away."

I went to the left side and rested my gun on the sandbags. Where were they? We had too few grenades to waste more. We would have to be patient and see whose nerve held. Once again the night was riven by the sound of a triple explosion. They had triggered the booby traps on the first machine gun and flak position.

Bill chuckled, "That sorted them sir. There are just moans now and no movement."

"Take Crowe and make sure there are none left."

"Right sir. Alan, with me. Bring your Colt."

I took Hay's place and I waited, listening. I heard Hay speaking but it was low. I could also hear voices but they were coming from the emplacement. There was a slit trench beneath the guns and I suspected there were men there. I waited until Hay and Crowe returned. "Well?"

"There are none left alive sir." He jerked a thumb at the emplacement. "It seems that the bloke who ordered our chaps to be executed is up yonder. Feldwebel Hans Arenz. One of the 6th Parachute regiment was dying and he seemed glad to tell me that they had killed a Commando officer. He said they were doing the Fuhrer's will. He told me that this Feldwebel hates all Commandos and then he died."

"Well at least we know the name of our enemy and that four of those who killed our lads are dead. Just sixteen to go."

We had silence for fifteen minutes. They were up to something but the question was, what? We had our answer when they came at us from three different directions. Their flanking moves had told them exactly where we were. They came as we would have done, moving and firing as a pair.

"Here they come!" Fletcher's German machine gun rattled out closely followed by the Tommy guns of the rest of my men. I waited until I saw a German rise. I did not move my position and I fired a burst in a semi-circle. As I had expected the two men working as a pair were close together. They both fell although I knew not if they were dead. My men were cool and calm. The Germans were angry and they rushed. We might have escaped unscathed had not Gordy's gun jammed.

"Shit!"

In the heart beat it took to drop the Thompson and draw his Colt one of the paratroopers had closed to within twenty feet and was already pulling his arm back to hurl his grenade. Gordy fired two shots into his chest. It would normally stop a horse but the paratrooper was made of iron and he threw it. As I shouted, "Grenade!" Bill emptied his gun into the German's chest. He was thrown backwards.

I crouched and saw the grenade land in the middle of our sandbags. Before I could react Shepherd had thrown himself on the grenade and covered it with his body. His body rose and then fell. I stood, for I was angry and, ignoring the bullets zipping like flies, I fired a burst and then rolled over the sandbags. I stood and emptied the magazine before dropping it and drawing my Luger and Colt emptied them like Billy the Kid!

I was suddenly pulled back by Sergeant Poulson, "Enough sir! We have lost one man! We can't afford to lose you too."

I stared up at Sergeant Poulson and then nodded. Fletcher had crawled out and retrieved my Thompson. "You don't want your pay docking, do you sir?"

I saw that my men had covered Shepherd's body with his cape. My wild counter attack had knocked the heart out of the Germans and they had retreated. No one said a word. There was little to say. Ken was a good lad. He did his job

161

well and quietly. We had not lost a man since before Normandy. It hurt. It would sink in later on when we were on our way home. It was then we would remember Ken and his life with us. Until then he would be a body covered by an oilskin cape. He had died a hero. An hour later I looked at my watch. It was 05.00. The Marines would be landing in an hour.

"Gordy, how many grenades do we have left for the launchers?"

"Six sir."

"Do you reckon you could put one into the gun emplacement?"

"I could try."

"Fletcher, load a fresh magazine."

"Right sir."

"Beaumont get those satchel charges ready. Wilkinson and I are going to leave a memorial for Ken Shepherd."

"But sir..."

"Polly, my mind is made up. If those guns are still operational in forty five minutes then they will blast the landing craft out of the water. They will be firing over open sights. What I want is for every gun to fire and for Gordy and Alan to try to get a grenade into the emplacement. If they fall short then they will hit those in the slit trench. Wilkinson and I will throw the charges into the aperture."

"Sir it is my bomb..."

"And Joe Wilkinson can throw further than you. You are game aren't you Joe?"

"Too right sir! It's why I volunteered for your section! Besides we owe it to Ken. They were his idea."

"Right, then show us what we need to do."

"They are simply made sir. You pull this piece of cord and throw the satchel. You have ten seconds, that is all. When it goes up, well you better be back here is all I can say."

"Right then we go in ten."

I reloaded my Colt and Luger and put them in my belt. I looked at my watch. There were five minutes to go. I knew why I was doing this. My dad had told me that an officer led from the front. *"You can always refuse a commission, son, but if you accept it then accept the responsibility."* I would not ask them to do something I would not do. The other reason was because I thought we could succeed. By now they knew our numbers and it would take an insane man to do what we were planning.

"Ready!"

"Yes sir."

"Give it to them. Ready, Joe?"

"Aye sir!"

The two grenade launchers fired first. They failed to get through the aperture but they succeeded in other ways. They hit the concrete above the opening and dropped. They exploded in mid-air and an air bomb of shrapnel shredded the trenches. My men opened fire as the second two grenades were launched and

Joe and I clambered over the sandbags. The second grenades were more accurate. One hit the barrel of the gun and then bounced to the side while the other hit the top of the concrete over the gun and exploded. By the time the third grenades were fired we were forty feet from the guns. I saw a German head appear. I drew my Luger left handed and fired blindly. I did not hit him but my bullets made him hide. I watched the two grenades hit the concrete and fall down into the slit trenches.

"Down!"

We threw ourselves to the ground as the grenades sent shrapnel to bounce off the concrete, into the trench and towards us. Had we been stood we would have been hit.

I rose and ran at the emplacement. Now that we were closer it seemed an impossible task. I threw mine first and, to my amazement and horror it wrapped itself around the barrel of one of the two guns. I watched Joe throw his and it sailed through the aperture.

"Run Joe!"

My satchel charge might be the death of us. Joe's would blow up inside the structure but mine would clear the ground around the outside. We almost fell over the sandbags and we were helped as the concussion from the explosion blew us into the middle. Pieces of masonry and metal flew overhead and I lost my hearing briefly. It was as though a whirlwind had blown over us. I lay, unable to move. When I did and turned I saw that one barrel had been bent and would not fire again. Inside the emplacement I heard the crack and crash as shells exploded. Something was on fire inside the emplacement and men were screaming. I saw a figure run, flaming, from the rear door. The 150 mm guns would not fire again.

"Well done, sir."

"Don't get carried away Beaumont. There is still the other gun. Get your weapons and let's clear this slit trench. I want a better position to enfilade the other guns. We can still make it hard for them to hit the Marines."

"Right sir."

"Shall I bring the German gun sir?"

"Yes, Fletcher. It is the heaviest gun we have. There are no grenades left for the grenade launcher now."

As he stood Beaumont looked at Shepherd's cape covered body, "We'll see to him after the battle eh, Roger?"

"Right sir."

We moved up the slope. Already the survivors were fleeing north and east. The other pair of 150 mm guns were their best protection. They still had machine guns and flak guns there. We threw ourselves down on the ground. "Sergeant Poulson, take Crowe and see if there are any survivors in the emplacement. Fletcher set your gun up in the trench."

"Sir, it's full of bodies."

"Then you are fine. They can't hurt you."

Just then I heard the rattle of fire from inside the emplacement. "Joe, with me. Gordy, take charge." I drew my Colt. I resisted shouting for Sergeant Poulson. If he had fired then there was danger. There was no point in announcing our arrival.

As we burst around the corner a handful of Germans opened fired with their submachine guns. Luckily Joe and I saw the grey and threw ourselves to the ground. I emptied the Colt in their direction and then Joe fired his sub machine gun. I saw bullets from a Thompson come from the back of the emplacement and then the Germans disappeared. We rose and ran to the rear of the gun. Sergeant Poulson lay with his left leg bleeding and inside the door lay Alan Crowe. He had been shot in the face.

Sergeant Poulson opened his eyes, "It was that Feldwebel, sir. He pretended to be dead and when Alan turned him over he shot him at point blank range. I moved quick sir but he still hit me in the leg."

Chapter 19

I took out a field dressing. "Joe, fetch Hewitt." As he ran off I cut Poulson's trousers and attached the field dressing to the wound so that it was tight. He would not bleed to death and Hewitt would be able to deal with it. Grabbing Crowe's Thompson I said, "I will be back!"

I ran through the dark towards the position the Germans had occupied. I saw that we had managed to kill just one. He was a paratrooper. We were whittling them down but we had now lost two men in a very short time. I nearly paid for my carelessness with my life. Bullets were fired from the dark. It was lucky that the man I was examining was a big man. The bullets thudded into his back. I could do nothing alone and I ran back to Sergeant Poulson. Hewitt was helping him to his feet and I lifted his arm over my shoulder. The Germans were getting bolder and bullets smacked into the wall above our heads. Joe Wilkinson went down on one knee and began to fire into the dark although, even as I looked, I could see the hint of grey. Dawn was not far away.

We lowered the sergeant into the trench. "I'll load for Fletcher, sir."

"Good." I looked at my men. We were down to eight of us. "Find German rifles. Today we become snipers. The other gun is a hundred and fifty yards away. The Thompsons and Colts are not accurate enough. We use German rifles and we fire at the gunners."

"We can't touch the big guns though, sir. We have no charges left."

"I know but they have a slower rate of fire. We just do what we can, eh lads?"

I walked down the slope to the sandbagged dugout we had used. I took the German rifle and the ammunition from the bottom where it had been dropped. It was the Mauser Karabiner 98 kurz. Not as good as the one I had had for it had no sights but it had a five bullet clip and was effective up to five hundred yards. The Germans were well within range.

I raced back to my man and, pulling a dead German in front of me for protection, rested my rifle on his battle dress. My men were already firing. We had plenty of ammunition and the light was getting better. We were in the west and they were in the east. We would see them before they saw us. We were also aided by the fact that we knew where they would be for the guns could be clearly seen even if the gunners were shadows. There was an 88 mm which had not been destroyed. I knew they had a crew of about eight. I aimed at the shadow close to the centre of the barrel. He was responsible for the elevation. If they could not elevate the guns accurately enough then they would hit nothing. I fired two shots. My second hit him. It had an effect as though someone had sent a jolt of electricity through them. They all ducked but not before Gordy Barker had hit another.

The two German 150 mm belched smoke and flames as they fired. The marines were coming. I could not see the fall of shot but I heard it whistle before us. Fletcher's machine gun continued to fire. I heard orders shouted and saw an officer point in our direction. I fired another two bullets but they were snap shots and I missed. A section of Germans ran towards us. Fletcher let them get to within fifty yards from us before he opened fire. The Germans dropped like stones. Fletcher managed to hit a couple more before they found cover and the rest began to fire from a prone position. I fired again at a shadow which appeared to be moving to the front of the gun. I heard a shout. I had hit him. The two guns fired again. They were taking eight minutes to fire a salvo. The landing craft had a chance now. I changed my clip and looked beyond the flak gun to the machine gun which enfiladed the beach which the Marines would attack.

It was lighter now and, as I peered I could make out a helmet. German helmets are good and can even withstand a bullet but concentration is hard when bullets start to hit it. I fired. My bullet cannoned off the top of the helmet. The head disappeared. I moved it to the right for I could see the barrel. I thought I had the feeling for the rifle and so I fired my next four shots at the barrel. I must have hit it for the black shape moved. My men were having more success with the crews of the larger guns.

"Sir, the landing craft! They are on the beach."

I reached into my Bergen and took out the flare gun. I had to let the Marines know where we were. I fired a red flare and then a green one. It was still gloomy enough for them to stand out in the half light of dawn. I hoped they would know that we were friendly. With the rising sun it would become easier to see but it also meant we could be seen more clearly too. Already the Germans were switching around their machine guns to fire at us. That was a good thing for it meant they were dividing their fire.

With both sides in cover our bullets were largely ineffective. I laid down the Mauser and picked up my Thompson. We had to keep our heads down as did the Germans. Our most effective weapon was Fletcher on the German MG. Having sighted it at first he could fire it from below the trench. When he shouted, "Reload!" then I put my Thompson above the dead German's body and fired a burst. It was stalemate but we had the Marines advancing up the beach; they would decide this battle. The two German guns were ineffective now. The landing craft were too close to the beach and the guns could not hit them. The landing craft had disgorged the Royal Marines. Attacking from the beach they were able to use their own mortars and grenade launchers.

I decided it was time to try to force the issue. "On my command I want you all to throw a German grenade as far as you can. Then everyone apart from Sergeant Poulson and Fletcher charge them."

They all shouted, "Right sir!"

We were ready. I smashed the porcelain and held the cord. "One, two, three!" On 'three' I hurled it as high and far as it could go. Those in the slit trench had less restrictions and theirs went further. It did not matter for the six grenades caused a wall of concussion which raced towards the Germans. I rose with my Tommy gun in two hands. I did not fire straight away but as soon as I hit the smoke I did. I sprayed in an arc before me firing bursts of three and four bullets. The gun was most effective when used that way. When I emerged from the smoke I saw that the Marines had breached the German line and the ones before us were fleeing. I fired at them and one dropped.

"Number 4 Commando!" This time it was not only a rallying call it was a warning to the marines that we were friendly.

A Royal Marine captain strode up to me. He crouched next to me, "Captain Howard of 41 Commando. Splendid job!" He pointed to the bent gun in the emplacement behind us. "Damned good job."

"Tell your men to be careful. There are some German Paratroopers. They are as bad as the SS. They are tricky."

"Thanks for the warning. We'll take it from here."

I shook my head, "We are going after these paratroopers. They have murdered Commandos and no one gets away with that."

He suddenly seemed to see me for the first time, "You are Captain Harsker, the chap who won the V.C. They say you are a bad man to cross and I can see why. Good luck old chap." Turning he shouted, "Come on Marines, let's show Army that we can destroy guns too!"

The company of Marine Commandos roared a war cry as they hurtled towards the one remaining emplacement. We returned to our dead and our wounded.

"Get Ken and Alan's bodies. We will take them down to the beach. John and I will bring Sergeant Poulson."

The two of us manhandled him from the trench. His wound and leg were now stiffening and I saw the agony etched on his face as he felt the pain race up his wounded leg. "Sarge, just let us take your weight. The Captain is a big lad, he won't bend will you sir?"

"No indeed. It's a nice hospital with nurses and clean uniforms for you my lad."

"I want to be there when you get that bastard sir! Poor Alan, he never stood a chance."

"Don't you worry, we will get him." Speaking like that in front of my men was like an old fashioned oath. It would be a blood oath. We would have vengeance for the dead the paratroopers had caused.

The beach seemed closer than when we had ascended it all those hours ago. Perhaps it was the incoming tide, I didn't know. Only one of the landing craft remained, he was just closing his ramp and pulling off the beach. I saw the officer on the bridge wave. He must have known we needed him! I was beginning to get annoyed when I spied the Motor Launch surging towards the beach. The wave from the landing craft had been to tell me that help was on its way. I turned and looked back. My men were carrying the two bodies on the dead men's capes.

The launch stopped and two dinghies were paddled towards us. Able Seaman Spalding stepped ashore.

"I thought I told Lieutenant Williamson to return home."

The sailor grinned, "He must have misunderstood but when we heard there were Commandos coming down to the beach we knew it had to be you, sir."

I nodded, "We have one wounded man and two dead."

The grin left his face, "I am sorry about that sir, who bought it?"

"Privates Shepherd and Crowe."

He looked grimly at the guns as he said, "Alan was a nice lad. He came from close to where I lived. We had been to the same dances. He had plans for after the war."

I hadn't known that. "That is why I don't make plans. Anyone who makes plans is deluding themselves." He nodded. I handed my Thompson to Sergeant Poulson. "Take this. I will stick with the rifle. We are hunting this time."

As we lowered Sergeant Poulson into the boat he said, "You will survive, sir. I can feel it in my bones. It's nowt, this; I'll be back."

"Well at least you will be safe for a while."

The first boat paddled back to the launch and we placed, reverently, the bodies of our two dead comrades in the second. The sailor said, "We will look after them sir; like they were our own. We are all in this together."

We watched them row back to the launch and only turned when the boat began to move away from the shore. The two bodies were laid on the after deck; they were a stark reminder of the dangers of our job.

"Right, back to the war."

"What do we do first, sir?"

"Get back to the trench and find more ammo, guns and grenades and then question the prisoners."

Up ahead we could hear sporadic firing but it was almost desultory, as though it was the last hurrah. It did not take us long to gather what we wanted. Fletcher looked longingly at the MG. Gordy said, "No chance, Scouse. That is too heavy to carry. These blokes we are chasing will be fast enough as it is. We travel light."

"Nice piece of firepower though Sarge."

I handed my spare magazines to Emerson and Sergeant Barker; they had the sub machine guns. The rest of us had rifles. I hung as many grenades as I could on my battle jerkin. "Take on water and food. We don't know how long this chase will take. I will go and find the Captain." Before I left I took a packet of cigarettes from a dead officer and two cigars.

I found the Captain. He was on the radio to Headquarters. I waited until he had finished. "Have you any prisoners?"

He pointed to the back of the emplacement where around thirty Germans sat disconsolately. "Headquarters complimented us on a job well done. It is now down to the process of mopping up. We have all but finished here."

"When those paratroopers are in the bag then it will be over."

"Do you have orders, Captain?"

"I don't need orders." I smiled, "Don't worry, if there is a court martial you will be safe."

"I wasn't worried about that Captain. How will you find them?"

I pointed to the prisoners. "I will ask them."

"What if they don't speak English?"

"I speak German. When the war started my German was average now I can speak it well! Come with me." We walked over and I took out my Commando knife. We walked along the line of Germans.

"You aren't going to use that are you? I couldn't allow that."

"Let's just call it psychological warfare. Jerry is afraid of Commandos and especially the dagger. I have rarely had to use mine but it might help." I stopped at the end. "No paratroopers amongst these. I thought not. Did you find any amongst the bodies?"

"Three or four."

I stopped next to an officer, "Where are the paratroopers?"

He sneered at me, "You can have my name, rank and serial number. No more!"

"It's funny, Lieutenant, I don't remember the Germans who captured me affording me that privilege. They wanted to put me against the wall and shoot me. And the men I seek flouted the Geneva Convention when they surrendered and then murdered their captors."

"You are a Commando! It is the Fuhrer's order!" I moved towards him and he pressed himself into the wall. He was not worth bothering about. I would find another to question.

I walked further down and saw a wounded sergeant, "You, sergeant, can you tell me where the paratroopers went?"

He shrugged and then patted his tunic.

"Do you want a cigarette?"

He smiled, "If you have one."

I took out the packet I had taken. They were better than the ones the average soldier smoked. "I have a whole packet."

I saw him lick his lips. "They are tough men these paratroopers, Commando. Are you certain you wish to go after them?"

"Tell me and you can have the cigarettes and these cigars."

He shrugged, "No skin off my nose. There is an E-boat base to the north east of the island at Vrouren Polder. It is not far from North Beveland. They will head there. The leader has a brother in the Kriegsmarine." I threw him the cigarettes and the cigars. He nodded his thanks, "I hope you catch them, Commando. They are as bad as the SS."

"I know."

As I turned to leave he said, "You haven't any food have you? We have been on half rations for weeks."

I shook my head, "Do not worry, you will be fed. We treat our prisoners well."

I rejoined my men. Captain Howard stood with me, "How will you find them?"

I took out the map. "Here is where they are headed. It is nine miles away. The land between us and it is flooded. You can get across but it is time consuming." I looked overhead as a flight of Typhoons zoomed low across the island. "These men are being hunted. There are Canadians to the east and Commandos to the west. They have been on short rations and they are hungry. We race them to their E-Boat base."

"But there will be Germans there."

"And...?"

He laughed, "And we are Commandos. Sorry, Captain, I have only been in the Commandos for six months. It seems I have a lot to learn."

I hefted my Bergen on my back and, gripping my map, said, "Right boys, let's see who is fitter us or these paratroopers."

I led and we began to jog north east. The first part was relatively easy for the Germans had built up the land around their defences and it was relatively firm. I could see the lakes, puddles, ponds and pools ahead. If we twisted and turned around them all then it would take forever. I headed for what looked like the shallowest pools and took the line of least resistance. The paratroopers were hard, fit men but they would be tired and hungry. I guessed there were about twelve or thirteen of them left. They were like us. They would not leave a man behind and that would slow them down.

We jogged. It was the sort of pace we had done each morning from our digs up to the camp at Falmouth. Now we had a good reason to put it to good use. I guessed they had a forty minute lead over us. We would keep going and, if needs be, we would eat as we ran. What we did not do was to sing as we ran. That was for training. Now we were at war and we would be silent and vigilant.

Half way to our destination we passed through the small village of Grijpskerke. We knew that they had been through when we saw the bodies lying at the side of the road. A grim faced Dutchman approached us. "You are too late for our friends, Englishman. Those savages came through twenty minutes ago. They shot these men and boys for sport."

I looked down at the three men and two teenage boys. It was a waste of lives and so unnecessary. "How many were there? Which way did they go?"

"There were twelve and they headed along the road to Vrouren Polder." He pointed to the open door of the nearest house. "They took food from there."

I put my hand on the man's shoulder. "I am sorry for your loss but this is almost over. The British and Canadians are coming and we will hunt these dogs!"

He nodded, "Kill them for us!"

We began to make better time for we were now on a road. In places it was flooded but it was only ankle deep. Now that we knew they were close we were even warier. As we ran I looked at the map. There were no more villages between us and the E-Boat base. There would be nowhere for them to shelter and nowhere for them to acquire more food. To the east I heard the sound of small arms fire and the crack of Canadian tanks. It was too far away to be our prey but it would channel them further west for they would wish to avoid our troops. It was this detour which brought them into our sights just twenty minutes later.

"Sir, I see them! Ten o'clock and about half a mile away!" Joe Wilkinson had good eyes.

I saw them too. They had been trying to cross a flooded field. It must have proved too deep and they were heading back for the road. I unslung my rifle and we ran. We made another hundred yards on them before they saw us. I saw the Feldwebel, at least I assumed it was him, pointing to the road. They cut their losses and ran across the flooded field to rejoin the road. I resisted the temptation to run faster. The object was to get there together. Now that we could see them we would not lose them. By the time they reached the road there was just two hundred yards between us. They stopped and formed a skirmish line. Before they could fire I shouted, "Break left and right!"

While the rest of my men dispersed I knelt in the road. Bullets came towards us but the German bullets missed me. It seemed I bore a charmed life. I took aim and squeezed off a bullet. It must have grazed the cheek of one of the paratroopers for I saw his head jerk to the side. The gun was pulling a little to the right. I corrected my aim and sighted the gun a little lower. This time the bullet hit him square in the chest. My men were all good shots and, against the flooded fields we were harder to hit. I saw a second and a third man fall.

I heard a cry from my right and saw Fred Emerson clutching his arm. "Hewitt!"

"Sir, a bunch of them are legging it!"

I looked and saw that Fletcher was right. Six of them had broken off and were now running down the road. There were still three men firing. They were being sacrificed.

"Hewitt, bring Fred along when he is fit. The rest of you, in pairs, move and fire. Wilkinson, you are with me."

"Right sir!" He squeezed off two bullets and said, "Move sir!"

I zig zagged down the middle of the road. Joe and I had the hardest job because there was no cover. I stopped thirty yards down the road, crouched and shouting, "Move!" fired three bullets. I changed my clip as Wilkinson reached me. I ran towards the three Germans. I saw one pitch backwards as Gordy Barker hit him. I lowered my gun to waist height and fired my whole clip, moving my gun from right to left. I hit one and Beaumont's bullet took the last man. As I reached them I saw that all had been wounded. That explained why they had been left. I saw that one had a Tommy gun. That had been Lieutenant Mulgrave's. I was just bending down to examine it when I heard the sound of Beaumont's Tommy gun. I whipped my head around and saw that one of the Germans who had been playing dead had tried to shoot me.

"Thanks, Roger." I examined the Thompson. It was empty. "There are six of them left and one has a Colt. Take no chances next time." I pointed at the man Beaumont had shot. "If we think they are dead put another bullet in them just to make sure. They got Alan Crowe like that and they nearly got me."

Emerson and Hewitt reached us.

"How is he?"

"I'm fine sir. It is my left arm. I can still run and I can use the Colt. Anybody want my Tommy gun?"

Hewitt said, "Give it to me Freddie!"

"Now let's run. We know where they are now!"

Chapter 20

Although they were briefly out of sight we were fitter and better fed. Within a mile we saw them again. They were running in a column of twos. It showed they still had discipline. I shouted, over my shoulder, "If you can't keep up, Emerson, we will come back for you!"

"Don't worry sir! I'll keep up! Alan Crowe was my mate too!"

My men also had discipline but, more than that, they had heart! We hit trouble at one of the few places we had seen with a bend in the road. Fortunately I was partly expecting it. I saw a hedgerow which faced a stand of weedy trees. It was the sort of place I would have chosen for an ambush. Equally the enemy could have decided to double bluff us. I knew that we were less than two miles from the E-Boat base. I didn't realise that I was slowing down as I approached it.

"Worried about an ambush, sir?"

"Yes Lance Sergeant Hay. Wilkinson and Hewitt head to the west. Beaumont and Fletcher head to the east. We four will see if we can trigger the ambush. Go!"

My four men sprinted off and the rest of us carried on down the road. The closer we came the more certain I was that it would be an ambush. It was Fred Emerson's eyes which spotted the trap. He was behind us and he shouted, "Sir, stop! Booby trap!"

Even as I looked down and saw the familiar parachute cord across the flooded road the Thompson opened up. My glance down saved my life. The Tommy gun had a tendency to pull up if you were not used to it and the Feldwebel was unused to it. Even so he tore the pips from my right shoulder. I did a forward roll over the trip wire and came up firing the rifle from the hip. I heard Gordy Barker's Tommy gun as he shredded the undergrowth then there was an explosion as one of my men, on the flanks, threw a grenade.

Joe Wilkinson shouted, "Cover! Grenade!"

I dived into the waterfilled ditch which abutted the partly flooded road. The second grenade exploded twenty feet from us. I heard a cry and, as I looked back, saw that Fred Emerson had had his cheek laid open by shrapnel.

"Hewitt, first aid!"

From my left I heard, "Sir!"

Ignoring the stagnant water in which I lay I rolled around and put another clip into the German rifle. I saw a grey leg and I fired two shots at it. I heard a cry and I saw the injured soldier drop. I put another two in his chest and then fired the last bullet to his left.

"Grenade!"

I covered my ears as Bill Hay threw a Mills bomb. It exploded above the hedge. I raised my head and fitted another clip. There was silence ahead. Cautiously I rose. Keeping my gun aimed at the undergrowth I stepped out of the ditch and walked towards the two German bodies I could see. We had been bitten twice before and I would not get caught out a third time. I fired a bullet into each of the bodies.

"Sir, Beaumont is hit!"

"And Fletcher sir!"

"Hewitt!"

"On it sir!"

I did not take my eyes from the undergrowth. Suddenly there was a movement from the ditch to my left. A burst from Gordy's gun ended the life of the German who had hidden in the ditch. There were three Germans left. We found the remains of one of the Germans just behind the hedgerow. He was not playing dead. Half of his head was missing. Of the other two there was no sign.

Gordy went around the bodies, "None of them is the Feldwebel sir." He gestured north, "And they have legged it again! That bastard has more lives than a bloody cat!"

"You forget, we know where he is going! We get to the E-Boat base."

"Sir, there will be Germans there."

"I know. Get three tunics from the dead Jerries. Try to find some that aren't bloody."

"Three sir?"

"Yes Gordy. I intend to take Joe and Bill with me. They both speak German and we need someone to look after the wounded."

He nodded, "And they are younger and fitter than me sir. Fair enough. I'll get the uniforms and field caps, sir."

I walked back to the three wounded men. Fletcher had been hit in the leg while Beaumont had taken shrapnel to the chest. Hewitt looked up, "He will live sir. His battle jerkin took the worst of it. I'll try and get the bits out before it is too dark."

"I am leaving you here with Sergeant Barker. I will take Wilkinson and Hay into the base. If that slippery Kraut thinks he has escaped us he can think again."

We just put the tunics over our own battledress and donned the field caps. It was late afternoon. By the time we reached the base it would be dark. I hoped there would be confusion and three more men making it back to safety would not seem unusual.

I turned to Gordy, "When Hewitt has finished, try to make it back to the village. It is only a couple of miles and the Marines might have reached it by now."

"Right, sir, and you take care eh? They are not worth it."

We set off at a jog. I knew we would not catch them. It was getting on for dusk as we neared the outskirts of the small port. The thick black clouds had made dusk come early and that suited us. There were papers in the paratroopers pockets and, as we approached the road block at the bridge over the canal I took mine out to glance at them. I needed to know my name! As we neared the town I heard, from the north and west, the sound of tanks and British artillery. The attack was moving closer.

The sergeant snapped, "Papers!"

I handed them to him as did the other two. He frowned as he read them. "Your feldwebel arrived not twenty minutes since. He said he was the last."

I shook my head, "We were separated at Zoutelande. He must have thought we were dead. We had better report to him."

"Then I would run. He planned on being aboard the last E-Boat out of the port. He said his brother was the captain. The Tommies are coming." He pointed to the men who were setting explosives under the bridge. "We blow the bridge now. We are leaving on the ship which is waiting. You can come with us if you like."

"Thank you Sergeant, we paratroopers like to stick together."

"That is strange considering he abandoned you."

"You can't know how much we owe him. We will find him. Where is the E-Boat moored?"

"At the western side of the quay."

Just then there was a flurry of artillery shells which dropped to our left. We ran. The shells were falling thick and fast now. They helped us as they created confusion. A pair of Typhoons zoomed over and a moment or two later I heard the sound of a two hundred pound bomb being dropped. Flames leapt into the air not five hundred yards from us. It was a godsend. Every German was now racing for the last ship in the harbour. That helped us for we saw it directly ahead and we knew that the E-Boat would be to its left. We turned down a side street, past a warehouse to the western side of the quay.

As we approached I saw that she was getting ready for sea. I waved and shouted, "Hey, wait for us."

One of the sailors waved and kept hold of the rope. We were twenty yards from it when the Feldwebel came from below. He shouted something and then fired four bullets at us. I heard Joe Wilkinson shout as he fell. I fired at the paratrooper but I missed. I did, however, manage to hit the man at wheel in the shoulder. He was an officer and I guessed the Feldwebel's brother. Three more bullets came in our direction. They missed. Bill Hay sprayed his Tommy gun in an arc. The Feldwebel dived below. The sailor at the stern fell as did the second paratrooper who was pulling his hand back to throw a grenade. The exploding grenade did our work for us and the six other men who were close by fell.

Just at that moment there was a huge explosion behind us. The second Typhoon had dropped its bomb on the coaster. The flames shot high in the air and I knew that the coaster would not leave the port. The ship was already listing from the fatal damage and men were trying to jump to safety.

I glanced at Joe Wilkinson. He was holding his upper left arm and he waved a hand, "Go! Go!"

I ditched my rifle and drew my Colt. It would be of more use in the confined space of the E-Boat. Our time aboard the *'Lucky Lady'* had stood us in good stead. We knew our way about an E-Boat; even in the dark. I waved Bill to the aft hatch and I went forrard. That way we could flank the Feldwebel no matter where he hid. I opened the hatch. I heard a movement. I took a grenade and dropped it below decks. I closed the hatch. There was a muffled explosion. The tiny passageway had funnelled the explosion. I opened the hatch and smoke poured out. I stepped down into an abattoir. There were crewmen and two soldiers who had taken the full force of the blast. As I stepped down towards them I saw a hand and a gun appear. I fired at the officer from the hip and two of my three bullets hit him. As I stepped over his body I saw that he was a lieutenant.

I heard gunfire from the direction of the stern. I moved cautiously. As I passed each cabin I glanced in. There was no one. Just before the mess was the engine room. There was just Bill and me on the boat. The two of us would have to do the job. There might be more of the crew hiding in the engine room. I took out a grenade and, opening the door, threw it down. I slammed the door shut. The explosion was followed by screams. Whoever had been down there was no longer a threat.

When I stepped into the mess I saw Bill Hay. He had been hit in the back. He lay, face down. The Feldwebel had just entered from the other door and was going to finish him off. He saw me and raised his Colt. It clicked on empty. Even as I raised my gun he grabbed Bill's body and pulled it in front of him as a human shield. He held his dagger to Bill's throat. I saw Bill's eyes open. He was alive.

He spat at me, "Drop the gun or I slit his throat." I saw the edge of the knife begin to dig into his throat and a tendril of blood dripped along the edge of the blade and fell to the floor.

I shook my head, "You slit the throat of one brave man you will not," I fired the whole magazine into his head, "do it with a second." His lifeless body fell to the ground. I ran to Bill, "How bad is it, Bill?"

"He managed to put a couple in my back. I feel so stupid. He must have hidden amongst the dead and waited until I had passed."

There was an explosion beneath our feet and I felt the heat from the fire I had started in the engine room. "Put your weight on my shoulder. Let's get ashore and then see if there is a way out of this mess."

It was hard work for he was almost a dead weight. The E-Boat was settling into the water and the fire was burning fiercely making the upper works hot to the touch as we reached the deck. I saw that Joe was sitting upright and his gun was aimed at the deck. His face broke into a grin when he saw us step from the doomed ship. "You are a sight for sore eyes, sir. I thought the pair of you were going down with the ship!"

"No but we are not out of this yet!"

The coaster had now sunk and I could see Germans milling around the quay. It would not take them long to investigate the sunken E-Boat. We had to get the two men fixed up and then find somewhere to hide. I took a field dressing out of Joe's Bergen and fastened it tightly around his upper arm. "You can walk, right?"

"Yes sir."

I replaced the clip in the Colt. "Then cover us while I see to Bill."

The bullets had been fired at such close range that they had gone through. The fact that Bill was not unconscious told me that the bullets had missed everything that was vital. However, I would not be able to apply a tourniquet. I put a dressing between his body and his tunic and then fastened a bandage as tightly as I could across his shoulders. I strapped his left arm to his body. He was ashen. I still had some sweet biscuits and chocolate. He could use his right arm. "Here Bill, eat this. That is an order." I shouldered my gun and put my right arm around his body and under his right arm. He chewed on the chocolate. "Joe, cover us and follow us west, along the quay. Let's get as far away from Jerry as we can."

"Yes sir."

We moved as quickly as two badly wounded men supported by one exhausted officer can. I knew that Joe, wounded or not, would guard our backs. Bill was out of it and it was up to me to find somewhere to lay up. I was under no illusions. There would be no more heroics. We would hide and hunker down. Up ahead I saw some scrubland. There was no shelter from the elements but there was shelter from prying eyes. I led us into the scrub and moved as far away from the road as we could get. When Joe said, "Go on without me, sir." I knew that we could go no further.

"Here will do." I laid Bill down. Opening my Bergen I put my oilskin over him and then his. "Joe, lie next to Bill. Your body heat will help you both." The fact that he did not argue told me how hurt he was. I laid his oilskin over him. I opened both their Bergens and found their spare chocolate and sweet biscuits. I forced them to eat. Bill was drifting off. "Lance Sergeant Hay, stay awake! That is an order!"

"Right sir but I could really do with a kip."

"You can have one when all of this is over. Right now I want you to talk to me."

"What about sir?"

"Anything! Tell me your favourite film. What is it?"

"I like Errol Flynn sir. Charge of the Light Brigade, Robin Hood you know."

"I know. Go on."

He and Joe chatted about the action films and westerns they both enjoyed and I kept a wary eye to the east. When they stopped talking I said, "Get the German tunics off. We don't want to get shot by our own side, do we?"

After taking off the tunics they both ate and I watched, fearfully, in case they drifted off to sleep. I knew that was dangerous. When I saw a little colour reappear on both their faces I breathed a sigh of relief. I made them drink some water. Taking my reloaded Colt I said, "Now stay here while I have a quick look around and keep talking."

It was a risk, I knew, but if there were allied troops around I needed to find them if I was to save the lives of my two men. I slipped back to the road. I could hear the sound of small arms fire now. It seemed to be much closer. When the shell from the tank exploded close by the quay I jumped back. Then I realised that a tank meant the allies. The trouble was the tank sounded like it was coming from the east and I had heard them from the west. Had the Germans mounted a counterattack? I headed back along the quay. It was, alarmingly quiet. The bodies of the men we had killed before we boarded the E-boat were still there and the radio mast marked the final resting place of the E-Boat. I could see the coaster; she was lying on her side but I saw no Germans.

I heard voices approaching and I lay down flat beside the dead Germans. I levelled my Colt as I watched the four figures approach. I had a full clip and I knew that I could shoot all four easily. Of course, that might bring their colleagues. I looked around for an escape route which would take me away from my two wounded men. I realised that it would have to be the sea. It was a chance and a chance worth taking to save Hay and Wilkinson. I levelled my gun at the nearest shadow which was ten feet from me.

"Well I can see bugger all sir. There's some dead Jerries and that is it."

I stood. They were English. "And one live Englishman."

I heard the Lee Enfields being cocked and then a torch was shone in my face, "Good God, it is Captain Harsker! Do you remember me? I am Lieutenant Ditchburn with the 11th Armoured!"

I held my hand out, "And damned glad I am to see you. Now bring your chaps will you; we have two wounded soldiers in need of some help."

By the time we had brought Hays and Wilkinson to the sunken E-Boat the column of tanks had drawn up. Major Dunlop climbed down. He did not shake my arm he picked me up in a bear hug. "You are a sight for sore eyes. We picked your chaps up down the road about an hour ago. They said you were heading here. Great news, Captain. We have Walcheren! The Battle for Antwerp is over! You and your men have performed a great service."

I nodded as the doctors and medics began to treat my two wounded men. The trouble is sir that there are just three of us left alive and unwounded. That is a pretty high price for a flooded little island, wouldn't you say?"

He shook his head, "No, Captain, for whatever sacrifices your men have made have shortened the war. How many men can say that?"

Epilogue

It took a whole day to get back to our base. I slept for most of the journey. The wounded had been taken by ambulance and that was a relief. They would be safe. We were back in Breskans when I began to write my report. I did it when I had written the letters to the families of my two dead men. I couldn't remember when I had had to write two such letters. Our wounded would all be back in England soon. With just John Hewitt and Gordy Barker we were no longer a fighting force. I made sure in my report that my men would be recognised for their valour. I put Ken Shepherd in for the V.C. My own award suddenly seemed shallow. Ken had given his life to save the rest of us. It was a true sacrifice and I felt humbled by it. I put each of my men in for the M.C. I doubted they would all receive one but, by God, they deserved it. I could think of no other men who could have done what they had done. I made sure that each soldier who had fought with me was mentioned in detail. The Colonel needed to know what they had done.

When I finished I felt exhausted. I was about to retire when Major Foster came into my quarters, "Well Tom, you have been promoted to Brevet Major." I nodded. "You don't seem very excited about the prospect!"

"Major, I just want this damned war to be over. We have the Scheldt; the Rhine can't be far away. Let's just get this bloody war over."

He handed me a whisky. "I can tell you are upset. Look take a week off and then it is off to Liege. No fighting this time. You have impressed everybody. They want you and your two chaps to talk to the Rangers and American Airborne commanders about how you operate behind enemy lines. After that you can go back to Blighty and have a Christmas leave. No more fighting eh? Just talk about what you do. It is getting on for Christmas. Everyone knows that the fighting stops in December. December 1944 could be the last winter of the war. Think on that!"

And that is how I was, as the Americans say, suckered in. That is how I came to be in the Ardennes in December 1944 when Hitler had his last hurrah. He would catch the allies napping, almost sipping the victory Champagne. But that was yet to come.

The End

Glossary

Abwehr- German Intelligence

ATS- Auxiliary Territorial Service- Women's Branch of the British Army during WW2

Bisht- Arab cloak

Bob on- Very accurate (slang) from a plumber's bob

Butchers- Look (Cockney slang Butcher's Hook- Look)

Butties- sandwiches (slang)

Chah- tea (slang)

Comforter- the lining for the helmet; a sort of woollen hat

Conflab- discussion (slang)

Corned dog- Corned Beef (slang)

CP- Command Post

Dhobi- washing (slang from the Hindi word)

Ercs- aircraftsman (slang- from Cockney)

Ewbank- Mechanical carpet cleaner

Fruit salad- medal ribbons (slang)

Full English- English breakfast (bacon, sausage, eggs, fried tomato and black pudding)

Gash- spare (slang)

Gauloise- French cigarette

Gib- Gibraltar (slang)

Glasshouse- Military prison

Goon- Guard in a POW camp (slang)- comes from a 19thirties Popeye cartoon

Hurries- Hawker Hurricane (slang)

Jankers- field punishment

Jimmy the One- First Lieutenant on a warship

Kettenhunde - Chained dogs. Nickname for German field police. From the gorget worn around their necks

Killick- leading hand (Navy) (slang)

Kip- sleep (slang)

Legging it- Running for it (slang)

LRDG- Long Range Desert group (Commandos operating from the desert behind enemy lines.)

Marge- Margarine (butter substitute- slang)

MGB- Motor Gun Boat

Mossy- De Havilland Mosquito (slang)

Mickey- *'taking the mickey'*, making fun of (slang)

Micks- Irishmen (slang)

MTB- Motor Torpedo Boat

ML- Motor Launch

Narked- annoyed (slang)

Neaters- undiluted naval rum (slang)

Oik- worthless person (slang)
Oppo/oppos- pals/comrades (slang)
Piccadilly Commandos- Prostitutes in London
PLUTO- Pipe Line Under The Ocean
Pom-pom- Quick Firing 2lb (40mm) Maxim cannon
Pongo (es)- soldier (slang)
Potato mashers- German Hand Grenades (slang)
PTI- Physical Training Instructor
QM- Quarter Master (stores)
Recce- Reconnoitre (slang)
SBA- Sick Bay Attendant
Schnellboote -German for E-boat (literally translated as fast boat)
Schtum -keep quiet (German)
Scragging - roughing someone up (slang)
Scrumpy- farm cider
Shooting brake- an estate car
SOE- Special Operations Executive (agents sent behind enemy lines)
SP- Starting price (slang)- what's going on
SNAFU- Situation Normal All Fucked Up (acronym and slang)
Snug- a small lounge in a pub (slang)
Spiv- A black marketeer/criminal (slang)
Sprogs- children or young soldiers (slang)
Squaddy- ordinary soldier (slang)
Stag- sentry duty (slang)
Stand your corner- get a round of drinks in (slang)
Subbie- Sub-lieutenant (slang)
Suss it out- work out what to do (slang)
Tatties- potatoes (slang)
Thobe- Arab garment
Tiffy- Hawker Typhoon (slang)
Tommy (Atkins)- Ordinary British soldier
Two penn'orth- two pennies worth (slang for opinion)
Wavy Navy- Royal Naval Reserve (slang)
WVS- Women's Voluntary Service

Maps

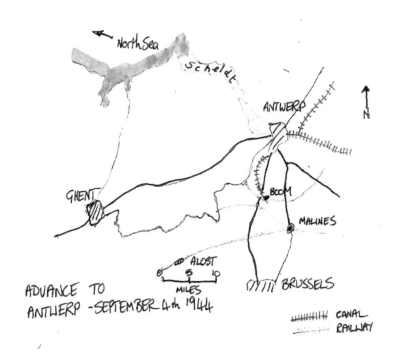

ADVANCE TO
ANTWERP - SEPTEMBER 4th 1944

Historical note

Readers of my books know that I incorporate material from the earlier books. Some of my readers have joined the series half way through and I think it is important that they know the background to my books. If you have the first books in this series, then you can skip down to the section marked Antwerp. It is 18 pages down.

The first person I would like to thank for this particular book and series is my Dad. He was in the Royal Navy but served in Combined Operations. He was at Dieppe, D-Day and Walcheren. His boat: LCA(I) 523 was the one which took in the French Commandos on D-Day. He was proud that his flotilla had taken in Bill Millens and Lord Lovat. I wish that, before he died, I had learned more in detail about life in Combined Operations but like many heroes he was reluctant to speak of the war. He is the character in the book called Bill Leslie. Dad ended the war as Leading Seaman- I promoted him! I reckon he deserved it.

'Bill Leslie' 1941
Author's collection

I went to Normandy in 1994, with my Dad, to Sword Beach and he took me through that day on June 6th 1944. He pointed out the position which took the head from the Oerlikon gunner who stood next to him. He also told me about the raid on Dieppe as well as Westkapelle. He had taken the Canadians in. We even found the grave of his cousin George Hogan who died on D-Day. As far as I know we were the only members of the family ever to do so. Sadly that was Dad's only visit but we planted forget-me-nots on the grave of George. Wally Friedmann is a real Canadian who served in WW2 with my Uncle Ted. The description of Wally is perfect- I lived with Wally and his family for three months in 1972. He was a real gentleman. As far as I now he did not serve with the Saskatchewan regiment, he came from Ontario but he did serve in the war. As I keep saying, it is my story and my imagination. God bless, Wally.

I would also like to thank Roger who is my railway expert. The train Tom and the Major catch from Paddington to Oswestry ran until 1961. The details of the livery, the compartments and the engine are all, hopefully accurate. I would certainly not argue with Roger! Thanks also to John Dinsdale, another railway buff and a scientist. It was he who advised on the use of explosives. Not the sort of thing to Google these days!

I used a number of books in the research. The list is at the end of this historical section. However the best book, by far, was the actual Commando handbook which was reprinted in 2012. All of the details about hand to hand, explosives, esprit de corps etc. were taken directly from it. The advice about salt, oatmeal and water is taken from the book. It even says that taking too much salt is not a bad thing! I shall use the book as a Bible for the rest of the series. The Commandos were expected to find their own accommodation. Some even saved the money for lodgings and slept rough. That did not mean that standards of discipline and presentation were neglected; they were not.

The 1st Loyal Lancashire existed as a regiment. They were in the BEF and they were the rear guard. All the rest is the work of the author's imagination. The use of booby traps using grenades was common. The details of the German potato masher grenade are also accurate. The Germans used the grenade as an early warning system by hanging them from fences so that an intruder would move the grenade and it would explode. The Mills bomb had first been used in the Great War. It threw shrapnel for up to one hundred yards. When thrown, the thrower had to take cover too. However, my Uncle Norman, who survived Dunkirk was demonstrating a grenade with an instructor kneeling next to him. It was a faulty grenade and exploded in my uncle's hand. Both he and the Sergeant survived. My uncle just lost his hand. I am guessing that my uncle's hand prevented the grenade fragmenting as much as it was intended. Rifle grenades were used from 1915 onwards and enabled a grenade to be thrown much further than by hand

During the retreat the British tank to Dunkirk in 1940, the Matilda proved superior to the German Panzers. It was slow but it was so heavily armoured that it could only be stopped by using the 88 anti-aircraft guns. Had there been more of them and had they been used in greater numbers then who knows what the outcome might have been. What they did succeed in doing, however, was making the German High Command believe that we had more tanks than they actually encountered. The Germans thought that the 17 Matildas they fought were many times that number. They halted at Arras for reinforcements. That enabled the Navy to take off over 300,000 men from the beaches.

Although we view Dunkirk as a disaster now, at the time it was seen as a setback. An invasion force set off to reinforce the French a week after Dunkirk. It was recalled. Equally there were many units cut off behind enemy lines. The Highland Division was one such force. 10000 men were captured. The fate of many of those captured in the early days of the war was to be sent to work in factories making weapons which would be used against England.

Germany had radar stations and they were accurate. They also had large naval guns at Cape Gris Nez as well as railway guns. They made the Channel dangerous although they only actually sank a handful of ships during the whole of the war. They did however make Southend and Kent dangerous places to live.

The first Commando raids were a shambles. Churchill himself took action and appointed Sir Roger Keyes to bring some order to what the Germans called thugs and killers. Major Foster and his troop reflect that change.

The parachute training for Commandos was taken from this link http://www.bbc.co.uk/history/ww2peopleswar/stories/72/a3530972.shtml. Thank you to Thomas Davies whose first-hand account of the training was most illuminating and useful. The Number 2 Commandos were trained as a battalion and became the Airborne Division eventually. The SOE also trained at Ringway but they were secreted away at an Edwardian House, Bowden. As a vaguely related fact 43 out of 57 SOE agents sent to France between June 1942 and Autumn 1943 were captured, 36 were executed!

The details about the Commando equipment are also accurate. They were issued with American weapons although some did use the Lee Enfield. When large numbers attacked the Lofoten Islands they used regular army issue. The Commandos appeared in dribs and drabs but 1940 was the year when they began their training. It was Lord Lovat who gave them a home in Scotland but that was not until 1941. I wanted my hero, Tom, to begin to fight early. His adventures will continue throughout the war.

The raid on German Headquarters is based on an attempt by Number 3 Commando to kill General Erwin Rommel. In a real life version of *'The Eagle Has Landed'* they almost succeeded. They went in by lorry. They failed in their mission. Commandos were used extensively in the early desert war but, sadly, many of them perished in Greece and Cyprus and Crete. Of 800 sent to Crete only two hundred returned to Egypt. Churchill also compounded his mistake of supporting Greece by sending all three hundred British tanks to the Western Desert and the Balkans. The map shows the area where Tom and the others fled. The Green Howards were not in that part of the desert at that time. The Germans did begin to reinforce their allies at the start of 1941.

The Dieppe raid was deemed, at the time, to be a fiasco. Many of the new Churchill tanks were lost and out of the six hundred men who were used on the raid only 278 returned to England. 3,367 Canadians were killed. wounded or captured. On the face of it the words disaster and fiasco were rightly used. However, the losses at Dieppe meant that the planners for D-Day changed their approach. Instead of capturing a port, which would be too costly they would build their own port. Mulberry was born out of the blood of the Canadians. In the long run, it saved thousands of lives. Three of the beaches on D-Day were assaulted with a fraction of the casualties from Dieppe. The Canadians made a sacrifice but it was not in vain.

The E-boats were far superior to the early MTBs and Motor Launches. It was not until the Fairmile boats were developed that the tide swung in the favour of the Royal Navy. Some MTBs were fitted with depth charges. Bill's improvisation is the sort of thing Combined Operations did. It could have ended in disaster but in this case, it did not. There were stories of captured E-boats being used by covert forces in World War II. I took the inspiration from S-160

185

which was used to land agents in the Low Countries and, after the war, was used against the Soviet Bloc. They were very fast, powerful and sturdy ships.

The first Sherman Tanks to be used in combat were in North Africa. Three hundred M4A1 and M4A2 tanks arrived in Egypt in September 1942. The war was not going well in the desert at that point and Rommel was on the point of breaking through to Suez. The battle of El Alamein did not take place until the end of October.

The Hitler order
Top Secret
Fuhrer H.Q. 18. 10 1942
1. For a long time now our opponents have been employing in their conduct of the war, methods which contravene the International Convention of Geneva. The members of the so-called Commandos behave in a particularly brutal and underhanded manner; and it has been established that those units recruit criminals not only from their own country but even former convicts set free in enemy territories. From captured orders it emerges that they are instructed not only to tie up prisoners, but also to kill out-of-hand unarmed captives who they think might prove an encumbrance to them, or hinder them in successfully carrying out their aims. Orders have indeed been found in which the killing of prisoners has positively been demanded of them.

2. In this connection it has already been notified in an Appendix to Army Orders of 7.10.1942. that in future, Germany will adopt the same methods against these Sabotage units of the British and their Allies; i.e. that, whenever they appear, they shall be ruthlessly destroyed by the German troops.

3. I order, therefore:— From now on all men operating against German troops in so-called Commando raids in Europe or in Africa, are to be annihilated to the last man. This is to be carried out whether they be soldiers in uniform, or saboteurs, with or without arms; and whether fighting or seeking to escape; and it is equally immaterial whether they come into action from Ships and Aircraft, or whether they land by parachute. Even if these individuals on discovery make obvious their intention of giving themselves up as prisoners, no pardon is on any account to be given. On this matter a report is to be made on each case to Headquarters for the information of Higher Command.

4. Should individual members of these Commandos, such as agents, saboteurs etc., fall into the hands of the Armed Forces through any means – as, for example, through the Police in one of the Occupied Territories – they are to be instantly handed over to the SD

To hold them in military custody – for example in P.O.W. Camps, etc., – even if only as a temporary measure, is strictly forbidden.

5. This order does not apply to the treatment of those enemy soldiers who are taken prisoner or give themselves up in open battle, in the course

of normal operations, large scale attacks; or in major assault landings or airborne operations. Neither does it apply to those who fall into our hands after a sea fight, nor to those enemy soldiers who, after air battle, seek to save their lives by parachute.

6. I will hold all Commanders and Officers responsible under Military Law for any omission to carry out this order, whether by failure in their duty to instruct their units accordingly, or if they themselves act contrary to it.

The order was accompanied by this letter from Field Marshal Jodl

The enclosed Order from the Fuhrer is forwarded in connection with destruction of enemy Terror and Sabotage-troops.

This order is intended for Commanders only and is in no circumstances to fall into Enemy hands.

Further distribution by receiving Headquarters is to be most strictly limited.

The Headquarters mentioned in the Distribution list are responsible that all parts of the Order, or extracts taken from it, which are issued are again withdrawn and, together with this copy, destroyed.

Chief of Staff of the Army

Jodl

The FW 190 had two 13mm machine guns with 475 rounds per gun. It also had two twenty mm cannon with 250 rounds per gun. It could carry up to five hundred kg bombs. It usually had just one bomb in the centre of the aeroplane

Faith, Hope and Charity were the nicknames given to the three Gloster Sea Gladiators which, for a time, were Malta's only air defence. These ancient biplanes did sterling work in actual fact there were more than three but it suited the propaganda of the time. To ascribe the success against the Italian bombers to just three aeroplanes. They were based at the Sea Air Arm base, H.M.S. Falcon.

The Royal Navy rum ration was 54.6% proof. It was an eighth of a pint. Senior ratings (Petty Officers and above) received their rum neat while junior ratings had it diluted two to one. *'Up Spirits'* was normally between 11 and 12 each day.

The Rangers under Colonel Darby were at Amalfi. The rocket launcher known as the bazooka was first used in North Africa. Italy was the first time it had a widespread use. It was limited to the Americans only at first but later was used by the Russians and the British. The Germans captured some and used them to make their own version, the Panzershreck.

The Commando attack at Vietri Sul Mare went according to plan and the only losses they suffered were when they attacked Salerno itself. Nine Commandos were killed and thirty seven wounded. The Commandos were opposed by the 16th Panzer Reconnaissance Battalion which they defeated before capturing Salerno. It was an impressive feat for a brigade of Commandos. Following this and Lord Mountbatten's departure for the Far East Major General 'Lucky' Laycock was appointed commander of Combined Operations. It was a position he occupied until the end of the war.

The Noel Coward play of 1936 was eventually made into the wartime film of 1945- Brief Encounter. *'Beau Geste'* was a popular film made in 1939. Brian Donleavy plays a particularly sadistic sergeant in the French Foreign legion. The film was very popular amongst servicemen.

Operation Bodyguard and Operation Neptune were the code names used in 1943 and 1944 although Operation Overlord was the umbrella name for the planned invasion of Europe.

The term tobruk was the name given by the allies to the concrete emplacements. They were first encountered in North Africa, hence the name. Frequently the Germans would use the turrets from captured tanks.

Operation Tiger was the name given to the practice attacks on the south coast. German E-boats did attack the convoy and almost a thousand Americans lost their lives. There were problems with signals as well as with training on life vests. Many Americans died because of incorrectly fitted jackets.

The Battle of Bréville was called one of the major battles of World War II. The Commandos and the Airborne Division had to fight off two infantry divisions and the 21st Panzer Division. The 21st had been part of the Afrika Korps. As such they were veterans. Until the 6 pounder anti-tank guns were dropped by parachute on the 90th of June they had to fight them off with PIATs and grenades. The counter attack of Bréville did take place. It was stormed and then the Commandos were withdrawn back to the ridge. Theirs was a holding action until the main attack could break out of Caen. The battle was won on June 12th. Had they not held then I wonder of the main attack might have been halted.

The slang was taken from an Imperial War Museum publication called service slang and http://www.oocities.org/faskew/WW2/Glossary/WW2-SoldierSlang.htm

Paris

Operation Bulbasket was an SAS operation in France in 1944. Thirty SAS were sent into France to help the resistance. They were highly successful blowing up fuel dumps and destroying railway lines. The Germans found them and shot them as spies. 34 men, in total, were executed. I have used those as the inspiration, in this book, for Tom and his men. There was no fuel dump at Trun but the town was heavily damaged in the fighting and its capture was crucial to the closing of the Falaise Gap.

This is the full transcript of the Charles de Gaulle speech after the liberation of Paris. Apparently, the Americans and British had little to do with it!

"Why do you wish us to hide the emotion which seizes us all, men and women, who are here, at home, in Paris that stood up to liberate itself and that succeeded in doing this with its own hands?

No! We will not hide this deep and sacred emotion. These are minutes which go beyond each of our poor lives. Paris! Paris outraged! Paris broken! Paris martyred! But Paris liberated! Liberated by itself, liberated by its people with the help of the French armies, with the support and the help of all France, of the France that fights, of the only France, of the real France, of the eternal France!

Well! Since the enemy which held Paris has capitulated into our hands, France returns to Paris, to her home. She returns bloody, but quite resolute. She returns there enlightened by the immense lesson, but more certain than ever of her duties and of her rights.

I speak of her duties first, and I will sum them all up by saying that for now, it is a matter of the duties of war. The enemy is staggering, but he is not beaten yet. He remains on our soil.

It will not even be enough that we have, with the help of our dear and admirable Allies, chased him from our home for us to consider ourselves satisfied after what has happened. We want to enter his territory as is fitting, as victors.

This is why the French vanguard has entered Paris with guns blazing. This is why the great French army from Italy has landed in the south and is advancing rapidly up the Rhône valley. This is why our brave and dear Forces of the interior will arm themselves with modern weapons. It is for this revenge, this vengeance and justice, that we will keep fighting until the final day, until the day of total and complete victory.

This duty of war, all the men who are here and all those who hear us in France know that it demands national unity. We, who have lived the greatest hours of our History, we have nothing else to wish than to show ourselves, up to the end, worthy of France. Long live France!"

Charles de Gaulle

Ernest Hemingway and Colonel 'Buck' Lanham were good friends and Hemingway did disappear to the forest of Rambouillet where he became a guerrilla leader for the local resistance.

During Operation Cobra over 50% of all German casualties came from the attacks by the 2nd Tactical Air force. Eisenhower said, "The chief credit in smashing the enemy's spearhead, however, must go to the rocket-firing Typhoon planes of the Second Tactical Air Force. They dived upon the armoured columns, and, with their rocket projectiles, on the first day of the battle destroyed 83 tanks, probably destroyed 29 tanks and damaged 24 tanks in addition to quantities of 'soft-skinned' Motorized Transport. The result of this strafing was that the enemy attack was effectively brought to a halt, and a threat was turned into a great victory."

There is an excellent web site with more information than I could put here. http://www.ibiblio.org/hyperwar/AAF/AAF-H-DDay/

General Montgomery is often lauded as a great general but Normandy was not his finest hour. He sent back Americans who had closed the Falaise gap because it was in the British zone of control. He could be petty and small minded. He did not like Patton. Had he behaved more reasonably then the gap would have been closed a day earlier.

I have simplified the liberation of Paris. Captain Dronne was sent by General Leclerc to liberate Paris. His regiment was from North Africa, the Regiment of Chad and they did name their vehicles. Many of them had fought in the Spanish Civil War. Major general Gerow forbade the French from going into Paris. General Leclerc flew back to speak with Omar Bradley in an attempt to get the order rescinded. When the columns did head for Paris it became a race to see who could get there first. Captain Dronne reached the Paris Hotel de Ville just before midnight. The Germans had wired all the bridges over the Seine but the majority were not destroyed.

There were no British involved in the liberation of Paris itself. This is a story after all!

Antwerp

I have used real events from the campaign and ascribed them to Tom and his men. They are an amalgamation of many people. The attack at Boom did happen but the part played by my heroes was actually a Belgian engineer who directed Major Dunlop and his tanks. Robert Vekemans was the real hero. I changed the bridges a little but the two tanks and the armoured car did race across the mined bridge before it could be exploded. Had they not done so then the Germans would have had time to bring forces down to the Rupel to hold up the advance.

Major Dunlop, Major Bell and Lieutenant Colonel Silvertop were at Boom and Antwerp.

*'We never closed the lids of our turrets, because we then became so blind and so deaf that we felt too vulnerable. We felt a lot safer with them open . . . But that afternoon I remember seriously considering closing down. However, this sporadic firing from above was confined to the out-
skirts of the town and later, rather more intensively, to some parts of the centre. Our biggest problem was with the crowds of excited civilians who thronged the streets and climbed on our tanks. We had no objection to kisses from charming girls, cigars or bottles of champagne. But we kept meeting bursts of small arms fire and an occasional grenade, and there were civilian casualties!'* (Major Dunlop)

As we dealt swiftly with the scattered and disorganised opposition, we could see ahead of us the main streets of the city densely packed with crowds awaiting us, and this spurred our efforts. Then came the great moment, as we entered the heart of the city to receive a welcome none of us had ever dreamt was possible. Our vehicles were unable to move and were smothered with people; we were overwhelmed with flowers, bottles and kisses. Everyone had gone mad and we allowed ourselves a few moments to take stock of the situation. (Major Noel Bell)

'The difficulties ... amongst this mass of populace crowding round still cheering, still flag wagging, still thrusting plums at you, still kissing you, asking you to post a letter to America, to give them some petrol, some more arms for

the White Brigade, holding baby under your nose to be kissed, trying to give you a drink, inviting you to their house, trying to carry you away, offering information about the enemy etc., had to be seen to be understood. (Colonel Reeves)

I have taken real events described by these brave soldiers and ascribed them to my Commandos.

Sherman as used by the 11th Armoured Division
(Repainted in American colours)

Source: File:Shermantielt 28-10-2008 18-10-52.JPG - https://en.wikipedia.org

German Defences at Walcheren
202nd Naval Artillery Battalion
(Batteries are given the target numbers allotted by 84 Group RAF and subsequently used by all three British Services: German numbers in brackets.)

W7 (91202) four 15-cm guns (S.9-inch) immediately west of Flushing

WI 1 (81202) four 15-cm guns in the dunes between Flushing and Zoutelande near Dishoek; close defence and flak not known.

WI3 (71202) four 15-cm guns with two 7.5-cm for close defence and three 20-mm flak in the dunes between Zoutelande and Westkapelle.

WI5 (61202) four ex-British 3.7-inch (9.4-cm) anti-aircraft guns captured at Dunkirk and now mounted against shipping with two ex-British 3-inch for close defence, mounted on the sea wall immediately north of Westkapelle.

W17 (51202) four 22-cm guns (8.7-inch) with one 5-cm gun for close defence, immediately west of Domburg.

WI9 (41202) five ex-British 3.7-inch guns in the dunes at the northern tip of the island near Ostberg.

Major types of Landing Craft used in the attacks on Walcheren
Landing Craft Tank - LCT Marks 3 and 4
A ramped beaching landing craft capable of carrying six Churchill tanks or nine Shermans and also used extensively for soft-skinned vehicles and stores. Marks 3 and 4 were both within a few feet of 190 feet in length, the latter having increased beam and shallower draft to give better beaching

characteristics on the flat Normandy beaches. Speeds: Mark 3, 9 knots; Mark 4, 8 knots. Seaworthy in seas up to Force 4. Originally unarmed, later 20-mm Oerlikons were added for AA defence. Very limited armour for wheelhouse, etc. The specification called for utmost simplicity to facilitate industrial production. Crew - 12.

Landing Craft Gun (Large) - LCG(L)
After the Dieppe raid of 1942 much greater emphasis was placed on the need for close support for troops landing on a defended beach. A total of 23 LCT 3 and 10 LCT 4 were in consequence decked over to take two 4.7-inch destroyer guns, mounted in gun-shields, and a number of lighter weapons. Their shallow draft enabled them to go close inshore, although they would not normally beach, and gave them a fair degree of immunity from contact mines. Crew, including RM gun crews, 3 officers and 44 men.

Landing Craft Flak - LCF
Another LCT conversion, intended as the name implies to give close AA cover to craft approaching a beach and landing troops and transport. Armament: eight 2-pdr Bofors and four 20-mm Oerlikons, or alternatively four Bofors and eight Oerlikons. Crew: 2 naval officers and 10 ratings, RM officers and 48 other ranks gun crews.

Landing Craft Tank (Rocket) - LCT(R)
Another LCT conversion intended to increase the weight of fire brought down on a beach immediately before assault. 800 to 1,000 5-inch rocket projectors were mounted on the decked over LCT to be fired electrically dead ahead in a ripple salvo on a radar range of 3,500 yards as the craft closed the beach. A second outfit of rockets was carried, but reloading took a long time. Rockets were normally HE, but smoke rockets could be fired. The idea was viewed with suspicion by the Gunnery Division at the Admiralty, but the first LCT(R), used in the invasion of Sicily, were reported on highly favourably and in Normandy 6-10 LCT(R) were used on the front of each assaulting brigade group.

Landing Craft Gun (Medium) - LCG(M)
A later and experimental design of LCG built as such, not a conversion, and intended to deal with thick concrete or similar defences by firing into loopholes and similar weak points at close range. The craft were armed with two 17-pdr anti-tank guns firing solid shot and were intended to beach and flood ballast tanks to give a steady aiming platform. The only two ever used operationally were both lost at Walcheren. As J. D. Ladd remarks, they broke the golden rule of combined operations - get off the waterline as quickly as possible either ashore or back to sea.

Landing Craft Support (Large) - LCS(L)
Early LCS were modified versions of minor landing craft (see below). When the demand came for much increased fire power, however, ten LCI(S) (below) were converted to carry one 6-pdr anti-tank gun in a turret forward, a power-operated twin .S-inch Vickers aft and a 4-inch mortar firing smoke.

Performance and vulnerability similar to LCI(S). Crew: 2 officers and 23 including RM gun crews.

Landing Craft Infantry (Small) - LCI(S)

Design adapted from coastal forces craft built by Fairmile with reduced scantlings to permit troop spaces between decks. Later some armour added, reducing speed. Landing by gangplanks launched by rollers over the deck. Originally intended for raids, the craft were much too vulnerable for beach assault. Speed: 12 knots (with armour) endurance 700 miles; load, 100 armed men. After their heavy losses in Normandy, which might have been still worse had the enemy used incendiary ammunition against their unarmoured tanks carrying high octane petrol, the wing tanks were filled with sea water for the Westkapelle assault.

Landing Craft Headquarters - LCH

A conversion of the Landing Craft Infantry (Large) to take headquarters at the level of naval assault group/brigade. American-built to an initial British specification, the LCI(L) was a steel craft with properly fitted landing gangways intended for the follow-up rather than the first waves of an assault. Speed 12 knots, load as LCI(L) 200 armed men.

Motor Launches - ML

These were not landing craft but a number of them acted as markers, guides etc. for the Westkapelle assault. Nos. 100 to 919 were Fairmile Bs, length 112 feet, speed 18 knots at sea; armament, one 3-pdr or 40-mm AA and four 20-mm Oerlikons. Crew, 18.

Minor Landing Craft

Landing Craft Assault - LCA

Speed -- 10 knots claimed, probably less in practice. Load 35 armed men and 5 crew. Endurance 90 miles. Designed by the Inter-Services Training and Development Centre in 1938-9 at 10 tons to be within the capacity of a liner's lifeboat davits and to land infantry in beach assault, a small number of these craft had been built by the outbreak of war and were used at Dunkirk and in Norway. They are said to have been inferior to the comparable LCV(P) in speed, manoeuvrability, and seaworthiness but to have the advantage over them in bullet proof protection, troop carrying capacity, disembarkation on a beach, silence and low silhouette.

This is the type of boat my father was on. LCA(I) 523 was his boat on D-Day and at Westkapelle.

Amphibians

Except for the DUKW, amphibians arrived late in the European theatre Those used in the Scheldt operations comprised:

Landing Vehicle Tracked - LVT

Buffalo

An American tracked amphibian which reached the -9th Armoured Division in August 1944. Water speed 5 knots, and speed 11 mph. Shaped grousers on tracks provided water traction. Limited track mileage ashore; some light armour in front of driving cab. The Mark 2 had no ramp and could take 24 armed men;

the Mark 4 had a stem ramp and could take a jeep, Bren carrier or 25-pounder field gun. The tracks gave the appearance and sound of a tank, but the LVT were much too vulnerable to be used as such. Maximum speeds: land, 25mph; sea, $5_{1/2}$ knots.

Weasel

A light. unarmoured, tracked snow-mobile with very limited water performance. Its light track pressure gave a degree of immunity against land mines, but it was very slow and unseaworthy in water and should not have been classed as an amphibian. Issued to the 52nd (Lowland) Division for mountain training in Scotland, it was found to have reasonable cross-country ability in skilled hands, but the steep dunes south of Westkapelle were too much for it.

DUKW - initials from maker's code pronounced 'duck'

An American six-wheeled load carrying amphibian. Water speed 6 knots, land speed 50mph. Unarmoured but very handy and seaworthy afloat.

Terrapin

British-built eight-wheeled load carrying amphibian, which appeared in the latter part of 1944. Generally considered inferior to the DUKW.

Kangaroo

Source: File:IWM-BU-2956-Ram-Kangaroo-Ochtrup-19450403.jpg -
https://en.wikipedia.org

It was a Captain Rewcastle and his men who captured the 26 Germans in their dugout. It happened almost exactly as I described it. It was the first action of the attack on Flushing. Major Boucher-Myers did lead the advance party of Commandos. I used Lieutenant Colonel Moulton's book to help me. He was in command of 48 Commando. As he wrote his book shortly after the battle I have taken it as an accurate source of information. The style of the book does not lend itself to reading but it is very factual. You can tell it was written by someone used to writing reports and not a novelist. It is worth reading to get the minutiae of battle. In the actual battle the Commandos managed to turn a 75 mm around to attack the troublesome hotel. The attacks on the W7 battery is fictitious as is the murder of the Commandos. The 6th Parachute Regiment were present. There is a good account of the battle at the Combined services website. https://www.combinedops.com/Walcheren.htm under the title of the actual operation: Operation Infatuate.

The street which leads along the breakwater in Flushing is now called Commandoweg. It is good to know that they have not forgotten the sacrifices the Commandos made in 1944. There are many streets in Antwerp and Boom also named after the men who led the forces in 1944. Colonel Silvertop has a street in Boom named after him.

Tom Harsker will return. The Battle of the Bulge is coming and Tom and his men will be needed again!

Source: File: HMS Warspite, Indian Ocean 1942.jpg -
https://en.wikipedia.org

Reference Books used

The Commando Pocket Manual 1949-45- Christopher Westhorp
The Second World War Miscellany- Norman Ferguson
Army Commandos 1940-45- Mike Chappell
Military Slang- Lee Pemberton
World War II- Donald Sommerville
The Historical Atlas of World War II-Swanston and Swanston
The Battle of Britain- Hough and Richards
The Hardest Day- Price
Overlord Coastline- Stephen Chicken
Disaster at D-Day- Peter Tsouras
Michelin Map #102 Battle of Normandy (1947 Edition).
The Battle for Antwerp- Colonel J.L. Moulton
From the Beaches to the Baltic- Noel Bell

Griff Hosker January 2017

Other books
by
Griff Hosker

If you enjoyed reading this book, then why not read another one by the author?

Ancient History

The Sword of Cartimandua Series (Germania and Britannia 50A.D. – 128 A.D.)

Ulpius Felix- Roman Warrior (prequel)
Book 1 The Sword of Cartimandua
Book 2 The Horse Warriors
Book 3 Invasion Caledonia
Book 4 Roman Retreat
Book 5 Revolt of the Red Witch
Book 6 Druid's Gold
Book 7 Trajan's Hunters
Book 8 The Last Frontier
Book 9 Hero of Rome
Book 10 Roman Hawk
Book 11 Roman Treachery
Book 12 Roman Wall
Book 13 Roman Courage

The Aelfraed Series (Britain and Byzantium 1050 A.D. - 1085 A.D.
Book 1 Housecarl
Book 2 Outlaw
Book 3 Varangian

The Wolf Warrior series (Britain in the late 6th Century)
Book 1 Saxon Dawn
Book 2 Saxon Revenge
Book 3 Saxon England
Book 4 Saxon Blood
Book 5 Saxon Slayer
Book 6 Saxon Slaughter
Book 7 Saxon Bane
Book 8 Saxon Fall: Rise of the Warlord
Book 9 Saxon Throne
Book 10 Saxon Sword

The Dragon Heart Series
Book 1 Viking Slave
Book 2 Viking Warrior

Book 3 Viking Jarl
Book 4 Viking Kingdom
Book 5 Viking Wolf
Book 6 Viking War
Book 7 Viking Sword
Book 8 Viking Wrath
Book 9 Viking Raid
Book 10 Viking Legend
Book 11 Viking Vengeance
Book 12 Viking Dragon
Book 13 Viking Treasure
Book 14 Viking Enemy
Book 15 Viking Witch
Book 16 Viking Blood
Book 17 Viking Weregeld
Book 18 Viking Storm
Book 19 Viking Warband
Book 20 Viking Shadow
Book 21 Viking Legacy

The Norman Genesis Series
Hrolf the Viking
Horseman
The Battle for a Home
Revenge of the Franks
The Land of the Northmen
Ragnvald Hrolfsson
Brothers in Blood
Lord of Rouen
Drekar in the Seine
Lord of Rouen

The Anarchy Series England 1120-1180
English Knight
Knight of the Empress
Northern Knight
Baron of the North
Earl
King Henry's Champion
The King is Dead
Warlord of the North
Enemy at the Gate
The Fallen Crown
Warlord's War
Kingmaker

Henry II
Crusader
The Welsh Marches
Irish War
Poisonous Plots
The Princes' Revolt
Earl Marshal

Border Knight 1182-1300
Sword for Hire
Return of the Knight
Baron's War
Magna Carta

Struggle for a Crown 1367-1485
Blood on the Crown

Modern History
The Napoleonic Horseman Series
Book 1 Chasseur a Cheval
Book 2 Napoleon's Guard
Book 3 British Light Dragoon
Book 4 Soldier Spy
Book 5 1808: The Road to Corunna
Waterloo

The Lucky Jack American Civil War series
Rebel Raiders
Confederate Rangers
The Road to Gettysburg

The British Ace Series
1914
1915 Fokker Scourge
1916 Angels over the Somme
1917 Eagles Fall
1918 We will remember them
From Arctic Snow to Desert Sand
Wings over Persia

Combined Operations series 1940-1945
Commando
Raider
Behind Enemy Lines
Dieppe

Toehold in Europe
Sword Beach
Breakout
The Battle for Antwerp
King Tiger
Beyond the Rhine

Other Books
Carnage at Cannes (a thriller)
Great Granny's Ghost (Aimed at 9-14-year-old young people)
Adventure at 63-Backpacking to Istanbul

For more information on all of the books then please visit the author's web site at http://www.griffhosker.com where there is a link to contact him or you can Tweet him @HoskerGriff

CPSIA information can be obtained
at www.ICGtesting.com
Printed in the USA
BVHW041255121119
563595BV00009B/47/P